Cabal Books

The Kitchen Witches
Copyright © 2024
ISBN: 979-8-218-35477-0

First paperback edition published by Cabal Books
June 22, 2024.

www.cabalbooks.us

Typeset by Ira Rat
Cover by Tod Foley

Cabal Books
DBA Thicke & Vaney Books
P. O. Box 223
Catlett, VA 20119

the Kitchen Witches

ELAINE PASCALE

Cabal Books

Acknowledgements

I would like to thank Bix Skahill for enjoying this story and encouraging me to enjoy it, too. Also to Bix for crafting the greatest author contract of all time. I would like to thank the family and friends that embolden me to take the time for creative outlets and I would especially like to thank the women who have taught me that I don't have to be a Melanie: Ruth Collins, Nina D'Arcangela, Kristi Petersen Schoonover, Nancy Kilpatrick, and Ygraine Hackett-Cantabrana. As always, the greatest amount of thanks to Christopher Costa and Sierra Costa for being the motivation for everything.

Prologue

A contract is a thing of beauty.

A contract stands for something in a society full of false promises and even faker compliments. It means that someone believes that you have something to say. And that both you and they will be held accountable in the telling of a story.

A contract is especially beautiful when the world surrounding it is ugly. So ugly that there are days that will eat you alive. So ugly that a publishing house of some merit contacts you to write about the murders that followed a very ordinary bracelet party. The murders would have been a bit more upsetting if the victims hadn't been so deserving. Despite the countless surgeries, expensive salves, designer clothing, and personal beauticians, the victims were the ugliest part of the already ugly world.

What follows is my end of the contract.

Attempt 1: Wishes

Months After the Bracelet Party

Prior to Melanie Voss's first experience with Time Between Time, she had been well acquainted with the phrase "be careful what you wish for." The Time Between Time was then prior to the sharp, biting pains in her abdomen that she visualized as a tiny, fanged animal chewing on her entrails.

Melanie had been in the middle of her third load of laundry, and her second sink full of dishes, when she had turned her attention to the recently acquired and much coveted Bracelet and the power had gone out. Having lived on Cape Cod for her entire life, she was accustomed to power outages and always had candles and flashlights at the ready. That the flashlight wouldn't work did not alarm her. That the matches would not light when struck, was merely interesting. That the phone had no dial tone was nothing to spend time considering. That the day had grown gray seemed startling, but not alarming. It had been the silence of her house which had made Melanie realize something was wrong.

"Kids," she said quietly, afraid of waking from this pleasant, noiseless, dream. She actually winced, expecting the maelstrom of requests and accusations that would pelt her as soon as the children realized that she was available. She had almost instinctively moved toward the pantry, knowing that hunger came first in the list of needs, boredom second. She waited for the feet to pound down the stairs from bedrooms or up the stairs from the basement. She waited and listened.

Nothing.

"Guys?" she called a bit louder. There were no sounds at all. No TV, no PlayStation, no iPhones plugged into speakers.

Nothing.

It would take some time, and some Time Between Time, before Melanie connected the *nothing* that she had experienced that day to the Bracelet. The nothing of senseless death, the nothing of fragile sanity, the nothing of Melanie's health—all were due to the glamorous and ubiquitous beads ringing a glittering metal of speculative origin.

But that revelation, as well as the day of *nothing*, reside in time past. The current time, the one that requires immediate examination, is of Melanie in a hospital gown, finding the table she sits upon to be unnecessarily cold. The specialist is seated on a stool and is looking at her x-rays with confusion, as if he were reading a menu in a foreign language. He is trying his best to project concern when he tells her she has inoperable cancer in her pancreas. He is trying his best to sound confident when he explains that he has never seen this particular strain of an already uncommon cancer before.

Melanie stares at his well-groomed moustache and seeks to project sympathy. She knows that what one sends out comes back threefold, and she could use some sympathy right now. She does feel badly for this doctor: his textbooks and mentors could only prepare him for so much. He has no concept of what could happen to bodies in other dimensions. He seems to want her to fill in the gaps, to provide some reason behind this diagnosis. Some reason other than that the world is simply an ugly place. When she had first seen her primary care physician and he had asked if there had been any changes in her life or in her daily regimen, she had answered "no." How could she have explained all that she had seen and experienced? What would have happened if she had tried to put the acquisition of the Bracelet into words? She could certainly describe how tempting it had been to buy or steal or win it. She could articulate this much better than she could estimate the location of her own cancer-riddled pancreas inside her body.

She tells the doctor she understands. She comprehends what

inoperable means and the impact it will have on her life. She tells the doctor she will fight the cancer because, as a mother, she has no other option.

The one thing she would not do is pray. That had gotten her nowhere in the past. All prayers had gotten her were phantom panties found floating amongst the suds in her washing machine, belonging to no one. People can lie about the ownership of underwear, but machines cannot. Just like the plastic cookie jar could not lie about the fact that it had been ransacked, even when Melanie dieted.

The panties had eaten away at her, appearing right after she received the Bracelet. There was nothing practical about the panties. They were red with white lace and a small white bow as if containing a present for some lucky man to unwrap. She knew they were not hers. The last time she had bought new underwear had been before Mathew was born and he was now in pre-school. Her husband had naturally denied knowing anything about the origin of the underwear. He'd become defensive, making her feel guilty having asked. That had led to excuses and explanations which finally led to her wearing the underwear. First, as a kind of triumph; later, she had nearly been able to convince herself that they belonged to her.

Now, as she sat panty-free on the examining table, contemplating the inoperable, she wished she could go back to a time when unfamiliar panties were her biggest problem. Almost immediately, she tried to eradicate the wish: she knew all too well what wishing begot.

A Month Before the Bracelet Party

There are no sounds to wake you by the water on Cape Cod. The houses are set far enough back on high dunes that the waves whisper meekly and with no effect. Any noise is muted by the continuous morning fog. And, when it rains, the curtain of silence grows thicker—from gossamer to velvet.

That was how the story wishes to begin: with the setting. Stories want to paint a place so that readers can feel situated. It is comforting to know where you are. That is why we have always loved maps. That is why we depend on GPS. That was how the story wanted to begin, but it needed to begin with the truth.

The truth is that Melanie lived at the bottom of the street of fortune: across the bridge, beside the marsh. The marsh is not like the ocean, and the house on the marsh where Melanie lived was constantly filled with noise.

Long before she visited Time Between Time, long before the doctor's office, Melanie had been the silicon packet that protects the precious jewelry that is her family. She was practical and made for use, while the others shone around her. She also secretly lamented that she was utterly discardable. She was known for being Graham— the real estate agent's—wife, and for being her children's mother. In fact, very few people called her Melanie. She was Mrs. Voss to teachers, pediatricians, coaches, and sticky-fingered play date companions. Her husband's old frat brothers even had the audacity to refer to her as "Mrs. Graham," relegating her to the role of appendage. She never feared death because her sense of identity was completely underdeveloped. It is impossible to die while those with whom you have a symbiotic relationship live. One cannot fear an expansive, empty abyss when one truly and simply craves a moment alone. Mostly, Melanie never feared death because she was so deathly tired.

It was Time Between Time that awakened her senses and reminded her of her happy childhood of summer memories and sweets. Even before Time Between Time, Melanie's back had been bent by loads of laundry and shopping orders and bedroom escapades meant to keep Graham interested and away from football on TV. Time had incredible meaning as it measured dryer cycles, naps, baking, and chauffeuring schedules to and from school and practices.

Melanie's time was not only devoured by her family. The women who resided on the street that stretched from the sea to the marsh often took a serving for themselves. If Melanie's children did not attend the same schools with these women's children, and if Graham did not occasionally go to the country club for a round of golf with the other husbands, Melanie would not find herself on the receiving end of invites to the ladies' luncheons and events. Melanie often felt that her presence was needed simply so there was someone to treat with open disdain, while their disdain for each other was more in the form of camouflaged backhandness. Recently, Melanie had been summoned to meet with some of these women at Michael's Pier—an exclusive sea-side bar and grille whose menu did not contain any children's items, and lunch selections could not be found under forty dollars.

Too early for cocktail attire, the women donned sequined blouses, slacks and four-to-six-inch heels. Melanie managed to shine the scuffs on a pair of Louboutins that were older than her youngest child and had been acquired through an estate sale.

Most attending the party had been recently tucked: eyes, chins, cheeks, and/or tummies. All except Melanie were wearing Tiffany or Chopard around their necks and false lashes on their eyes. Their lashes were transformed into mystifying tarantulas that nearly tapped their foreheads when they winked and batted them widely.

One of the most coiffed, most adorned, was the one who had called the meeting: Nashville DeCota.

Nash, as usual, was the last to arrive. She enjoyed making the others wait. She entered like a cat, sashaying between tall pub tables and bar stools, pausing to enjoy the view, as if the only time that mattered was hers.

Nash would not be so infuriating if she were not right; most of the women seated around the only large dining table in the establishment had nothing better to do than wait for her. Some were practically chomping at the bit for her to take a seat.

Which she finally did, plopping her large, Birkin "all business" bag on the table, without acknowledging anyone. She had once been asked how she could afford to treat the Birkin so casually to which she had surprisingly responded that it was uncouth to discuss financials. Everyone who knew Nash knew that her mind was running numbers even in her sleep and that those numbers felt no shame when they fell from her frosted lips into conversation.

Nash dug around, pulling out little baggies, then pushing them aside, apparently in search of some sunken treasure that had been swallowed by her leather tote. Some of the baggies contained pills or powder. Others contained Cheerios, pretzels, candies, and trail mix. Before she could stop herself, Melanie eyed the bag of M&Ms lustily and asked, "How do you stay so thin with all of those snacks around?"

Nash, lifting her head, offered a smile of superiority. "It is precisely because I have *so* much that I don't need to eat it. I suffer no anxiety about running out, about being hungry." She flipped her fiery red hair and returned to her tote.

A few of the other women murmured in agreement. Melanie secretly wished she were at liberty to order real food, but they had met for drinks only, and she was too insecure to eat before the scorning eyes of the other women with their exotic and demanding food regimens. Besides, she was unsure if her monthly budget could handle the pricey menu. She would do what she often did: drive off Cape where she and her car would not be recognized and luxuriate in a quick drive-thru run before rushing home.

Nash paused in the middle of her purse diving, as if struck by an epiphany. "We need to throw another party. A benefit. The school has called me for help. They usually do, seeing as how I can bring them the greatest… return on investment."

The other women nodded encouragingly.

"They want additional funds for the afterschool programs. I was thinking we could sponsor a sale. It's the perfect time; people are completely over the gifts from the holidays and are looking for the next big thing. Half of the money from the party can go to the Community Center. You know, for those who can't afford fancy camps or their own swimming pools." She, perhaps unintentionally, glanced at Melanie. "The rest goes to… cover the cost of the party, of course. Catering and what not—"

"—I have an idea," Jacqueline interrupted and was shot a nearly fatal glare from Nash. Jacqueline was the only one who gave Nash a run for her money—so much money. Jacqueline was infallible, off limits. Initially, she insisted that the others call her "ʒakleen" ("it's French," she sniffed) but they christened her the Porcelain Princess, or P.P. because she never had a spot or an imperfection. And she was so bloody cold.

Inexplicably—because she never approved of anything that did not self-originate—P.P. took a liking to the moniker, and it stuck. "Even though I doubt the school really wants another benefit so soon. I mean, they would have contacted me." She glared at Nash through the superfluous cat's eyeglasses she habitually donned. Very few of the women actually _needed_ anything: they purchased perfection in surplus. "There is a new protein shake. It comes in these cute foil packets. With different colors so you can coordinate with your wardrobe. The best part: you drink one shake, ladies, and you won't feel hungry for _days_."

Melanie was dying to ask if the packets were expensive but knew that question was social suicide.

The other women at the table, who will be introduced in good time (and Melanie knows all about the importance of time), appeared excited about the excuse to hold another party. There had been no charity events in over a month and they were growing restless and bored. They were not bored because they craved good deeds, but because they thrived on the competition the events brought into being. They competed over outfits and accessories and amounts of contributions. While the competition was far from admirable, it was much less dangerous than their boredom.

After deliberations and martinis, after plans had been laid and duties delegated, Nash shot the idea down, claiming that "shakes" were too pedestrian for their usual crowd, and that there was no way that she would invest an afternoon in the company of anyone who would drink from foil. Melanie remembered that Nash's children had never been allowed juice boxes or juice pouches. Their cadre of nannies had been required to master a juicer, a liquefier, and a strainer for their all organic, sugar-free drinks that were served in crystal with garnish.

Nash held up a glittering business card. "This is what I had been looking for." She laughed with faux embarrassment. "It was nowhere to be found at first, and I truly am sorry that I allowed you ladies to prattle on about... shakes... but here it is." She turned it away from the women and read it, as if discovering it anew, "Jewelry. Bracelets. And not just any bracelets. The man who makes these, well, he is a true artist."

"Is he from the Cape?" Someone asked. This was important information. Artists and entertainment needed to be homegrown. All other services were more valuable, more enviable, if they came from off-Cape—the closer to Boston or Providence, the better.

"Of course he is. He is the loveliest man and, I hate to admit, he seemed totally smitten with me. I am sure he would give us part of the profits for our cause." She winked. "I can be very persuasive."

The women began firing questions about the man and his exact origin. Nash was frustratingly vague. At times, it seemed as if she truly were stumped for an answer.

After another round of drinks, several of the women claimed

to have a sudden recollection of knowing the artist. Their intimacy with the master craftsmen grew as the sun began its early descent. As daylight disappeared, so did Melanie's dreams of French fries and fattening, non-foil shakes. She had no interest in winning the contest of fake connections to the Bracelet man and realized she would have no time to herself as her children would be done with after school activities soon.

While the others had nannies and maids to keep their children and homes in order, they wrapped up the meeting as most had other social appointments to attend. The final result: there would be a party. One of Nash's approval, and one that would threaten Melanie's life and sanity in unimaginable ways.

⌛

The Day After the Bracelet Party

Remember: there is no GPS down the rabbit's hole, or on the other side of the looking glass.

It was after Melanie picked up the kids at school that all hell broke loose. The fifteen-minute drive from school to home was an orchestral movement of complaints: mean teachers, bullies, unsympathetic friends, toxic school lunches, insurmountable mounds of homework, and sibling rivalry.

By the time Graham came home, it was out and out war, replete with hostages (toddler Chloe, one of the cats, and a wireless gaming headset). Graham entered the house; removed shoes, socks, and tie—all of which stayed where they fell; grabbed a handful of nuts and a chocolate-chip muffin and retreated to the asylum of the master bedroom. Melanie was tempted to yell "sanctuary" and high tail it after him but was not willing to sacrifice the structure of their home.

As she stirred the cheese into the macaroni, she wondered how Graham had perfected his invisibility act. Melanie secretly believed that it was easier for fathers to leave, to abandon. She had seen many men do it. They had moved onto second families with barely a thought for the first. She knew Graham would be capable of replacing them. His hours away at work, his weekends away at conferences, were all in preparation for some final escape.

A final punishment.

She didn't know how she knew this—call it intuition, call it reality—but she knew that her marriage would not last forever. Her aunts and uncles and cousins all had what she would classify as "solid marriages." Divorce was not believed in or practiced and the same was true for Graham's family. But she had the feeling—call it a premonition, call it "eyes wide open"—that she and Graham would break the cycle. That one day, Graham would leave and, after the fear subsided, she might be glad to see him go.

But what would that mean? Would she still live with the kids (and animals) in the house by the marsh? Would she have to fight Graham for the house? For custody? He rarely expressed interest in either, but his penchant for punishment made courtroom battles highly plausible. Would she have to work to support herself? Would she re-enter the dating world? She felt sick to her stomach at the thought. She had hated the game playing, the insecurities, and she had been so much younger then. She would hate to be dating at the same time as her older children. Her son, Skyler's love life didn't bother her so much—he seemed to have less to lose—but she felt a great deal of anxiety for her eldest daughter. Melanie dreaded the cars that would pull up to take Marjorie away for an evening. She always pictured them as demon-mobiles with flames shooting from the headlights, fetid smoke billowing around the tires. The driver, a pimply, horned incubus wanting to slide greasy fingers beneath her daughter's clothing. That world was definitely something which she, and her imagination, wished to avoid.

This from a woman who was well acquainted with what wishes wrought.

As she stirred noodles, her thoughts stirred conflict. Then, she remembered the laundry and ran to fetch it, swapping one load out for another dirty load, toiling as if in a race with the clock.

It was when she was in the middle of her third load of laundry (and her second sink of dishes) that Melanie saw the panties floating in the soapy water that refused to drain from the bottom of the conspiring machine. They were red, with white lace, and a small white bow. Later, many days after the Bracelet, she would convince herself that they belonged to her. For now, all she could do was turn them over in her hands, looking for clues, as if some careful mother had stitched the name of her child on the tag.

She began to feel even sicker. How had these panties found their way into her home? There was only one possible explanation, and while she had just been contemplating divorce, she was wholly unprepared for this unholy proof of infidelity. How dare that man bring adultery into her home? Didn't he have the decency to be disloyal in some shady motel? Anywhere but in her house on the marsh.

She felt angry and betrayed. He had brought a woman into her house. Into the house she scoured and scrubbed. Into the house where she wiped noses, checked homework, and made meals. Into the home she had fought so hard for when her husband had wanted something better, something different. And now she had this confirmation that he still wanted something better, something different. All her fears of Graham leaving solidified into a sour rage. Her fury brought hunger. Did she have any mallow bars tucked away? She had won Plasticware at one of Nash's parties; she knew she had stored some goodies in them.

She brought her dried laundry (including damp scarlet panties) into the kitchen and saw the box containing the Bracelet. It felt heavier than when she had brought it home; heavier and warm. There was a heat, a pulse that resided more in the air around it than within the closed box. As she opened it, the power in the house went out. She was accustomed to power outages, but not to the unearthly silence that had accompanied it.

"Kids?" she called, afraid of an answer that would slaughter this blissful silence. The quiet was both exasperating and soothing to her rage.

Nothing.

"Marjorie?... Sky?... Matt?" She waited for a litany of wants and desires, ranging from juice to taxi service, to converge in a storm front where the stairs to the separate floors of her house met.

Nothing.

Absently, she slipped on the Bracelet and reached for the always ready flashlight, which, stocked with fresh batteries, refused to shine. She then struck match after match to illuminate the candles that were scattered around her house, but there was no sulfur spark, no scratch, no flame.

Hunger forgotten, she folded laundry in the dark and called for her children again. There was nothing. No TV, no PlayStation, no iPhones synched to speakers—all explainable due to the lack of electricity, but where had her family gone? What had happened to all the commotion of the late afternoon and why weren't they complaining to her as if she were the cause of the outage? Had Graham taken them somewhere? Usually a blackout brought cries from Chloe, accompanied by wails from a few of the dogs. Even the animals appeared absent. Melanie continued to fold laundry because, even in a blackout, time waits for no one.

It was as she carried the overflowing laundry basket through the kitchen that she realized that the red LED light on the stove, and the matching one on the microwave, were blinking. No other power in the house, just those two mini clocks hearkening the same time over and over: 0:00.

"I wish such a thing existed," Melanie muttered, forgetting

the dangers of wishes. "Zero time. Forever and ever."

The two clocks continued to blink. Together, they sent a hellish pattern, drenching the vicinity in blood-red, followed by empty black.

<Blink>

Red

<Blink>

Black.

Melanie became mesmerized by the lights and by the concept of zero hour. She imagined the dripping clocks painted by Salvador Dali and somehow this image felt right. In the darkening, empty house, time was melting away. It was what she always wished time to be: inconsequential.

The kitchen faucet chirped in unison, creating a soundtrack for the impromptu laser show.

<Blink>

Why was the kitchen the only room with power? In the empty, dark house, this space felt alive. It felt electric in defiance of the power outage.

<Drip>: a silver thread, knotting from the nozzle to the drain.

<Blink>

Only on one side of the kitchen? In the blackness that erased the scarlet panties, relegating them to the status of phantoms that could be spirited away…

<Drip>

Only where the stove and microwave are?

<Blink>

And the deadly silence? It was as if the world's mute button had been activated.

<Drip>

Melanie felt anxious.

<Blink>

The air stirred around her, funneling like a tornado.

<Drip>

Melanie felt a rush of vertigo and the kitchen moved far away.

<Blink>

It was between the drips in the blackness that Melanie was able to escape.

The Day of the Bracelet Party

On the day of the Bracelet party, Melanie stuck to her usual routine. She tried to catch up on all the baskets of laundry that either waited to be cleaned, or sorted, or put away. She drove to the grocery store where her youngest saddled-up in the cart. It was an overcast day with a great deal of electricity in the air. Melanie had forgotten to brush her stick straight brown hair and it whirled around her, taking on a life of carefree flying that she envied. It was a day when Melanie could not help but feel that something was going to happen. She welcomed something, whether good or bad, just for the uniqueness of something.

Once in the store, Melanie consulted the list in one hand while steering the cart with the other. The broken laces in one of her Keds, gnawed to uselessness by one of her dogs, slapped the floor and threatened to get caught in the cart's wheel. She was so engrossed in the list and the cart and the shoelace that she nearly ran over her son's basketball coach, who was equally engrossed in the caloric content of anisette cookies.

"Oh! So sorry," Melanie spat out as she swerved and missed his heel by a fraction of a fraction of an inch. Her proximity permitted her to enjoy a waft of his cologne, making her wonder who would put on cologne to go to the grocery store. This then led her to remember that she had neglected to brush her hair or put on any makeup before leaving the house. She was wearing an old gray sweatshirt that bore a lacrosse print, even though she had never played, and competing stains. The spaghetti sauce stain seemed to be winning in terms of its brilliance.

The man tore himself from the nutritional facts label and smiled at her with recognition. "No problem. I should really watch where I stand… Melanie." He looked as if he were going to turn back to the shelf but changed his mind. "Sky's been really working hard this season."

"Oh, sure," she lied. The last time she had seen Skylar move for something round was when he was diving into a bag of Oreos. She hadn't realized how young the coach looked: she had only ever seen him from across the basketball court. Up close, he appeared vibrant and handsome, and his cologne—a dusky, sexy scent—suited him.

"His game really improved last year." It was the coach's turn to lie, and Melanie wondered why two adults were wasting time spinning webs about an adolescent's athletic prowess, or lack thereof.

Her curiosity was satisfied when he smiled, and it was her turn to recognize him—as more than her son's coach. "I never put it together, I am so sorry." She blushed in a way that she hadn't in a long time. "I mean, Sky just always refers to you as 'Coach' and I can be horrible with names, especially last names… and I think I have had pregnancy brain for the last seventeen years…" She was rambling and she knew she was rambling, but she could not stop herself.

He laughed. "Not stupid. I was a lot younger than you; there's no reason for you to have remembered me."

She felt herself blush again. "H-How is Dash?" Silently, she cursed her nervous stutter.

"There it is. That's what they always want to know, how the former prince of the Cape is doing. He's fine. Really." He leaned against a shelf of instant noodle packets and smiled again. "Big business guy, big home, big cars, big everything."

Melanie found herself growing warm. In high school she had desperately wanted to know about the equipment that Dash Royce was carrying, but he had been a few years older than she, so they had little opportunity to interact. She remembered his younger brother Don as being very hyperactive and fun, but not even close to containing the charm of Dash. It now seems he had caught up in the charm department. Or was it simply that she was thrilled that another human being had remembered her name and thought of her as someone besides "Mrs. Graham?" Why hadn't she bothered to brush her hair before leaving the house? Or at least thrown a decent looking jacket over her ratty sweatshirt? Why couldn't she be more confident, like the horrible Porcelain Princess or Nash? She tried to invoke the positive qualities of her frenemies. As she smiled and struggled to think of something compelling to say that would extend the conversation, the fluorescent lights in the supermarket flashed twice, the second flash resulting in a lengthy stretch of darkness.

"Uh-oh," Chloe gasped from the carriage, and Melanie was reminded of her motherly duties. She took the girl's chubby hand and whispered, "It's ok…"

"Great." Don glanced at the low-level emergency lights. "I wonder if the registers will be working now." He glanced at his watch and Melanie realized that she, for once, had not been concerned with the time. "I need to hightail it back to the school—"

Many shoppers began moving toward the check-out, trying to beat the storm home. Cape Codders are accustomed to sudden blackouts and storms, and when threatened with either, the natural instinct is to shift into an ego-centric survival mode.

"It will be slow going," Melanie concurred. There was an awkward stretch where neither moved nor spoke. There was a part of Melanie that wanted this blackout to linger. It was the same part of her that wanted to continue in Don's company. For what purpose, she asked herself, and why couldn't she think of anything to say? They had grown up just a few houses apart. Should she ask about his mother? Her mind raced to recall if Mrs. Royce had been the main subject of an obituary in the local paper. What could she and Don have in common? The return of the lights offered a reprieve. "Oh, shoot. I had been planning to use the power outage as an excuse to order out." Melanie grabbed a can from Chloe's hand before the toddler could throw it to the ground.

"Have you tried that new place... across from the old church?" When Melanie met his eyes, he glanced down at his feet, "That might be a place to try for take-out." He rubbed the back of his neck nervously and looked at the noodles that were stationed at cye level.

"I'll try anything that frees me from cooking. I don't think I've had a break since Mother's Day." She returned her attention to her failing shoelace. "And even then it was only an hour break for lunch."

He smiled conspiratorially. "My birthday passed with my mowing the lawn and practicing minor car repairs."

"Eww." She made a face. "I am not big on grease under the nails."

They both glanced at Don's hands which were clean and well kept. "It all washes off eventually." He shrugged.

"Tell that to the stains on my carpeting," Melanie countered. Again, she was baffled by the excitement generated by this exchange of the mundane. The topic was completely dull, yet neither seemed in a rush to end the conversation. It was the first time in a long time that she was not in a rush.

Don broke eye contact to look at his watch again, pushing a button in order to shed light on its face. His face looked suddenly serious, as he consulted the numbers measuring the time. "Don't you wish you could get one free day? One day out of the millions that count?"

Melanie stared at Don, surprised that men felt that way too. He became embarrassed by his sudden confession and the store lights mercifully dimmed again.

"Yeah." Her voice had dropped but she knew he could hear her. "That is exactly what I would like. One day extra, nothing piles up, nothing counts."

"And nothing you do that day matters, because it's like the day doesn't exist… it's off the record."

How did he know that that was what she wanted more than anything? That that was what she wished for even when she knew that wishing led to disappointment.

"I'd love to catch up... about the old neighborhood... Maybe sometime... I don't know... did you want to go get a cup—?" He was interrupted by a loud groaning sound that seemed to emanate from the back of the store. Melanie was about to prod him into continuing his invite when the store began to shake as if it were attempting to stand on two drunken legs.

A woman from the next aisle over began to yell loudly, "What is that? Were we hit?" and a cashier got down on her hands and knees and covered her head with her arms. Melanie clutched the cart tightly, attempting to keep Chloe still. She slid closer to Don, who put a protective hand on her shoulder.

"Earthquake?" she asked, even though they were unusual on the East Coast. He replied that he was not sure.

The store became still again, but Chloe had started a keening wail. Don told Melanie that she had better get home before the storm got worse. Melanie, always obedient, agreed, deserting her groceries, and bundling Chloe in the car so that she could pick up the school-aged children before heading home.

While Melanie chauffeured, she remembered a story (sparked by thoughts of Dash Royce) that had kept her awake at night when she had been in the fourth grade.

Melanie's bus had always dropped her off on the short concrete bridge that bolstered the highway. The bridge covered the marsh lands that ran between the ocean and its tributaries. The marshes were a thing of beauty to Melanie. In the summer, they were a dried brown, with long clay walls that appeared crunchy-soft, like a properly toasted marshmallow. In the fall, they were wild and green, like long shoots of peppermint flavored licorice. In the winter, they had a short trim of snow-like frosting, and in the spring, they yellowed like a lemon Italian ice. She often dreamed of exploring the marshes when she was older, of building a house right on their banks, of somehow owning the marsh and letting it own her. She was truly happiest on the marsh. Her classmates loved the ocean and the promise of sandcastles, waves, and ice cream from the snack bar. Melanie was always the odd one out, preferring the stiff mud, the slashing reeds, the scuttling crabs, and fishy smell of the marsh.

She was often late walking home, as she found ways to get closer to her beloved marsh. In the warm weather, she would remove her uniform socks, tuck them into the band of her plaid skirt, and walk through the shallows, scooping the occasional empty crab shell, searching for minnows and tadpoles. When it was cold, she would toss fallen leaves, sticks, and pinecones onto the water, charting the ripples. And if there were ice… if there were ice it was the best time to test how close to the center, or the heart, she could get. The center was a place removed from the world, where the noise of the highway failed, where no one could reach her and make her go home. She often dreamed of winding her way through the marsh's maze and finding a hidden castle, or a type of Atlantis, at its core.

One day, while arriving home late, she saw a police car parked in front of a neighbor's house. Some of her neighbors stood on the adjacent sidewalk murmuring stuffed words from the backs of their throats. Melanie scanned the group of adults until she found her father.

As she approached, he grabbed her by the arm and reprimanded her for being late: "You are to come home directly from school. Do you understand me? You cannot go on worrying me every day."

Worrying? Had she been worrying her father by taking her time coming home? She never wanted to be disobedient, but she had a difficult time seeing the marsh, and the time spent there, as *bad*. She remembered another little girl who had been told not to dally, not to leave the chosen path, not to talk to the wolves that she might meet. But that had been a forest, peered at from beneath a red cloak, not a mesmerizing marsh, singing its siren song to foggy bus windows.

Richard "Dash" Royce, the target of piercing crushes of all women ages three to sixty-three, had found his way to the group of gossipers as well. Even though he was only in junior high school, he was already tall and broad shouldered and showing signs of manhood. He pushed his way over toward Melanie.

"What happened?" Melanie asked in a breathy way that she would later learn to wield and control.

"I heard that Kaila never came home last night," Dash answered solemnly.

Kaila Johnson was a pretty high school junior who had babysat Melanie only a few years before, on the occasions when Melanie's father had to work late.

"What happened?" Melanie repeated dumbly. She couldn't understand what all of this meant.

"She just never came home." Dash's patience was just one of his endearing qualities. That, coupled with his green eyes and stunning smile that was framed by dimples. "No one knows, but…"

She leaned in because his voice had dropped. She realized that he smelled better than the boys in her grade. "But what?"

"I think it was the Marsh People."

Melanie, who believed she knew her beloved marsh intimately, was surprised at this new revelation, and a bit hurt by this imaginary betrayal.

Dash painted a quick picture: The Marsh People could be either male or female, sometimes they were found nude, especially when the tide was high. Other times they were seen in long, watery robes. From a distance, they were very attractive, especially their bodies. It wasn't until one caught you in its hook-like nails that you saw the mouth, the terrible mouth like a steel-trap that contained bits of flesh and gristle. Their eyes were fish eyes, large and glassy; and their tongues were like one long thick leech that would suck you in if it could grab you. And the smell: the marsh naturally smelled of its floating inhabitants' decay, but the smell of one of their mouths, this was the most putrid scent on earth. Even for an older boy like Dash, it was indescribable.

"If they, you know, the *Marsh People*," she superstitiously whispered their name, "If they got her, wha-what would they—"

"We won't find her," he interrupted, "Remember how Dawgie went missing?"

She did remember. The Royce's retriever had last been seen chasing crabs along the marsh. She shivered as her mind traced the fate of the lovable dog. Melanie had wondered how the Marsh People did it; did they drown their victims or use their horrible mouths?

There was a bend in the marsh where a narrow stream ran and hid inside a long copse of trees. No one ever went back into that forested area, not even teenagers seeking privacy. The water that ran back there was a deep black and it never drained. The tide in that little, hidden part, ebbed from high to higher. That was where the Marsh People lived, and others met their end.

Despite these rumored dangers, or maybe because of them, Melanie had managed to convince her husband to buy the smallest fixer-upper there was on the canal that bordered the marsh. She was on the other side of the cement bridge, but it was the property closest to the marsh. Nash lived closest to the ocean on the canal and furthest from the marsh. The value of the homes, and their inhabitants, were easily identified by nearness to the ocean and distance from the marsh.

Melanie's thoughts were snatched from the past and returned to her drive home when a figure appeared in the middle of a road near her neighborhood. The storm was successfully forcing people inside, and her van felt like a tomb—encased in the smell of wet children and filled with flying papers and wrappers that were escaping from backpacks. Her oldest, Marjorie, had just begun the 3:15 ritual of asking what was for supper and then waging a war against the answer, even if the reply was the young woman's favorite meal. It was while Marjorie was compiling her arsenal that the figure stepped into the middle of the road.

Melanie stomped on the brakes hard, and the sudden cessation of movement quieted the children.

The figure remained in place, obscured by a long gray coat that was the same color as the rainy sky. She could make out an eerily familiar face on the person but could not place where she had seen it before. While the car idled, the figure raised a hand and swept a pointed finger at the passengers, one at a time, as if it had a perfect view of the interior, even though the windows were darkened. The finger paused on Melanie, separating her from the group, its talon-ed end seeking access to her, singling her out.

It was Skylar who broke the silence. He looked confused and asked his mother, "Why did you do that?"

The figure continued to point. A breeze from the storm rustled its long coat so that a taut, naked body was exposed. With the aid of her headlights, Melanie could see that the figure's skin was crawling, covered with crabs and minnows and other creatures from the marsh, but it was mostly ensconced with leeches. There was also an appendage on the creature that tugged at a memory she had worked hard to repress: the figure had a serrated tail.

Melanie turned her face away from the road and looked at her son. "...I didn't want... I couldn't run over that... that p-person, could I?"

Skylar leaned forward and squinted into the raging rain. "What person?"

When Melanie turned and pointed, mimicking the figure's earlier gesture, she saw that it was gone. "I... thought I saw... it must have been the storm, playing tricks on my eyes." Her head suddenly felt very heavy, and she rested it against the steering wheel while the icy rain's weighty onslaught pounded the windshield. "I am just so tired."

Marjorie's tune had changed. "Do you want me to drive home, Mom? I have my license with me...?"

"No, honey. I can make it, but thanks for the offer."

Melanie knew that fatigue could do funny things, it could even make you hallucinate. That must be what had happened on the road. She was just too damned tired.

They were so close to home that she forced herself to lift her head and drive the remaining distance, thinking all the while of the Marsh People who, years before, had taken a neighborhood girl and plunged her into the murky depths near Melanie's house.

While they had terrorized her sleep as a child, it was later, during the days after the Bracelet party, that the Marsh People, and others, significantly horrified Melanie.

Days After the Bracelet Party

Melanie's visits to Time Between Time cry out to be recorded. Time Between Time was a blank cocoon: a padded white room. While there, the blood crashed around inside Melanie's head, making the sound that the "ocean" makes when trapped inside of a large conch shell. All it took was to set the kitchen appliance clocks to 0:00, while wearing the Bracelet, and she could be transported to this transcendent place.

Her first visit, on the day after the Bracelet party, had been frightening. One moment she had been in her kitchen, fuming over glamorous panties and unglamorous chores. The next, she had been somewhere else: a place with no landmarks, no structures, nothing at all. How quickly her fear had evaporated. She thought that perhaps she had suffered a stroke and that this was her mind's way of leaving consciousness. Only she felt very much "herself," very cognizant of the issues that were waiting in her kitchen. She found that the more she remembered her problems—the more she allowed her anger to return—the less substantial her footing felt. When she let go, the blankness around her solidified, protecting and supporting her, cradling her with a comfort she was not sure she had ever felt before.

It took several trips and some internal exploration before she began to trust Time Between Time. Instead of being an explorer, she was a sovereign being in this place. She began to develop the ability to manipulate her trips to match her desires.

She suspected that Time Between Time had expansive properties. It seemed to grow and spread, like the universe grew and spread. What she didn't know was whether it would reach a breaking point. Would the space fall in on itself? Would it burst? Why was it snug at times and at other times freeing? What was it made of?

She found herself in a white smog like the kind that routinely obscures the canal and the marsh, only this whiteness did not have a salty smell. It had no properties of odor at all. It was like a blank screen.

But Time Between Time was not still. It was soft like a mattress and vibrating. Graham had once paid for a spa treatment for Melanie after Marjorie was born, but before Skylar had been welcomed on this earth, and the massage she had been treated to then could not compare to the feeling this blank space was giving her. Her flesh tingled and felt alive. Her entire being was alive in ways she had never experienced before. The feeling was overwhelmingly powerful. She could touch the impossible. She felt both invisible and invincible.

Mostly, there was no hunger in Time Between Time. It was the first time that Melanie could remember when she wasn't planning a meal, shopping for food items, snacking, grazing, eating, or denying herself sustenance. She could no longer calculate time via her hunger. Melanie had always had a finely tuned inner clock: she never needed to set an alarm to awaken, or a cooking timer to know when a casserole or lasagna was done. *Here*, wherever here was, had an entirely different rhythm and it wreaked havoc on her punctual mind mechanisms. The limited visibility of the place slowly dissipated, but her senses remained blanketed, warm and snug beneath a protective psychic quilt.

She believed that her energy allowed for the sensory deprivation to dissipate when she was ready to slowly return to life. In these instances of being in an in-between, when the fog cleared, she was able to see her house on the marsh, as if viewing it on a television screen. From her vantage point, she felt no connection to the home; it was like watching the movie of a stranger's life. She was able to shift her focus, to zoom in and out and satisfy her curiosity. For instance, if she saw that someone had left the cap off the toothpaste in one of the bathrooms and that the sticky green gel had taken up residence amongst the grout between the mosaic on the sink, she could ignore it. In Time Between Time, she could leave spills where they lay. How often had she wished she could live in the present and ignore the past and future? Once, she had visited a spiritual mentor who had suggested meditation and yoga. Who knew that a bracelet would provide the solution?

If Melanie shifted her attention to the yard, no swans or animals would be visible. In her first visit, she turned to the porch and saw an airplane flying overhead, leaving twin plumes of exhaust. It did not move in the sky, but stayed flickering, like a cursor on a screen, waiting for words and inspiration. "Waiting to be filled up," Melanie breathed and realized that that was exactly what she had been waiting for. Like the clear beads on her Bracelet, she was transparent: without babies inside of her, and children to need her, she was afraid she was nothing. She had always thought she had wished for more time when she had actually been terrified of the prospect of having to fill time on her own. In her world, time had stretched onward, like an old, dirty carpet. She could clean and patch it endlessly; it would remain shabby. In Time Between Time, the limitlessness of the future offered hope. Having a space to catch up, to plan out possibilities, to perhaps get a step ahead in the game: this was sublime.

During that first visit, she thought she could see movement in her house, but the fog closed in again and pushed any worry from her mind. She decided she wanted to nap. She wanted to forget about everything, so she closed her eyes. From time to time, her eyes reopened, but she was still tired, so she drifted off again. It was only when she was completely caught up on her sleep that she was transported back to her kitchen. It felt as if a great deal of time had passed, but Melanie soon found out that her disappearance had been of little consequence and had not been noted on the clock at all.

What was noted was a frustrated P.P. foraging through Melanie's kitchen. The woman looked perfect: her hair was twisted into a stylish chignon, she wore an expensive suit and heels, and her glasses were properly placed at equidistance from the end of her nose and its bridge. She looked perfect, for a trespasser.

This appearance of P.P. finally gave Melanie the upper hand. P.P. had a way of continuously and publicly pointing out Melanie's shortcomings. The perfect example of this would be the dialogue from P. P.'s tea party, hosted only a few months before the appearance of the Bracelet. The occasion of the tea party had been the new tennis court that was to be put into the elementary school playground the following spring. The women were not raising money for the tennis court, nor aiding in its construction, but the party would set the collaboration in motion that would ensure that they had a vast amount of input into its design and use.

Most of the women residing on the street from the sea to the marsh attended. There was friend Gwynnie who collected children as one would collect marbles or trinkets or Plasticware or bracelets. She had managed to adopt many children, more than anyone could bother to count. They were all purposefully ethnic looking, so the world would realize that they were adopted and that Gwynnie was a "giver."

That was the common denominator for most of the women in Melanie's circle: they did not do anything unless it was for display. They were like the bracelets they would learn to covet (and kill or die for): completely decorative. Charity works were rarely charitable, but more like public pats-on-the-back. Marriages were arranged with holiday photos in mind, and children came with press kits.

While P.P. tried to strong-arm all events, as well as the people involved, Gwynnie was much more passive-aggressive. Small in stature, she would fly under the radar during planning sessions. Then, during the actual party, ball, tournament, or auction, she would voice her "concerns" over decisions that had been etched in stone months prior. She would look up at her audience (she always had to look up, even in six-inch heels) with doe eyes and claim to have been railroaded into participating in a failure of a venture. Anything that went wrong could not be pinned on her; she had had the foresight bubbling silently in a brain that was covered with perfectly frosted hair. Doubts were always percolating behind brown eyes, but never articulated. When anyone, especially P.P., would confront Gwynnie about why she did not forewarn the ladies of impending social doom, she would claim that she was so busy with her children, that she *thought* she had said something, and by the time she realized she hadn't, it was too late.

Also in attendance was Fiona, who was nicknamed Wi Fi for her ability to broadcast gossip via any number of hotspots. She had four children with husband number one. Husband number two brought four of his own into the marriage. Together, they had twins. By all counts, they had Melanie beaten by a few, depending on how Melanie was counting her own brood, and they were putting the squeeze on Gwynnie. Large families were worn like a badge of courage, even when women like Wi Fi had enough nannies to assure that she never had to wipe a runny nose or smelly rear.

Wi Fi had been forced to endure an emergency hysterectomy around the time that Melanie had been pregnant with Chloe. That had caused a spiral of depression for Wi Fi, followed by a period of complete dementia. For example, she had stolen Melanie's travel-sized breast pump, even though Wi Fi had not breast fed in years. Everyone was aware she had done it, but no one could produce evidence, and Melanie was far too meek to confront the woman. The pump had been a gift from a baby shower and Melanie had been unable to convince her husband to allow her to replace it. The loss had made her days more difficult and had forced her to remain closer to home. Melanie was sure it was only her imagination, but Wi Fi had seemed smug with delight each time they had met following pump-gate.

Melanie was still young enough to have a few more children if she wished. While wishing was no good, she did miss being pregnant. More than that, she missed nursing. She missed the intoxicating pull on her breasts and the sugary smell of the babies' heads as they drank her milk. She missed the rush of it. She wondered if the shifting hormones of producing and nursing children had been her drug of choice.

She also wondered why she appeared to wear the largest dress size in the group. All the women wore the same cookie cutter shape: large breasts, flat stomach, dainty in the hips, twig legs. Melanie knew for a fact that P.P. was low-to-no carbs. Wi Fi was rumored to subsist on the glue from her children's art set, and nothing more. Had the others had surgery, or cleansings, or eating disorders? Or, as in the case of finances, was Melanie cursed compared to her peers?

Once the women had taken their seats, the Porcelain Princess had nodded toward the tea set, asking, "Melanie, would you *pour?*" She intentionally dragged out the final word which hung on her plum lipstick so that everyone at the party could read the homonym: poor.

This was met with a snicker from an unidentified source, and Melanie blushed and ducked her head into her cowl-necked sweater, reaching for the daisy painted tea pot, and distributing the steaming liquid. She knew that she hadn't been invited to proffer ideas about the tennis court. She had been asked to the party for gratis servitude. She knew she would be expected to help clean up after, along with P. P's live-in maid and the others who had been hired to guarantee an afternoon of perfection. Melanie would then be offered leftovers and scraps to share with her troops at home, as a final slap in the face.

The Princess had begun a well-rehearsed speech about the importance of physical activity for their children. She also mentioned that tennis scholarships usually go untouched, offering an incentive for some parents to encourage their children to take up the sport. She conspicuously addressed this latter information in Melanie's direction.

But the Princess had underestimated Melanie. While P.P. tried to lead the conversation, Melanie would interrupt, offering guests napkins and suggesting honey or milk for their tea. While P.P. would try to wax dramatic with a show of fluttering hands and lashes, Melanie would lean over yet another woman's shoulder, refilling the tea saucer and blocking the view of P.P.'s theatrics. P.P. was barely able to finish a sentence, and the death ray glances she shot at Melanie from above her superfluous glasses confirmed that Melanie's assault had been on target.

It was after the teacups had been drained, and the tennis court plans fully violated, that P.P. loudly asked Wi Fi to accompany her on a weekend trip to Vegas. All conversation stopped while the women waited for the outcome of this glamorous invitation. Wi Fi nodded demurely and suggested that they make a group affair of it. She turned to Melanie first, smiling genuinely, her face full of friendship. P.P, still hurting from the intrusion on her tennis lecture, seized the opportunity for a volley: "She can't get away..." She simultaneously raised her eyebrows while lowering her voice to a conspiratorial stage whisper. "She can't afford it."

This had certainly not been the first occasion during which P.P. had taken a jab at Melanie's smallish bank account and tiny house on the edge of the marsh. One time, when the school had been having a white elephant sale, P.P. had made sure to tell Melanie, loudly and proudly, to donate only whatever she could truly spare. No other mother had been treated to that kindness. Melanie had made sure to make several high-end donations, hiding the purchases from Graham and slipping the receipts to their accountant in a battered envelope bearing the name *Gifts to Charity*. She had found herself smirking as she had passed the "gently worn" tables, feeling superior and hating the joy that feeling bought.

Despite these memories taking up prime real estate in her mind, she did not lose her cool at the sight of P.P. in her house; she merely asked what the woman wanted.

P.P clutched at her chest, looking alarmed and very confused. Her third finger was clad with an engagement ring, a wedding band, and a diamond encrusted ten-year anniversary band. All the women, except Melanie, collected similar be-gemmed tokens as if they were merit badges and, in some cases, they were arduously earned.

"Melanie? I… what happened?" P.P. looked about with genuine surprise—and a little disgust at where her feet had landed. "I… how did I get here?"

"I don't know, Princess." Melanie decided the safest bet was to go along with the ruse. "I just got back… from errands and found you here. Do you want to sit down for a minute?"

P.P. pushed past Melanie and walked toward her living room. Melanie realized that the laundry was still spread across the couch, folded and in piles, but in plain view. She quickly directed P.P. to the dining room which she knew to be clean and toy-free. The woman sat on an embroidered side chair and raised a hand to her forehead. "Don't freak on me, love. I hope I didn't startle you. It's just… I have been doing a cleanse and it can make one disoriented. I don't think you've ever done one, but cleanses are particularly rigorous."

"I can imagine." Melanie snorted, then remembered the rule about the energy one sends out. As she looked at P.P., she noticed a small blood stain on the woman's blouse. "You're bleeding."

Melanie watched as P.P. quickly unbuttoned her blouse, revealing a leech. It was thick and black and fully erect, engorged on blood, yet it continued to suck, blood spilling from around its suctioning jaws. Seeing the leech suckle, Melanie discarded any remaining breast-feeding desires. P.P. reached into her purse, removed a vial of eucalyptus oil, and applied it to the leech. This caused the leech to unhinge from her chest and fall to the floor. From where Melanie stood, the leech appeared to have a jaw like a small trap, like the jaws of the Marsh People. She looked at P.P. with horror.

"Don't freak on me, love. Angelina Jolie uses leeches all the time. Many actresses do. It detoxifies."

"Y-you p-put that thing on yourself?"

"I didn't say that. I just said not to freak. Just toss it into your little marsh or have one of your hundreds of kids do it." P.P. was standing and refastening her shirt as if nothing out of the ordinary had happened.

"Should I get you to a doctor?"

"Oh, God. I said, not to freak. I have my own private doctor; I will speak to him when I get around to it. You know I don't see anyone on the Cape!" P.P. stood and glanced into a mirror above an antique wash basin that Melanie used as decoration in her hallway. She smacked her lips together, refreshing her lipstick, and tucked a stray strand of hair back into her chignon.

"I will be fine. Of course I will." P.P. smiled icily. "Sorry for any bother."

P.P. made as if she were going to leave and then stopped suddenly, placing her raised index finger to her lips. "Now I remember." She tapped her head in what she must have thought was a cute show of forgetfulness. "I came here, Melanie, for a very good reason. You see… it's funny, really… and also sad, really." She sighed dramatically.

"What is it, P.P.?"

"I had… how can I even say it? I had promised the *exact* Bracelet you won to Gwynnie's oldest African daughter."

Melanie frowned. "Gwynnie's oldest daughter is from India."

"Yes, I know. Of course I know, I am much closer to her than you are. I meant the oldest one that is from Africa. There are several from Africa."

Melanie knew she was being presented with a pointed distraction. "How could you have promised her my Bracelet?"

P.P. shrugged. "Nash had provided me with a catalogue."

Melanie shook her head. "But the man said that it was one of a kind and not shown before."

"Melanie, if you want to disappoint a little girl, then go right ahead. I simply thought that you, of all people, with your maternal instincts—I mean, you practically lactate at pictures of babies—I thought you would understand."

If the Bracelet had not been connected to Time Between Time, Melanie would have relented. Because it was magical, she refused. "No, P.P. I am sorry, but I promised it to *my* daughter."

She would later regret those words.

The Bracelet Party

The party itself, its setup and overt agenda, was not unusual in the women's neighborhood. They often invited product representatives to demonstrate the latest and greatest in conveniences. Sometimes these speakers were parents from the school—the mothers who had to earn and could not afford to live anywhere near the sea.

These parties were a ritual. Everyone vied to arrive with the newest bag, the most fashionable shoes, the latest 'do, the thinnest waist. Everyone prepared stories of their husbands' and children's successes. They purchased more of what they didn't need or registered for classes they had no intention of attending. Then they would return home and silently hate each other until the next party.

But this one would be different.

This party would introduce the next big thing. They'd done cigar bars and yoga, mommy and me scuba lessons, CBD, and adultery. Each fad dropped swiftly, each waning from hot to cold like everything else in their lives. It was difficult to sustain a healthy passion for anything.

Except for their competition with each other.

But this jewelry party would be different. The bracelets were beautiful, affordable, yet priceless. Something to collect. The mommy version of trading cards. The bracelets were crafted of special metal and contained beads in every shade and hue of red, pink, or purple imaginable. Each unique, each a treasure.

Nash greeted her guests and seated them in the cleared-out room beside her sunroom. The overall affect was of one large room, rivaling any ball room found in any palace anywhere in the world. Premium lighting created an optimum ocular setting to display the prisms of the bracelets. All the women wore silk and sequins, except for Melanie who wore a green-ribbed turtle-neck sweater accompanied by a brown suede skirt and matching boots. She was appropriately dressed for the weather, but not for the event.

"Not even last year's outfit," sniffed Wi Fi to Gwynnie, as the former tugged at the straps of her heels to reduce dreaded swelling.

Gwynnie loudly interjected, as she scanned the room, "It *is* nearly impossible to keep these older style windows clean." Wi Fi snickered, seeming to agree that it *would* be more fun to take Nash down a few notches. Melanie knew that she provided no challenge to the women; with her clothes and shabby house, she practically invited others to take swipes at her.

"Ladies." Nash held up her palms, as if warding off something besides the painted, manicured, and jeweled women before her. Her hair was in yet another tight bun, tighter than her lifted and treated face. "Ladies, I want to thank you all for coming." She smiled at the room, the decency of her smile raining down on her guests, "I am always so… comforted… when we have our little get-togethers." She emphasized the word *little* with a wink. "While in the past we have attended community building benefits, this soiree intends to benefit us all, personally." She looked around the room, imitating a friendly admiration of her guests, mocking genuine care. "Please make sure that you have enough to eat. And let's begin." After clapping her hands together, her front door blew open and a man could be seen at the threshold, pushing a dolly loaded down with boxes upon boxes of jewelry. A silence followed the man into the room. Each woman had an expression on her face as if she had seen him before. Some had. His was the face of the figure blocking Melanie's road. His was also the face she had repressed from an event years before. His was a face that could launch a thousand ships and Melanie sensed that the women all felt it. They leaned in, as if they wanted to touch him. Whatever he was selling, they were buying.

The man began to speak to the rapt audience. He told them that he had something just for them. His pitch was simple: he promised them ownership and independence. They were free to sell the bracelets themselves—and to keep whatever fortunes they made. And they wouldn't have to tell their husbands, they could keep the bracelets hidden.

It would be a secret.

Better if it were a secret.

But no one wanted to sell. They only wanted to consume.

"What I recommend… my best advice to you, ladies, is tonight you treat yourselves. This jewelry makes anything possible." A collective breath was taken, each woman seeming to enjoy the tantalizing scent of the man. Melanie later learned that as the man spoke of possibilities, the women imagined themselves in his embrace, on his bed. Some of the party guests imagined doing things that they never dared to suggest to their husbands.

"Ladies, for one of you, tonight will be extra special and filled with luck." His eyes flickered, like a candle, entrancing those in the room. He turned his back to them and bent over the dolly. When he stood, he held a jewelry box in his hands. The box glowed in the light of Nash's chandelier.

"We are going to play a game to see who wins this exquisite Bracelet." He popped open the lid to display a glistening cluster of beads. The women let out a sigh of contentment—they loved being judged against each other.

The man handed out slips of paper: each a different shade. Melanie noticed that hers matched the beads on the Bracelet. He then asked them to write down their biggest wish. "I am like a genie," he said with great charm, "One wish will win!"

"What if we all wish for the Bracelet?" Gwynnie asked, lips pursed.

The man's face darkened. "That's not very original, is it?"

With that admonition, the women quieted and began to write. Melanie did not have to stop and consider her answer—she wanted more time. It is what she had always wished for: more time for herself, more time to indulge. She noticed P.P. whispering to the man. The Porcelain Princess leaned over him, her breasts pressing against him, and slid her paper into his hand. She let her hand linger inside of his for a moment before he pulled away. Melanie had witnessed this exhibit before. P.P. always won.

The man collected the papers, glancing at them briefly before placing them into a bowl. Without looking, reached his hand into the pile to grab one. Melanie saw right away that it was hers.

Shortly after the presentation of her Bracelet, the party disbanded, mostly because P.P. was in a funk over not winning. She also refused to extend Melanie's moment in the spotlight. As Melanie turned to leave, thrilled that she had been selected and finally had something to laud over the others, she looked back toward Nash's festive room. P.P. had her hand on the man's shoulder, flirting dramatically, while he offered her a tight-lipped smile and repacked his wares. As he bent, his pant leg lifted, Melanie could swear that she saw a spiked tail peeking from beneath the perfectly hemmed slacks.

⧗

While under the guise of loving husband, Graham routinely and subconsciously punished Melanie. Whenever she had something that was totally her own, there was an organic repercussion.

When the local newspaper had done a small write-up on Melanie's part in organizing a winter coat drive, that very weekend Graham had volunteered to clean their bedroom, including the long-overlooked closet, while she played with the kids at the park. He had been so endearing with his offer, that she immediately was reminded of why she had fallen in love with him. He had even resembled the man of many years earlier who had promised her backpacking trips through Europe, garden strolls, and weekly dancing. None of which had come to fruition due to their fruitful multiplying.

She had spent an argument-free day in the sun and had come home to find the room immaculate, the bed made, the closet spotless. Oddly, there had been a trash bag left behind, in the center of the room. It appeared displaced and shabby considering all the neatness around it, and she had asked Graham why it had been orphaned.

Graham—a man who consistently forgot to leave the garbage on the curb, although it was his only household chore, and even when the Christmas tree was completely needle-free, or the fish dinner was generating new levels of reek—became defensive. "I took all of the trash directly to the town dump. There was too much to leave for pick up." When she looked at him quizzically, he pouted and made a face she had long ago labeled "wounded soldier" in honor of all the times she had beaten him at Stratego and chess. "I was trying to surprise you."

"I appreciate that," she carefully worded, unsure of his sudden protective posturing. "I'll set that bag out on the curb tomorrow night for you." She smiled and patted his shoulder.

"Oh." He slapped his forehead. "*That* bag. That one isn't trash." He laughed. "Well, you and I may differ on the value of what is in the bag, but it is definitely not trash."

"Graham." She was even more cautious now, suspecting that he was up to something. "It really is a bag of trash."

"No, it isn't." He was becoming angry. "I vacuumed the closet floor, I wanted it to be really clean for once—"

She recognized this as a jab at her housekeeping skills.

"—so I put your shoes in a bag while I cleaned. That is the way to really get the closets clean, to take all the shoes out, you know. It's not enough to just rearrange the hangers and refold the sweaters, and dust around everything else."

She nodded but still didn't understand what this had to do with the obvious bag of trash in their bedroom. He began to pick at lint and cat hairs on his sweater, avoiding her eyes.

"So, I left the shoes in the bag because I didn't know how you wanted to arrange them. I know how women are about their shoes."

A part of her desperately wanted to believe this. The same part that wanted to believe in happy endings and fairy tale princes. The same part of her that wanted to ignore all the strangeness and enjoy Time Between Time. She wanted to have seen shoes when she had opened the bag and she wanted her husband to be the good guy of the story. The hero, not the villain. Melanie went with whimsy and double-checked the bag. It was definitely trash, meaning he had *accidentally* thrown her shoes away at the town dump.

Accidentally.

Later, when the ladies had convened at the Bats in the Belfry, which was an old church, restored and renovated into a multi-level restaurant, Melanie had let the incident slip from her lips. P.P. had been consumed with the gardens and statuary outside the large window, but Gwynnie and Wi Fi had christened Graham the Anti-Christ. Didn't he know how laborious it would be to replace all those shoes?

"And on Melanie's tight budget?" P.P. had not missed the opportunity to add.

"Leave him." Nash had waved her hand, as if it were that simple to erase a man from one's life. Either that, or she was simply in a hurry to order and wanted the conversation to end and menus to be opened and read. This simplistic waving gesture was how she usually conjured the waiter. The ladies ate (or pretended to eat) there often, but always went through the motions with the menus, just as they went through the motions with their husbands and children. It was habit. Ritual.

Ritual was a large part of Melanie's life. Performing on autopilot. When she did take the time to consider her motives and feelings, her life felt mostly unhappy. Sometimes, she wondered what would happen if she left or threw Graham out. She just never knew what that would accomplish or where either of them would go.

Since reconnecting with Don, she had begun to wonder even more.

She had almost believed in the shoe accident, just as she forced herself, later, to believe that the red panties with the bow had been hers. She almost believed in the shoe accident, until her son had written an essay for school, full of accolades for his mother. The essay had prompted another punishing incident. Graham had commented that it sounded as if she were a single parent based upon the litany of all she did and provided for the household. Instead of pointing out the veracity of the essay, Melanie had laughed off the comment. While it had never been funny, it was even less humorous when it had been time to put out the Easter decorations the following weekend. Every year, she put up a large picture frame that contained several small shots of each child's first turn on the Easter Bunny's lap. There was Chloe, in her onesie with a runny nose and one small tooth gleaming from a mouth of gums. There was Skylar, with sticky fingers red from the lollipop given to him so he wouldn't cry on the strange, costumed man's lap. There was Marjorie. There was Mathew. Only this year, there was no frame to be found.

She had tried to convince herself that she must have misplaced it, that she hadn't packed it away with all the other Easter decorations. Until she noticed that Graham's mood was decidedly lighter. He no longer moped over the essay or called her "the children's pet."

Another piece of evidence: when Melanie had taken it upon herself to landscape the front yard, as a surprise to Graham, she should have foreseen the damage. She had put in a small retaining wall and flower bed. She had mulched over bald spots and planted the most persistent perennials she could find. The neighbors heaped praise on Melanie and—some of the men—a few jabs at Graham. The most common being about his wife making his job easier as he'd have less to mow. The insinuation was that she had usurped him, had emasculated him—publicly (who could even begin to guess how she must emasculate him behind closed doors?). Before Melanie could begin to enjoy the fruits (and flowers) of her labors, Graham "accidentally" ran over some of the front hedges when he was coming home late at night. And, he "accidentally" poisoned some bushes when spraying for wasps. And he "accidentally" paved over her flower garden to install a basketball hoop so Skylar could practice his free shots for a sport he barely enjoyed playing.

Melanie searched for a means to understand Graham's behavior. Was he jealous of her? Was he competing with her? Was he putting her in her place? Her father had never shown this type of behavior; therefore, Melanie was not well versed in marital rivalry and wanted to reach harmony with Graham.

Her desire was left unquenched. When a former high school friend, male, had found her on Facebook and had sent a Christmas card, her class ring had found its way into the garbage disposal. True, her rings had been piled along the kitchen sink as she had gone into the bathroom to retrieve some hand cream. But it was entirely suspicious that none of her other jewelry, all precariously on the lip, had managed to fall in.

She could never forgive Graham for these incidents, nor, later, for the red panties.

Fully aware of his penchant for punishment, Melanie secretly contacted Don, and knew she had to keep the Bracelet hidden.

Time Between Time

Thump

The whiteness of Time Between Time reverberated with a loud noise, one that Melanie had heard in this place before.

Thump

At times, it sounded frighteningly close. So much so that Melanie counted seconds between sounds, just as she used to do with thunder to convince herself that the lightning that it heralded was far away.

Thump

When the sounds were "closest," Melanie felt them deep inside of her. They were cloying cramps. The threatening noises and painful shocks did nothing to diminish her longing for the place. She had quickly become addicted to having extra time, to having a space where nothing counted. It would take a grave misfortune to get her to turn her back on Time Between Time.

Thump

But, eventually, she would.

Days After the Bracelet Party

Melanie's house overlooked a thin finger that reached out from the marsh and pointed toward the salty, roaring sea. From the highway, her house looked like a piece of a dream: waterfront, walking distance (albeit considerable) to the beach. The sunken yard had formed a small pond which dried just in time to reach the boating dock. Around the pond were a variety of flowering shrubs, a small bridge, and steppingstone walkways. The back end of the house showcased a colony of Great Blue herons, their froggy clucks becoming a normal soundtrack to Melanie's days. The back of the Voss house truly appeared utopian. The front told a different story. Seasonal cabins and year-round trailers fought for patches of land that randomly appeared, like acne, between groves of trees. Melanie was not sure which she liked least, the renters who shook the cabins with their parties and barbecues from April until October, or the trailer inhabitants who shattered the woods with their desperate lives the rest of the year.

As with her children, Melanie was the sole caregiver and nurturer to an uncountable, indefinable brood of animals. The menagerie contained the predictable cats and dogs—some that lived in the house, others that hunted the marsh but came to the Voss porch for meals during the lean months—and also fish, eels, turtles, and a pair of swans that had decided that Melanie's flooded, sunken yard was their Hilton.

The animals were initiated into the family with the traditional agenda: to teach the children about responsibility. Maintaining further tradition, the children grew bored with the pets and their care was left to the person who took on all undesirable chores. To her credit, Melanie was quite fond of a few of the cats, and one of the dogs, and she enjoyed looking at the swans as she sipped her morning tea.

But the animals were sometimes more than a burden—they were obtrusive. They interrupted her days when Chloe was finally napping; they interrupted her sleep with scrapping. The dogs would often hump her, taking advantage of her leg, or even her back, when she stooped to feed them or to pick up toys. The animals were habitually rowdy and vocal. The cats would frequently appear spooked, darting from room to room as if being chased. The eels would engage in a twining dance, making their tank water roil and roll over the edge, staining her floors with silt. Yet this evening, just as in the Time Between Time following the Bracelet, all the animals, even the herons, were eerily still and silent.

She was accustomed to feeling alone in a room teeming with people. Melanie felt loneliest in the company of her children. This was because she was not herself around them, not Melanie, simply Mom. She had been Mom for so long that she had lost touch with what her dreams used to be when she had had an internal life.

She felt even more lonely in Graham's company. When she spoke to him, his eyes turned a glassy gray as his mind drifted to places she was not allowed to visit. When he was physically away, she enjoyed their relationship more, as she had control over the house. Melanie was not dumb; she knew that he was not required to attend as many conferences as he did. She also knew that some conferences were not really conferences, and that he was not traveling alone. Such was the silent compromise of life in the house directly on the marsh.

Melanie felt very insignificant: more so than usual. Recent happenings with Marjorie and other girls at school had disturbed repressed memories that she tried to battle into submission. She felt that she was not awake nor asleep. She was in an in-between state, like the undead, like a ghoul.

"Ghoul Girl," she tried it out and liked the moniker. She pictured herself in full armor, with a cape unfurled, wind blowing through her thick, glossy, curled, parlor-polished hair. The image was not particularly ghoulish, and most likely, the only time her hair would be coiffed would be in her coffin.

In reality, Ghoul Girl had distinctly non-glamorous jobs such as: picking up underwear and socks left *beside* the clothes hamper, picking up Kleenex and cotton swabs thrown *beside* the bathroom trash can, picking up clumps of animal hair, cereal and potato chip crumbs, hair clogs in the shower drain, pacifiers tossed beneath the couch, pajamas kicked beneath the bed, building blocks, dolls, fast food toys, video game controllers, pencils, corrected homework assignments and exams, half full (or half empty?) water bottles, tooth paste caps, phone charger blocks, coins, paint brushes, assorted balls (foot-basket-soccer-ping pong-billiard-golf), fishing lures, hats, jackets, boots, gloves, and candy wrappers. She suspected that her house was the receiving end of a vortex for some messy universe that continuously spat its refuse at her. It was this constant deluge of busy work, these constant chores, that had relegated her to a zombie-like state, long before the figure in the road, and Time Between Time.

Ironically, she was more of a zombie/Ghoul Girl during the day than at night. During the day, she haunted grocery stores, she spirited sports equipment and computer parts that required repair, she conjured and cast doctor and dentist appointments. She washed baskets of laundry that, empty in the evening, magically replenished themselves by morning. She pictured a Rumpelstiltskin-style elf, weaving socks and towels from straw and dumping them into the empty hamper in the darkness of her home.

The only activity that broke her undead trance was picking up Skylar from basketball. She felt excitement about seeing Don again, despite her insecurity about the source of her excitement. She had been married for too long to remember, or have, these feelings. More than feelings for Don, it was the way *she* had felt talking to him. She had felt interesting and... human. As if she were her own person and being viewed as such. A few years ago, she had tried her hand at writing a "musings" column for the local paper. The editor had asked her to add another column to her portfolio before committing, but he had reviewed her skills positively. She had never followed through with the request. She had told herself that her large family would not allow her the time for creative hobbies. Recently, she had begun to wonder if she had used them as an excuse. Had she ever asked Graham to take over for an evening so she could write? She had simply assumed that he would refuse and belittle her interest. Was that fair to him? Maybe a part of Melanie felt safer hiding behind her husband and kids. She was judged less harshly in her role as wife and mother than she would have been as a stand-alone woman. Plus, Graham might have found her interesting had she become a columnist. How would that shift in dynamic affect their marriage? Placing all the blame of her inertia on Graham was not fair, nor was it fair that she invited Don to meet her to discuss plans for the silent art auction charity event that she had been asked to chair. She knew that staff were obliged to participate in community service; yet she was thrilled when Don enthusiastically committed to join her. She was equally thrilled that he did not question that they were meeting in a pub a few towns over.

The place was noisy, which suited her purposes. She was not sure of where the conversation would lead them and there was one important thing that she needed to discuss.

"I wanted to ask you about something, Don, that is probably going to sound pretty silly."

He sipped his beer and shrugged. "I spend my day with adolescents. Nothing could surprise me."

She took a deep breath. "When we were little, a girl from our neighborhood disappeared. And your dog did, too."

Don nodded. "Kaila Johnson. They never found her. We never found Dawgie either." He took another sip of beer. "I still miss him. He was my buddy."

"At the time, Dash had said something about what happened to them." She paused, not sure if she really wanted to chase the man away with supernatural talk. Especially not on the first... whatever this was. "He said that he thought the Marsh People did it."

Don nodded again, but with no more incredulity than his previous head toss. "Dash used to terrorize me with the Marsh People. When we would swim in the creek, he would go under the water and tug at my feet, trying to scare me."

"Do you think…his description of them to me was very detailed… do you think he thought that maybe he saw one?"

Don considered this for a moment. "Dash was always kind of a mystery to me. Still is. He doesn't really confide in anyone much." He pondered her question further. "I guess what I am saying is that, if he did see one, he wouldn't have told anyone."

When the quiet between them became uncomfortable he asked, "Is there a reason you brought this up?"

She toyed with her drink napkin. "There have been some weird things lately. I have seen some weird things lately." She leaned across the small table, lowering her voice, "And I keep having glimpses of a memory… I don't know, maybe it was all a dream, but I think that maybe, when I was a kid, that I saw one, too."

He reached across the table and put his hand over hers. It was comforting, and it felt normal, as if they always touched each other in this way. "I am not saying it's impossible, Melanie. I mean, Kaila was never found so who really knows what is out there?"

His gaze was very direct. So much so that she moved her eyes up to the television bolted into the corner of the pub. Clips of an old football game were being discussed on a sports show. The one being shown featured a quarterback slipping back into the pocket, with the defense on him almost immediately. A phantom pen marked the film with x's and o's while the commentator narrated his analysis and replayed the clip. "What he wouldn't give for a few extra seconds," she thought, feeling anxiety for the quarterback while being aware of the weight of her Bracelet. She continued to think of what an effect Time Between Time would have on this game: it would eradicate all rivalry. Unfortunately, since acquiring the Bracelet, she had felt more rivalry from her circle of "friends" than ever before.

As she turned her attention back to their table, she realized he had not removed his hand.

She wondered if her husband had ever traded his confidences with another woman. She thought of all the times that Graham had abandoned her for his "conferences." Her heart then sunk: had he met someone at a conference that had filled him with this same confusion? Someone that he could not chase from his thoughts? Someone he dressed especially for? Someone who made him feel better than the way Melanie normally made him feel?

She glanced down at her heeled boots and noted the marked difference from the scrubby Keds of her grocery store meeting with Don. She had managed to brush her hair today and put on earrings and a necklace that belonged to Marjorie; her Bracelet did not match, but that did not prevent her from wearing it, knowing it could only transport her when paired with the appliance clocks set to 0:00. She had even taken care to put on a matching bra and underwear set, which embarrassed her when she thought of it, sitting in a pub and discussing the Marsh People.

It would be easy to be a man and just cheat. What did she want more, Don or to simply cheat, to loosen the hold that Graham had on her, to separate herself from her family? Cheating would make her an individual, a person with needs. It would be selfish, and, for the first time in a long time, she wanted to be selfish.

Her thoughts were interrupted by her cell phone. As if on cue, it was Graham. She had said she was going to be at the library and the sounds from the pub would give her away. Graham sounded too distracted to notice. He told her that Marjorie had been in an accident and that he was at the hospital waiting to speak to a doctor. Melanie was hit with instant guilt, not only for not being where her daughter needed her to be, but also because of the genuine love and concern in her husband's voice.

Graham calmed her by saying that it did not seem to be serious. They simply wanted to check for a concussion. It had been a hit and run. He then added a detail that struck Melanie as odd but would make more sense later. He said that it was also a hit, steal, and run. As Marjorie had sat, stunned and shocked at the wheel, someone had taken the jewelry from her left hand: her class ring and a beaded bracelet.

Time Between Time

Sometimes the space in Time Between Time felt stifling, like being inside a linen closet filled with large, white towels. In those moments, Melanie could not push through, could not see anything but a small space around her. She attributed this limited visibility and limited room to her moods. When she approached Time Between Time with a closed mind, the space was smaller, tighter. When she approached as an explorer, the possibilities were limitless. The impact this was having on her philosophy of life was amazing. The fact that this heightened awareness was born from a bracelet (and the clocks on her appliances) was even more remarkable.

She had shut herself off from so many opportunities. The reason had never been Graham or the kids, she realized, it had always been her choice to turn her back on any experience that did not revolve around them. "Take a little time for yourself," her mother-in-law had insisted during one visit. The woman had wanted to spend time alone with her grandchildren, in their home environment, enjoying their games and toys with them. Either that, or she had wanted to spy on Melanie and prove her to be an unfit housekeeper. Either way, Melanie had had no idea of how to fill time when it was not filled by her family. She had spent that day wandering through the local mega-mart, consulting her watch to see if she were permitted to return home.

She was reluctant to approach Time Between Time in the same manner. She did not want to assign obligation to this sacred place. And that was how she had come to consider it: divine. Even though it came from a bracelet, even though her recent abdominal pain felt connected to it, even though she should question her own sanity *here*, she felt a reverence, and intimacy, for the blessing of her (now routine) escapes.

Melanie pushed against the blankness of Time Between Time and it shifted, relented, and gave her more empty space—more room to breathe. Her entire life she had been plagued by dreams of finding a hidden room, a secret space that abutted first the small house she grew up in, and second the smallest house on the marsh. An on-line dream interpretation dictionary claimed that the dream was about sexual fulfillment, and the room was the g-spot: hidden, yet within reach.

Now she knew the dream of a secret room was simply a hint of this marvelous Time Between Time. She could make this space what she wanted and within it, she had total control. The Bracelet party she had dreaded attending had given her more than she could hope for (and she had grown tired of superstitiously worrying about wishes and hopes).

She wanted to have her cake and eat it, too. Literally. She selfishly wanted to eat an entire cake. She did not want to have to promise the piece with the flower on it to Mathew, or the biggest piece to Skylar, or the piece with the most frosting to Marjorie. She did not want the piece that Chloe had discarded: fingerprinted and barren of all but the slightest remnants of icing. She wanted her needs met first and fully before fulfilling the needs of others.

For once.

Pushing aside her worries over wishes, she admitted to herself that she also wanted to have Don.

Just once.

Her worry-free approach had its advantages. Apparently, it made her attractive. The pub meeting with Don had graduated to dinner. The flirtation between them was mostly innocent, but the undertones were becoming more and more suggestive—just as the Time Between Time molded itself more and more to Melanie's preferences.

It seemed inevitable that they would have an affair.

Just once.

Just to satisfy her.

In Time Between Time, nothing counts. And no one would judge. And no one would look at her with scorn or pity or a combination of both. Here, she could wear the red panties and *own* them. Here, she could be fully in charge.

In the distance, she heard a thump, like a car door shutting under water, but she was too entranced to care. Perhaps it was her own heart beating happily for the first time in a long time. Perhaps it was her rusty brain wrapping itself around the notion of freedom.

The thump did not concern her. She was convinced that this strange world was created for her and she was safe here. Nothing counted so nothing bad could happen. Despite the strong cramps she felt when returning, she trusted this space.

Her trust would not be long-lived.

Days After the Bracelet Party

Melanie remembered being with Marjorie that first time in the hospital. She had become a mother then, her world changing in ways she could have never dreamed. Her life suddenly belonged to someone else. Her time, her energy, her heart were no longer her own.

There had been a few hospital visits in between: a bout with the flu that had Marjorie toddling the line of dehydration, a sprained ankle in soccer, and the times the girl had accompanied Melanie with another child's misfortune.

This visit was cloaked in a source-less guilt. She could not help but link P.P.'s desire for the Bracelet—and Melanie's lie about the intended ownership—to the accident. But why did P.P. always have to win? Why couldn't Melanie have one moment when she was lauded?

The doctor said that Marjorie would be released later that day. She suffered a concussion and bruised ribs but was fine otherwise. Melanie almost made a wish that the concussion wipe away memories of the accident, but then she remembered what wishes wrought.

⧗

Time Between Time

The sun's gravity is pulling us in. Slowly. So gradually, it's unnoticeable. Melanie, in particular, is beyond noticing the dangers around her. She is like the proverbial frogs in pots that allow themselves to be boiled to death. She is like moths who dance directly into the molten heat of light bulbs. She hides within Time Between Time, not realizing that the cramps it gives her, and the noises it makes, are clear warnings.

Melanie has had plenty of practice in ignoring warnings. She turned a blind eye to her husband's "conferences"; she ignored red-eyed and hung-over teenaged children. She overlooked strange figures pointing to her car from the middle of a storm. Most importantly, she ignored P.P.'s strange appearance in her house and blatant longing for her Bracelet.

Despite the cramps, despite the *thumps* she heard, she still loved Time Between Time. On this particular visit she had the suspicion that she was not alone. The *thumps* continuously grew closer, the air around her stirred with the heaviness of a presence. She was convinced that if she reached out behind her, that she would be able to touch someone. She was also reasonably confident that the someone was not entirely friendly.

Time Between Time was not a place for fear; it was a place for introspection. The impression of being stalked took her to another time, to the incident she had mentioned to Don. For a brief period, she had believed she had encountered one of the Marsh People. Later, she convinced herself that the heat had been playing tricks on her. Her insecurities had always caused her to doubt herself; the Bracelet and the Time Between Time were giving her confidence and in that confidence she could re-examine the past.

The day had been humid and busy, and all the more humid because it was so busy. A young Melanie had been busing tables for the lunch crowd at Chrysalis. People like P.P. ate at Chrysalis and they had treated her with the same level of disdain. The absence of fans around the steamy sinks where she delivered dirty dishes had caused her requisite polo shirt to stick to her skin like a plaster cast. Bicycling home, her body begged for a dip in any available cooling balm. Of the two beaches nearby: one required passes for its exclusive members, and the other had been quarantined by a crew filming scenes for a movie about an ocean-based zombie curse. That left her beloved marsh, and Melanie peddled feverishly in that direction.

As usual, the marsh was deserted. Most of the local families were too snobbish to sit on the muddy banks when sand was within reach elsewhere. And the marsh was too "off the beaten path" for tourists. It was however, perfect for a fifteen-year-old who needed to cool every crevice but would rather die than commit public nudity.

Melanie swore she could hear a sizzle as her steam-scorched skin sank into the cool water. She imagined the bluish crabs that scuttled around her turning pink from proximity to her hot flesh. Her mind toyed with this idea, shifting from crabs to clams to lobsters, until she heard a noise that sounded like someone throwing pebbles into the water.

She was not alone.

She had had this nightmare before, of being caught naked in public places. But this was real, and she didn't know how she could get to her clothing scattered on the shore.

There was another smooth "plop" accompanied by the distinct feeling of being watched. Oddly, the eyes that were boring into her, that were making her feel all sorts of self-conscious, were coming from the water and not the shore.

There weren't sharks in the marsh, were there?

Her question was answered by a humming—a human humming. It was a siren song, a seductive lullaby. Her face red, Melanie turned to find an adult man standing behind her. Very close behind her.

This was another type of nightmare. He could touch her, if he wanted, he was that close.

Melanie took a deep breath, to scream, but was stopped by the sight of him. His skin shimmered, like glossy scales. His hair was the color of crisp autumn and it glistened with drops of water. His body looked warm and flawless, as if it were capable of capturing rays of sunlight. He appeared to be naked, too. She could not believe she was this close to a real, live naked man.

She had never seen this man before; he was not a parent or older sibling of anyone she knew. Yet, he looked at her as if he knew her, as if he had plans for her.

The water that had been so refreshing now felt heavy. Moving through it would be like moving through molasses. The man reached for her, putting his hand on her shoulder. She wanted to scream, she wanted to run, but the touch felt strangely electric.

All her life she had been told not to let strangers touch her. She had never been told it would feel good.

The man stepped even closer. He had a smell to him that was not at all pleasant and that was at odds with his handsome features. His face was quite beautiful, except for the eyes which, up close, looked like fish eyes. Nervously, Melanie tried stepping back, but the man had a firm grip on her. The man moved even closer.

How could he be any closer?

Melanie looked down to see that she and the man were sharing space, were sharing her body. He had somehow stepped inside of her legs and was now pulling himself into her groin—not in a sexual way—he was not a seducer, he was a colonizer.

A cold chill ran through her. This man wanted to possess her. And he wasn't a man; he couldn't be a man. As terrifying as the other gender was to her, Melanie had never heard of any that could co-opt a woman's skin.

She could hear voices inside of her head, voices warning her of terrible things, asking her to submit. She seemed in a trance, and she feared that she could do nothing but let this man, this creature, inhabit her. She was terrified of losing herself, of being lost to him, until she saw his tail. Through the water, she could see it. It was long and thick and spiked. There was something about that tail, something so prehistoric and alarming, that she yanked herself backward and away from it.

Melanie felt a ripping sensation, like Velcro being torn apart, and she realized that she was free. She could not remember grabbing her clothes or peddling home. She could barely remember anything that followed, with the exception of sitting sullenly at dinner, afraid that if she opened her mouth the whole story would tumble out. How could she have had told anyone? How could she have applied words to the violation she had experienced?

As the days inserted time between Melanie and the experience, she had been able to convince herself that she had suffered heat exhaustion, or even sunstroke. She had never mentioned the incident, or hallucination, to anyone. While the body in the road and the man at the Bracelet party threatened to expose what she had worked to repress, she found a sanctuary by setting her appliances to 0:00. In Time Between Time, the cramps that were eating away at her insides were halted, and the feeling of being possessed felt as if it belonged to a separate lifetime.

Everyone has a secret life. This does not signify a life of evil, or even minor sins. Everyone has an internal life. Some fantasize about dream jobs, some imagine fantastic romance. Some travel to a Time Between Time where the world stands still and nothing that happens counts.

It didn't take Melanie long to recognize the inconsequence of her travel. She could do whatever she wanted without the fear of repercussions. She could overindulge on chocolates (her favorite contraband in this unusual world), but the scale would show no difference on her return. She could tie her hair into knots, only to find it tangle-free when she returned. She could strip naked and delight in the feel of the cool mist against her skin. No one was watching, no one was waiting for her to tend to their needs. She was experiencing the most blissful solitude that anyone could imagine, save, perhaps, for the emptiness of the grave.

The only price was the nagging cramps that periodically surfaced after she returned home.

Once she adjusted to the constant fog and seeming lack of temperature that the all-white, scentless, Time Between Time offered, it became a very pleasant place. In fact, it reminded her of being on the Sagamore Bridge during a thick fog, when visibility was limited to a few feet, and it felt as if you were flying over the invisible canal below.

Even though she had learned how to push through the white, to navigate and open the space and see her own home, she preferred to remain in that empty slate. If she could see home, she would feel guilty, noticing laundry waiting to be folded, or beds needing a clean set of sheets. She preferred to concentrate on the emptiness which was available as long as she cleared her mind of strong wants and wishes. The Melanie who had feared introspection had died, without grief, during the earlier travels.

She had learned to control her travel, and to not take advantage of this newly found power. She would escape when the kids were engaged in battle. She would return refreshed, the sentence she had departed during culminating as she reappeared. She left when she was exhausted or stressed. Once, she left while Graham awaited her in the bedroom. It humored her to leave him when he needed her. Since he hadn't realized she had gone, she didn't suffer any punishment. Life with no consequences was liberating.

She had confiscated a bag of marijuana from Skylar. After the requisite "just say no" speech, she had transported the baggie, along with rolling papers and lighter, into the white mist. The empty space had been cut through by the sharp scent of pot. She had held her inhalations until her throat burned, her eyes watered, and her head roared. She had floated on the gentlest of clouds, lungs heavy and head light. She had not been able to remember the last time she had felt so relaxed or good. She had never stopped to question how this was all possible or what the connection was between the travel and the Bracelet. She had focused on enjoying the moment, living in the present, and on how sober she would be upon her return. No red eyes, no munchies, no lingering odor. This was the best of all worlds.

After successfully smuggling food and magazines, she began to consider other things she could do in this space. She remembered that having her cake and eating it too was not all about food and drugs. Melanie was aware of the irony of desiring company during her "alone time," but she was equally aware of the importance of the time not counting. She recalled Don asking her about this very scenario inside the possessed (as she had come to think it) supermarket. This led her to think about Don and the things that she could do with him, and to him, in the Time Between Time. If there were no ramifications, if actions that occurred between time did not carve out a future, what would be the harm in bringing Don here? Since finding the panties, she no longer felt she owed

Graham her fidelity.

Even though nutritional hunger did not officially exist in between time, Melanie felt another type of craving. She felt a selfish need developing that she wasn't sure had ever been quenched before. That was what led her to consider Don and the possibility of his joining her here, where they had all the time in the world, and nothing counted.

Was it possible to feel guilty over actions that would remain as secretive as a dream? Melanie didn't think so, which was why the next time she traveled, as a test, she tucked Mathew's hamster into her jacket pocket before setting the clocks back to 0:00.

Days After the Bracelet Party

Melanie finished the dishes from the casserole she was preparing for dinner and went to turn off the small TV on her kitchen counter. A commercial was playing featuring a man hiking and ruminating about his love for protein bars. He sported a silly man bun that made Melanie smirk, but there was something familiar about his face. She knew she had seen him before but was powerless to place where.

"Without the bun, he is pretty hot," she said aloud since she was alone in the house, "I would buy whatever he is selling."

The sky was darkening quickly, forewarning a storm and a potential power outage. The air provoked meditation with its thickly quilted ions. But meditation required stillness and stillness begat introspection and that was a levee that Melanie was afraid to break unless she was in Time Between Time.

Instead, she opted to fix, to spruce, to adjust her home to approximate orderly bliss. She began with the inside and, by the time the sky had darkened like an angry bull, she moved to the outside to bring in wood in case they lost power and she needed to start a fire.

Once outside the screen door, she was confronted by a heaving cloud of mosquitoes. She swatted and tried to move quickly, wondering how the bugs were surviving the cold weather. A largish mosquito landed on her forearm and unabashedly penetrated her with its proboscis. In a part of her mind, a part that was tempted with non-Time Between Time introspection, Melanie was concerned about all of the sucking that had gone on as of late: the leeches, the mosquitoes, her life. She was concerned that she was not more concerned about her own well-being during weeks littered with gyrating grocery stores, apocalyptic figures in the road, and a bloody Princess. She simply could not amass the energy required to be fully afraid. Instead, she was mildly annoyed and mostly curious.

From the corner of her eye, she spied the green kayak that Marjorie had left tied to the dock. The girl had been told several times to wrap the kayak and stow it in the small shelter beside the dock. Instead, she had stubbornly left it, roped to a post, riding the waves that knocked it against the planks of the dock that, on warm summer days, the babies had run down prior to their water-winged jumping into the creek.

Now Melanie kneeled on those planks, pulling the small vessel from the water. As she had always been able to dress wriggling toddlers, she was able to grasp the writhing boat and pull it onto the dock. It was when the boat had cleared the water, that she saw the figure that had been sheltered beneath it.

There was something familiar about the blue-faced, drowned girl.

Something about her heavy hair and full lips that Melanie recognized. Something about the thin hips and long legs that made Melanie taste far-away chocolate chip cookies and hear a very old-fashioned tape recorder playing a mix tape that had been produced by holding the recorder up to the radio.

"Oh my... God..." Melanie felt sick and frightened. The marsh was tugging on her, but, this time, it was forcing its watery fingers into her brain, promising mental collapse and haunting terrors. She was stunned and still too tired for direct fear.

The body in the water belonged to Kaila, the babysitter who had been spirited away, years ago, by the Marsh People.

Melanie, the grown woman, and Kaila, the adolescent girl, stared at each other with matched expressions: horror mixed with grief. As Melanie watched, the girl tried to reach for her, lifting a water-logged arm just enough to clear the surface, but that was all.

Melanie could not move. The girl's arm hung in limbo, then collapsed again beneath the water. She looked at Melanie expectantly.

"You used to sing to me and bake me cookies..." Melanie was not sure of why she needed to tell Kaila this, but it felt therapeutic. The girl's face softened when she heard those words. At the time of Kaila's disappearance, Melanie had considered her a part of the adult crowd. One of the women's club. Now she saw that Kaila had not been any older than her Marjorie.

At the time of Kaila's disappearance, Melanie had sympathized with the girl—and had been afraid. Now, she felt a kinship with the girl's parents. She imagined what they must have felt—their hopes thwarted. She could recall all the dreams she had held (and still had) for Marjorie—desires for the girl to accomplish all that Melanie had been unable to bring to fruition.

The girl was able to lift her head from the water. Her skin fell slack and the bones of her skull became apparent. She floated in place, asking Melanie, "Why?"

"Why did this happen to you? Oh, Kaila, I have no idea and I am so sorry…"

"No," the girl gurgled. Her tongue was black and thick, like the leech on P.P.'s chest. "No, why…why do you do it? Why do you let them treat you so badly?"

Melanie was at a loss. "Who?"

"Them. The women." The girl dipped her head back beneath the surface before lifting it again. It seemed to be a struggle to hold it aloft. "You have no need to be around them. There is no reason to see them. They only take you to a dark place.

When I babysat you, we would read books about confidence and liking yourself. I never read you those horrible fairy tales about submission. Where does this need come from?"

Melanie knew that Kaila was right. She was the doormat for family and friends alike. How had that happened? What had happened to the girl who had fearlessly wanted to explore the marsh? What had happened to the girl who encountered a Marsh Person and survived? What had happened to the girl who had wished for so many things?

Like Melanie's dreams, Kaila drifted away, unwillingly, but powerless to remain in Melanie's view. Melanie did nothing to help her, nothing to keep her. It was Melanie who felt as if she were adrift, as if the salty marsh water were perfectly still and the dock and her yard behind it, even her house, were rocking with waves. She had felt this feeling before, when Graham was away and she realized that she would have to face any hurdle, any broken appliance or household issue, on her own.

As always, Melanie was the one left on shore, alone.

Melanie was drifting on the dock. She felt as if she were swaying and spinning. She felt as if she were wandering on and on and on. Just as the piles of laundry in her house went on and on and on. Just as the school events (chorus recitals, awards assemblies, bake sales) went on and on and on.

It was Melanie who felt as if she were beneath the water: darkness above and darkness below. She could trace glimmers of hope, as one might spy glittering foam dancing on the crests of waves. This was the same hope that had come after the kids were in bed and Graham was away and she was left to live inside her own body—moving at an unhurried pace, enjoying her home and a good book. When one was accustomed to constantly doing for others, it was nothing short of miraculous to do for oneself.

The blood crashed around inside her head, making the same sound the "ocean" did inside a large conch shell. Somewhere in the noise, a voice told her that it would be quiet in the water. The voice said that something bad was in the air, but that the water was safe, and the marsh was safest.

The voice seemed to hang in the air behind Melanie. It seemed to form a wall between Melanie and her yard, banishing her from retreating to her home, compelling her to move forward. The voice told her that it would be different in the water. The voice reminded her that the marsh belonged to her and she to it. The voice implored her to jump in. The badness was coming, better to escape it. Better to escape everything.

She knew that if she slipped into the water, she would metaphorically be swept along with the crowd. It would be so easy. No more loneliness, no more feeling as if others were whispering about her, gossiping with gossamer tongues. She would be light, weightless in fact.

And free.

Melanie put her hand in the water. Her fingers cut through,

slicing the surface open, only to have it close instantly. When she pulled her hand back, it was as if her fingers had never been near the surface, as if she had never touched it.

There was no place for footprints on the ocean.

Maybe drowning in the water would make her important. She would be part of a legend, just as Kaila was forever intertwined with the Marsh People. Perhaps the water would not be so bad. She could just—

Droplets of water splashed and licked Melanie's face: enough to break through the hypnosis. She remembered Kaila's words and their truth. Melanie did not mind being lonely and alone. There was good reason why she had never felt she belonged. She did not want to become one of them. Let the badness come. In the badness, she would find herself.

Days after the Bracelet Party

Once Melanie had successfully traveled with a variety of animals, each returning unscathed and apparently unaware of any difference in their existence—as far as this could be measured—she began to plot a special trip. Was this delicious deviant feeling the same that Graham felt when he planned his "conferences" with, presumably, whatever flavor of the month?

Now that she had the Time Between Time for repose, she found she could accomplish more for others during the day, allotting more quiet moments for introspection. She felt prettier than she had in years. If only for the biting cramps, she would say she was the picture of health.

The hunger within her was growing. She had been spending nights on the couch in the den, not wanting to snack on Graham when she was planning a feast. Graham, for his part, did not seem to notice. He had developed the habit of falling asleep while Melanie was still chipping away at chores, and when he awoke, she was already in the kitchen beginning breakfast. He had no idea where, or if, she slept. Melanie could recall a time when they had stayed up most of the night, talking and laughing, before falling asleep, one curled in the crevices of the other. Now, those memories felt more like a documentary she had watched about other people's lives. And, it had become depressing to be a mere witness to marital contentment.

After too many nights on the couch, Melanie sent the kids to school, put Chloe in her crib, and called Don. He agreed to come to her house for a cup of tea and a discussion about the basketball raffle that Melanie had agreed to oversee. While waiting for his arrival, she changed clothing—slipping on the red panties beneath her jeans and a low-cut sweater—curled her hair and applied make-up. She wondered if there would be enough Time Between Time, if she could be sated. Would she have regrets when she returned, or simply regret that she had to come back? And what about Don? Would he even remember their tryst? Did she want him to?

As his car pulled into her driveway, she dabbed some perfume on her wrists. As he rang the bell, she walked into the kitchen and called out that the door was open. As he walked to where she stood, hand offered in greeting, she set the clocks for 0:00.

⧗

Time Between Time

A loud thud shook Melanie awake. It was much louder than the previous sounds that littered Time Between Time. The sound came from a fugitive beach umbrella, touching down on the patch of mud where Melanie lay. Another thud followed: this was a dissevered half of a boogie board which looked as if it had been gnawed on by some tooth-challenged shark. Something had happened during this travel. This time, Melanie was not cloaked in fog. She was at the marsh, at its heart. The air smelled rotten, and it felt thick and swollen. There was a malevolent stickiness that permeated the sharp spiked grass and made Melanie feel as if she were on foreign turf instead of her beloved marsh. She caught movement in the reeds around her from the corner of her eye. This could be attributed to paranoia, or to nerves. Or to something much worse.

By the time the third item, the handle of a fly-fishing rod landed, Melanie realized that someone was throwing things at her. She heard something, a whisper. She turned to Don, only to find him deathly pale, blood trickling from his nose and ears and mouth.

"Oh, God," she breathed, and reached a tentative hand to him. He was not moving, his body hard and still. She put her hand on his neck. It felt solid and stiff. She could not make out a pulse. Nor could she see any movement of his chest to denote breathing. "Don," she whispered, hoping that whatever it was that was throwing things at them would leave them alone. The man remained motionless. Had she done this to him? Why had the animals survived the travel, but not Don?

What could she do for Don? If this place did not count, then this injury… this death… would not count. When she was ready to return, she would take him and they would both find themselves in her kitchen, ready for tea and talk.

She reminded herself that this did not count.

Just as one cannot leave a footprint on water, one cannot muse deeply at the marsh. Not when a figure was emerging from its depths. It was a young man. His hair was the color of early autumn. His skin was pale and without freckles. He was slowly walking to where she rested on the shore, rising from the water and revealing himself to her. Even though it was evening, the marsh was lit by the stars and moon reflecting off the water.

She was not afraid of this man. She was still afraid of what had happened to Don, but not of this man. She recognized him from the Bracelet party. And also from her encounter as a teenager. Had he waited all this time for her? For what purpose? She tried to take her eyes off him but found she couldn't. She was spell bound. He was naked in the water and his body was perfect and appeared warm despite the chill in the air. In fact, he looked like a young Dash. A part of her nearly mentioned this to Don before she could remember that they would not be speaking again. She was embarrassed that the young man had captured her attention and concern away from Don.

Then again, this did not count.

She allowed herself to watch the mystery man without conflict. The way he moved through the water was captivating, like a slow strip tease. Melanie found herself becoming aroused. He was holding her eyes, moving slowly, beckoning in a way that clearly demonstrated his intent. She *had* wanted to be selfish. She *had* wanted to cheat, and this beautiful creature was obviously willing to comply. And if he were part of Time Between Time then he most definitely did not count. Mostly, he made her feel special. He had been following her, waiting for her, and this time, she would know how to handle it. She couldn't be bothered to question who he truly was or where he came from. He was in her Time Between Time and activities here could not harm, would not count.

She continued to watch him. The tightness of his body both surprised and alarmed her. What would he think of her stretch marks and of the excess skin she carried from where her babies had expanded her flesh to the breaking point? It was this same self-consciousness that had always prevented her from having a fully enjoyable sex life. She could never abandon the mental mirror that warned her of how ridiculous she looked, whether on all fours or with her legs akimbo in the air. She would force herself to abandon worry while she was in between time.

This did not count. She had all the freedom of dreams.

She could feel a pulse: a heart beating between her legs. She felt as if the entire world, everything of importance, was being consumed by the need between her legs. She could swallow the earth's water and never quench this thirst. This achy ravenous desire.

This Time Between Time was freer and more sublime than the trips prior. Melanie was losing herself completely, without fear. She wanted nothing more than to remain in this space and to not have to return to the issues of family, and home, and Don.

As she watched the man, a voice said, *You can stay here, with your marsh, forever.*

Forever. Melanie could not fathom what that meant.

You can be one of them. The Marsh People. They never have to leave this place. They never have to worry.

What would it be like to be one of these seductive creatures forever? To belong? To only be concerned with her own needs?

She forgot the terror and discomfort she had felt when she had met this man years before. He was possessing her mentally, prior to possessing her physically, and that meant that she was free from guilt, too. There were no worries, no trepidation at all.

The man freed himself from the water and crouched near her

feet. She found herself shivering both from the cold and from the excitement.

"I know you," she told him, "I have seen you before. Did you wait for me here?"

He opened his mouth, perhaps to answer her, perhaps for something else. She could see that the inside looked like a steel trap and this vision combusted the siren's song.

She screamed and tried to urge her feet to run. The man jumped on her lower legs, his weight surprising her. She struggled against him, her cramps returning and intensifying. The man was causing the discomfort: his hands moved over her torso, creating waves of pain. It seemed as if he were trying to reach inside of her.

This was the bad thing she had been warned about. She had been so busy wishing that she had ignored the warnings.

His tail wrapped around her ankles, the spikes digging into her flesh. One wrong move and her hamstrings would be cut. Then, she would be immobile.

The awful, leech-like tongue was unleashed and moving toward her face.

Despite the pain and disadvantage in terms of strength, she knew she had to fight. Somewhere outside of Time Between Time, she had a family that needed her. If she were alone in the other world, as she was in this one, she would be able to quit. She would be able to believe that fighting didn't matter. Being alone meant being able to give up.

But she wasn't alone. A voice was calling to her, screaming her name with anger.

Someone else was here. One part of her was thrilled that she would be saved. Another, irrational part was jealous that someone else had discovered Time Between Time.

Once she realized who the voice belonged to, this imagined defeat made perfect sense. It was P.P. She was perfectly coiffed but shaking and her face was red. She was pointing at the man and instructing Melanie to move away from him.

The man seemed shocked at seeing P.P. and this allowed Melanie to pull herself free. "P.P. please help me!"

"I will, once you move away from him."

"But... how are you here?"

The other woman composed herself. "I grabbed onto your boyfriend there and hitched a ride." P.P. was brushing imaginary dirt from her clothing.

"Don? Is that why—did you kill him?"

P.P. snorted. "I did nothing of the sort. Melanie, please don't freak on me. Go get him some help and give me that Bracelet.

It's the right thing to do."

"I can't do it alone." Melanie kept one eye on the man, who was staring at P.P. "I need your help, P.P. Don is... and this creature... "

"Melanie, please do not lose it on me. You can take that— that person—back with you. Leave the Bracelet, it's the way it's supposed to be."

"This is still about the Bracelet?"

P.P. smoothed her hair. "You know I always win, Mel. It might not be right away, but eventually, I will always win."

Melanie was beside herself, «You don›t understand. He is not what you think.»

"What I *think*, Melanie, is that I saw him first. He is my find, so leave him alone." She winked at the man. "He and I have an understanding. After the party I told him what I wanted. Why he wasted time messing with you, I will never know... "

"P.P., his tail. Do you see his tail?" She could not believe the expense this woman would go to in the name of social rivalry.

"Melanie, you are so... pedestrian. You wouldn't know a good thing if it came up and... bit you on the ass!" P.P. slipped off her shoes and stepped closer to the naked man who was lurking on the shore, apparently baffled by the change of events. "That is why I am here. At the party, when we made our wishes, I wished for the best. And I want that Bracelet, and I want him." She pulled her shirt out from the band of her skirt and loosened her hair. "Now, hand me that Bracelet."

"I can't, P.P."

P.P. let out a long sigh that sounded more like a growl. "I came to get it from your house, the day after the party, but no one was home. Not even that husband of yours. Had he known I was in your house alone, I am sure he would have rushed home." She smirked. "And I couldn't find the Bracelet anywhere." The woman slid her skirt down over her hips, kicking it away playfully. She raised her eyebrows at the man and tested the water with her toe.

Melanie stared at P.P.'s panties: they were identical to the ones Melanie had found, only purple with a small pink bow.

"Then I came back that other day, but still no Bracelet. What do you do, sleep with it on? I would think that even you would know that you don't wear jewelry all the time. Not in the shower, not to bed. Even you should know that." P.P. began unbuttoning her blouse. The man smiled, with his lips tightly sealed. He seemed to be saving the sight of his trap as a surprise for later.

"P.P., you've got to listen to me," Melanie pleaded, "he is not a man, not at all. You are in danger— "

"Listen to you? Since when have I ever listened to you?"

The corrupt couple took a step into the water. It was difficult to determine which of the two was mesmerizing the other.

"Please listen. Look at his tail!"

"It's not his tail I am interested in." P.P shimmied lasciviously. "My friend here and I are about to get started. So, why don't you give me that Bracelet and beat it."

Melanie shook her head. "I wouldn't give this to my worst enemy."

P.P. entered into the man's embrace, smiling. "That's exactly what you are going to do."

P.P.'s confidence, her self-righteousness, her smugness, finally broke Melanie. That and the fact that it was P.P.'s panties that had been floating in her washing machine and that had sparked this tragic trip. She knew that P.P. was under a spell, but she also knew that the horrible words from P.P.'s lips were the same words and the same tone that she used in real time. Melanie watched the two figures walk into the water, the man holding P.P. impossibly close. Melanie was finished with Time Between Time, knowing that it had never been meant for her or for her happiness. Like the mouth of the Marsh People, it had always been a trap.

Melanie threw the Bracelet which the man caught with one hand, while dragging P.P. beneath the water with the other.

Months After the Bracelet Party

Melanie slid on the red panties and prepared herself for the results of her recent tests. The cramps never left after she returned home from her final trip to Time Between Time. Because the final trip had been so different, she had been able to return without the help of the Bracelet. She brought Don home but was unable to bring him truly back. The EMTs who retrieved him said it had been a hemorrhage. They said that even though Don was very young, there was nothing Melanie could have done, and they called her efforts courageous.

Melanie was no longer wasting time with the women who lived by the sea. Without P.P. and Nash's rivalry, there was no one to wrangle them and their efforts were unorganized and surprisingly petty. No one could believe that P.P. had actually been the motivator behind most of their activities. Furthermore, no one could believe that someone with as much power and prestige as P.P. would simply disappear. It seemed she had run away, but who would run from a perfect life?

Who would run from a good life? This is what Melanie believed that she had unwittingly done.

As Melanie sat on the uncomfortably cold table, she no longer wished for a quantity of time—she knew that was not in the cards, just as much as she knew to be wary of wishes.

Instead, she hoped her remaining time would count.

Attempt 2: Death and Taxes

Here is something you'd be wise to never forget: as Victorian woman were relegated to the kitchen, they became dark kitchen witches, using food to kill. These women, without the benefit of Plasticware, without bracelet parties, went after their own families. Motherhood as a natural occurrence does not, in and of itself, create loving mothers.

For example, Mary Ann Cotton (1832-1873) killed at least twenty-one loved ones, including several husbands and nearly all her children, using arsenic. Mary Ann Britland (1847-1886) used arsenic on her husband, child, and lover's wife. Amelia Dyer (1829-1896), pretended to be a foster or adoptive mother for illegitimate babies whom she later smothered or poisoned, pocketing her caregiver's fee. She may have killed up to twenty-five infants. Amelia Sach (1873-1903) and Annie Walters (1869-1903) played the same baby farmer game as Dyer, using poison. Margaret Waters (died 1870) and Ada Chard Williams (died 1900) were also baby farmers, feeding their children death.

All of these women were hung.

Belle Guiness (1859-?) murdered possibly 49 people, mostly husbands, suitors, and children, earning the name "Lady Bluebeard."

Belle may or may not have substituted a charred body for her own, while escaping to freedom.

This is what wives and mothers are capable of.

And this is why we have to respect Nashville DeCota.

Nashville DeCota lay chilled and dying on the operating table. She would have died even faster had she known that Melanie had the chance to tell her story first; she was also deprived of the assurance that her special frenemy, P.P., was no more. This is not past life regression, or a near-death experience. This was an actual case of dying coupled with an actual case of having a story that was dying to be told.

"We're losing her…"

Losing? What did that mean? How could she be lost when she could still feel the cold, steel table beneath her naked butt? A part of her remained glad that she was covering said butt with her body weight, as she would hate for any cellulite to be exposed to strangers. The other part of her had concern for the strange fingers that were being shoved into the side of her neck. How were those fingers getting in—getting through her skin? How was it possible that her throat was a gaping, open wound? She couldn't turn her head; she couldn't move. She could feel some pressure on her arms—perhaps IVs. There was definitely something covering her mouth: a sweaty, cold mask that had a minty smell. Was she breathing through the mask? Was she dead? Is that what *lost* meant? Maybe being lost would not be so bad, as long as it wasn't as cold as this steel table.

If Nash were being honest with herself (a luxury she had never been able to afford) she would admit that she was hungry. Lying on the table, evolving from Cape Capo to corpse, Nash was hungry. She would have eaten anything in that moment, even non-organic, carb-laden, fried, chocolate coated, anything. Vainly, she hoped that her cheek implants were holding up well despite the recent trauma she had undergone. The implants were her newest surgery, and she would never be able to trust some mortician to fix them if they were drooping. She also hoped that the harsh hospital lighting was kind to her expansive forehead which had recently been botoxed. Her Plasticware empire, that she had used to stash secret supplies of snacks and secret supplies of secrets, had nothing on the silicone and toxins inside of her.

Nash wondered where the light was. The one they all mentioned being at the end of some tunnel that was populated by deceased loved ones beckoning you to the other side. Didn't that tunnel lead to heaven? Or some good place? Was the lack of light attributable to her still being alive or to the activities she indulged in before ending up on this table? Either way, this did not feel scary or bad, it simply felt like nothing. And nothing was good, especially after all the chaotic, catastrophic somethings of recent. Nash could resign herself to nothing.

Was this what it had been like for those she had watched die? Had there been no pain, only nothingness? If she had ever felt guilty, she would have assuaged herself of that feeling, due to the nothingness, as she lay on the cold, steel table with fingers penetrating a slit in her throat.

Nash, with her flare for the dramatic, remembered her wound and considered it a near decapitation. While a deadly blow, much too much of her Cartier-wearing neckline remained intact to warrant such a description. The assault had been intensely painful, but this death might not be so bad. Nashville, as well as anyone, knew that the world was an ugly place. Leaving it, along with the memories, could be counted as a blessing. Nash also knew, better than anyone, that there was something to be said for killing your personal monsters. And, death—the final finality—could certainly cement those skeletons in her closet and prevent them from rattling their bones further. But, if she died, who would pack the lunches? Who knew, as well as she, how to disguise the protein she magicked into one plain brown bag and one Patriot's lunch box for the kids' consumption at midday? And who would help Dinah survive high school? A girl needs her mother for help with boys, and the mean girls, and the make-up, and the manipulation. As she lay on the cold table, hungry, Nash recalled Dinah and the blood and the gun. She remembered all she had done to cover up all Dinah had done. She could not abandon the girl when she so clearly needed help. Who else could provide motherly advice? Who would pick up Riley from soccer? More importantly, who would embarrass him by becoming his own private red-headed fury of a cheerleader? And the taxes. Who would do the taxes?

Death and taxes. They were right: those two items were eternally intertwined. Even when one was on the path between worlds, taxes loomed large. If anyone saw her private papers, if anyone knew what, and who, she had buried over the years... she had to force herself to live in order to make sure her tracks were firmly covered.

"Blood Pressure?"

"90 over 40."

Was that bad? She couldn't remember. She knew her husband's blood pressure was always 130 over 90 and that is why she gave him Kashi for breakfast. His claim, that does not appear on tax statements, is that his blood pressure would be much lower if he could afford the luxury of being unemployed. He claims that his commute (Appendix A of form 1040), which sandwiched a stressful job, had wreaked havoc on his system. *The big provider.* If only he knew about the other items that could not be deducted on Appendix A. If only he knew about all the income that did not fit perfectly into any of the categories that were provided on a W-2. If only he knew that for all these years, she had kept them afloat. He honestly thought his paycheck not only covered bills and household expenses, but also paid for vacations and clothing and the salon and the gym and her SUV. He fatally overestimated himself.

If she died on the table, she would be leaving them to a poorer life. To a life of coupon cutting and school loans and yard sales. More importantly, to a life of not fitting in and of not having as much as, or more than, the next person. How would Derrick afford Riley's braces without her? The poor sap would honestly try to pay the orthodontist instead of making the doctor *pay* for all his indiscretions. They'd be sunk for sure: all that precious money wasted on teeth. Teeth are so easily knocked out, so easily ripped from the roots, so easily separated from skulls. It's a crime to allocate household funds to them.

As Nashville thought of crime, she began to remember how she got here. Worse, she remembered that Derek had not been around to bumble through their tax accounts, or to believe that he was floating cruises and canapes, Jimmy Choos and champagne, Ferraris and filet mignon. He had not been around at all.

A few weeks prior, she had gotten everyone off to school and then had gone to the Ecco Organic Mart for a reasonably large grocery order. Even though she had very, very recently done a medium-sized order, and even though her kitchen refrigerator and basement freezer were drowning in sustenance. This trip was about acquisition and abundance. Her food regimen, at that time, required that she purchase food items daily, and then practice self-denial.

Nash had always employed immediate gratification, so this delay of satisfaction, coupled with the possibility of never eating the food and with disposing of it—wasting it—would, hopefully, shock her metabolism into sacrificing some calories, bringing her from a small dress size to the *smallest dr*ess size.

This habit of suffering might, ultimately, suit her.

She stored nonperishables in glass jars like some ancient apothecary. Crystal vases held bouquets of cheerios and pastas. Vials contained spells of rice, flax, and beans. And her

Plasticware—that contained the most precious things she owned or acquired. Everything had its place, but little had a purpose. Her house was overstocked, but she had long ago stopped seeing excess.

In certain circles, she would have been called a "hoarder." Yet, her staff of cleaning people kept the household manageable, and helped keep secret her obsession.

After stashing food on shelves, she had taken a break, choosing to sip a cappuccino at her breakfast nook table in her sunroom: a pretty glass room that jetted over her flower garden some three feet below, and faced the roaring ocean that met her property. She had specified that it be built that way, so she could walk on a bed of roses each morning.

It was the only window that received morning light, the large trees and shrubs of the yard protected much of the house with perpetual shadow. Not that she minded the darkness: it kept her secrets hidden.

First things first, Nashville DeCota was not the Island Impaler. Everyone who was anyone had been to The Landing that summer—picnicking, sailing, sipping fruity drinks—and leaving traces of their DNA everywhere. It is true, she had known all the victims. Furthermore, the three women whose bodies had been found had each hosted a Plasticware party as part of

Nash's multi-level marketing LLC, and each had been robbed of her individual profits at some point in the time following the party but preceding her impalement. And it is also true that the instrument of impalement was none other than the sharpened drivers that matched the golf sets that were offered as prizes in the "putt for the butt" auction to raise money and awareness for pre-prom liposuction. None of this proved anything, and Nash had been able to explain her innocence over afternoon tea with the chief of police.

While Nash sipped her cappuccino, she noticed a piece of Plasticware trapped amongst the thorns of one of her rose bushes. This was not her special container; this was not the exact one that had made her who she was today. But she valued her Plasticware nonetheless. Feeling independent, she did not call for her gardener, but went into her yard to retrieve it herself. Had it been another item, and not the prized Plasticware with matching lids—each set comprised of twenty pieces, from colanders to cups to cereal bowls to freezer squares to dessert containers and Jell-O molds, each container nestled inside one just slightly larger, with leak-proof, water-tight, freezer-safe, microwave compatible lids—she would not have been so motivated.

This particular container was meant for sandwiches. It had a diagonal divider down the middle to prevent separate halves of the meal from touching the other. It also had minuscule holes in the lid to allow for the color-coordinated toothpicks that were included. Instead of spearing deadly carbohydrates, lettuce, tomato, and deli meats, these picks held down a note which read:

Winning is not everything

It is the only thing

If you want to see Derrick again

You will lose it all: heads and tails

Nash was no stranger to blackmail, but kidnapping was new. She would have never sunk to that level. There was a certain hierarchy to crime and holding someone against his or her will for profit announced a lack of class and creativity. Nash considered herself to be highly creative. Like an artist or an inventor or a genius. That was why she was so often bored with those around her, even Derrick. She loved him tremendously, but his sheltered and ordinary life paled next to her own. And the fact that he was so clueless about her clandestine endeavors...

She knew everything about the man but could not remember when she had seen him last. How dare someone take him and then attempt to terrorize her in his absence.

First things first, Nash was not about to lose, heads or tails.

She would win by rescuing her husband and making his kidnapper pay.

At that time, Nash believed she would tackle this trial flawlessly. Looking back, from the benefit of hindsight on a hospital operating table, she was willing to admit to a modicum of defeat.

For a woman so consumed with control, the weeks that had led up to the hospital had been beyond nightmarish. Not only had she been forced into a husbandless state, but she had also been faced with catastrophe incarnate.

First, the spiders…

Dueling is a sport that does not belong exclusively to the patriarchy. One of the most famous "petticoat duels" took place between two ladies over a comment about the true age of each. They dueled first with pistols, one woman sending a bullet through the hat of the other, then switched to swords. Another famous female duelist, La Maupin, took on an entire room of men. To support herself and her husband, La Maupin fenced in taverns while dressed as a boy. She donned male fatigues not as a disguise, but for convenience, as it is difficult to swash a sword in a skirt.

There are times when one is so preoccupied with getting ahead in life, that one ignores the cement shoes that are being strapped to one's feet. This was the case with Nashville DeCota, who sat in all her splendor, like a fairy tale princess in a glass tower, while suffering the onslaught of eight-legged beasts. It wasn't that she didn't see the spiders, she simply did not recognize what they represented. Before becoming judgmental, ask yourself if you would correctly categorize an arachnid invasion. Before hopping on a high horse, ask yourself if, having the power and prestige of Nashville DeCota, you would be alarmed by mostly minuscule pests.

The spiders came down the chimney like some collective blaspheme of Saint Nick. They came in a variety of sizes. They crawled over carpet and floor. They touched pictures of Riley and Dinah with their alien arms. Some were fanged, and some were hairy. Some were almost beautiful in their ethereal grace, as they slid down glass panes and landed flawlessly on shag, straddling strands of rug with sovereignty. The spiders were unique. Not only because of their number and compulsion to break into Nash's psyche, but because this had been an "off" year for seasonal insects. The honeybees had been nowhere to be found, and the Cape beetle, which resembled a cicada, had not swarmed the early days of fall. The beetles typically presented a winged mosaic on football bleachers and pumpkin patches. People pretended that squished bug fluid on clothing was the new black, as it was unavoidable. This year, the people and the bleachers went unmolested.

Nash (Nashville) DeCota, nee Mitchell, decades prior to the spider attack had been born to confederate-phile/rebel lovers. Her mother had read *Gone with the Wind* dozens of times, claiming to have married a long-lost relative of the author, and had even memorized Miss Melanie's death bed speech to Scarlett. Nash's mother had warned her about flaming plantations and devilish suitors but had failed to give her any indication of what the true threats to womanhood were. There had been little talk of monsters, or monstrous competition, and no indication that the world was anything but beautiful.

They had named her Nashville, but her original birth certificate had read Graceland. That had been a typo, they later explained. A bureaucratic error. Perhaps some other poor girl, named after the home of the King, now had in her possession a birth certificate listing the home of country music. Wouldn't that be poetic? Nash's parents had almost named her Sabbath Lily after a Flannery O'Connor character. But their distaste for O'Connor's Catholicism prevailed. They decided their daughter was a southern belle. They felt that Nash's fiery hair reflected the flames of burning Tara and her graceful long fingers were simply made for tea parties and holding gentleman callers' hands as they pranced the Virginia Reel. If only they had known that Nash would grow to be a character who fought waves of spiders as opposed to Yankee conversion. If only they had known that she considered herself a Cape Codder at heart. If only they had known who she had been, before the Plasticware and the bracelet party, and who she would become when she grasped her very own Pandora's box after killing an indecent young woman named Virtue, she probably would have been christened without so much southern gentility.

The spiders knew her and were very aware of where she sat. They moved purposefully toward her, blocking her exit from her sunroom sanctuary. They took possession of that part of the house, the part she had always considered "hers." She observed them, in the same snobbish manner that she observed her human community, while she sipped her morning coffee.

First things first, Nashville DeCota was not the "Tooth Snatcher."

While many suspected her of being a criminal of the serial killer persuasion, there was simply no substantial proof to convict her, or even to tie her to the murders of several schoolgirls. The only evidence happened to be pictures, and everyone knows that photographs can be doctored.

Just because Nash figured prominently in photos with the girls at the time when they disappeared did not mean that she had anything to do with their deaths. Just because the girls had jack-o-lantern smiles that displayed a newly missing tooth—and the growth of the new tooth—or lack thereof—in the skulls found later gave scientific substance to the hypothesis that they were killed shortly following the photographs, did little to warrant a trial. Just because Nash held a vendetta against the girls' parents, was nothing to build a case against her. And because the photographs were found in Nash's possession, in a small Plasticware container that later became a playground for spiders, did not prove, beyond a reasonable doubt, that she had anything to do with the murders.

First things first. Nashville DeCota was not the Tooth Snatcher of criminal fame, but she did have a penchant for pulling teeth. Nash had used tongs and kitchen appliances to torture, and, while the Plasticware did its own damage, by both turning her into a marketing guru and by turning the women against each other—while they competed over limited-time-only sets—she had never been above the appropriation of storage containers to fulfill the roles of urn and coffin.

If we were to examine the hidden parts of Nash's conscience, the parts that lurk beneath the water, while only the iceberg tips are displayed, we would learn that she believed she only killed the deserving (and the economically disadvantaged who were contributing nothing). This alone would preclude any non-adults. She never killed for pleasure, except once. That first time is always sublime, and, unlike sex, the first time is always pleasurable.

The first time Nash had ever killed someone, actually stolen a life with her own hands, it had been an epiphany—a window into her true nature. She had been driving home for winter break from college. A girl who lived on her dormitory floor had asked for a ride. This wasn't just any girl, this was Virtue Degloria. This was the head duchess of the school, the girl all the others envied and vied to befriend. Nash's own roommate had stood Nash up on occasion to wait around in the hopes that Virtue would be free to attend some event, any event. Virtue had the best wardrobe, the most stylish haircuts, the best taste in *everything*, and, somehow, due to some twisted, demonic intervention, absolutely no way of transporting herself home for the holidays.

The fully adult Nash, the one you are acquainted with, could have been persuaded to admit that Virtue bore a resemblance to the Porcelain Princess, the enemy she assumed to be alive as she lay on the hospital table dangerously close to death herself, and whom Nashville detested in ways that there are no words to describe. Nash had grown up just one town over from Virtue, but they had not crossed paths until college. Even then they rarely interacted, much to Nash's displeasure, so she leapt at the chance to squire Miss Virtue home. She even cleaned her car and made sure that only the eclectic CDs by the most unusual bands were on display in her console. She hoped that this would be a bonding experience, and that, when school reconvened for the spring semester, Nash would be in Virtue's inner circle.

The three-hour ride began smoothly enough. The girls gossiped about people in their dorm, about faculty (careful to avoid mentioning the dashing Brit. Lit. Prof who was rumored to have been seduced by Virtue the first week of her freshman year). When Nash suggested they stop for a bite to eat, Virtue declined, choosing instead to suck at the fading polish on her days old manicure.

They drove the dark highway, passing fast food on either side, and Nash felt herself growing more and more irritable. In the past, she had never been one to skip a meal, and Nash could not understand the hurry to get home. Why couldn't they just go to a drive-thru? Was this precious princess too good for Nash, or too good for food?

As they cleared one of the last large towns before a lingering stretch of nothingness, Virtue surprised Nash: "We could stop for a while here. Some place… off the beaten path."

Nash sighed to cover her rumbling belly. "For food?"

Virtue smiled and took a deep breath, stretching her arms up and over the back of her seat, forcing her chest forward. "No. For fun."

Nash was not sure what that meant, but she knew that, socially, she could not say no to Virtue Degloria. That would be unheard of. She slowed the car and began to look for something that would be unusual and quaint and that would suit some mysterious purpose. She was hoping that Virtue would direct her, but the girl was mum—looking out the window and chewing on a straw-colored lock of hair that was able to free itself from her perfect bob in order to reach her lips. The only instructions Virtue gave was "not near the streetlights."

A dirt road caught Nash's eye. She turned the wheel and the tires bumped over the tell-tale divots that revealed the route of four wheelers and dirt bikes. The dirt road was the type that had always reminded Nash of the story of the Headless Horseman; it led into darkness and shadows. The trail took them into the woods.

When they were concealed from the road, Virtue said, "That's far enough." Her tone was as if Nash were pushing her or doing something that she had not ordered. Nash cut the motor and peered into the darkness beyond the headlights. The night seemed animated and energetic, as a light snow was falling. Virtue had unfastened her seat belt and pulled her purse onto her lap. She began digging through it, examining items as if she were shopping at fine retailers.

Virtue wore a lavender cashmere sweater that somehow managed to look as if she just removed it from protective wrapping even though they had been sitting in the car for quite a while. There was not one snag or nub on the sweater. She always made Nash feel shabby, even when it was just the two of them on a deserted dirt path. Her dangerously long eyelashes reminded Nash of spiders, and Nash had worked so very hard to repress her fear of the creatures. Virtue was breathing heavily as she inspected her purse, her breasts rising and falling quickly. Nash tried not to look at the girl's sweater, but her breasts were perfectly symmetrical, and she couldn't help but wonder if they were naturally like that or if that were the benefit of a special bra or surgery. They were round, despite the girl's small frame, and had the look of a cartoonist's drawing: just too perfect.

Virtue had slipped off her shoes and she was rubbing her toes together, possibly to keep warm, possibly from anticipation. Nash waited quietly as the excavation continued.

"Have you ever dropped acid?" Virtue asked without turning to face her. A lock of bangs covered half of her face and made it difficult to ascertain if Virtue was serious or joking. Mostly, Nash was unsure of what the cool answer would be.

Nash looked at the girl's small-boned hands and long, sharp nails. The adult Nash, the one you are acquainted with, would admit that the nails looked very similar to the serrated spikes that had accessorized a scaled tail that had slunk by her garage following the spiders. But Virtue did not look demonic. She looked very clean and completely at odds with the image of a drug pusher. She looked like the kind of girl that your parents hoped would befriend you in Sunday school, one of the model kids that they put in classrooms to inspire the others.

"Have you?" Virtue half turned so Nash could see the uncovered eye and its raised eyebrow.

"I... acid? N... uhmm." It felt safer to be noncommittal.

Virtue pulled a small, plastic pill box from the depths of her purse and peeled off two small tabs. "You can take a whole one or just a half... depends on your level of experience... and how much fun you want to have."

Nash watched as the girl put the colorful tab onto her tongue, taking it in as daintily as a communion wafer. She handed Nash the other. Nash's familiar car suddenly felt warm and confining. She tried to gauge if she could palm the tab and only pretend to swallow, but then she feared she would absorb the drug right into her sweaty palm.

"Mmm." Virtue returned to the archeology of her purse. Nash saw some baggies and pills that Virtue moved to the side of her bag. Then, a small bottle appeared: one that would store shampoo or mouthwash during travel. "Wash it down with this," Virtue instructed after knocking back a large pull herself.

Nash nodded and did as she was told. She was equally afraid of ingesting this drug as she was of disobeying this reigning royalty. The drink was sweet and dry, and it hit her suddenly, like pure grain alcohol, or like the pain from sunburn once day turns to evening.

"I should… will I be able to drive the rest of the way?" Nash could not prevent her naiveté from showing. Virtue made a "tssk" sound with her mouth and snapped together the confectionary delight of her glossed lips. Nash realized how foolish she sounded and tried to think of something else to say but was at a loss.

Virtue commanded her to turn on the radio, which she did, and also the heat, so they could sit and relax and enjoy the effects of all they had imbibed. Nash leaned her head against the window on the driver's side door and waited. Time was moving but she was not sure of how quickly. It was so dark outside that she could not trust her internal clock. She could not trust anything: instincts, intuition, even hunger. What was she supposed to be feeling? She felt slightly warm but thought that that was the result of the alcohol. Her lips felt a little tingly, but that might simply be due to the dryness of the air inside the car. She wondered if the entire experience was going to be anticlimactic and she was becoming impatient.

Virtue stared straight ahead, mesmerized by the falling snow.

Nash, too, turned to the snow and thought that she saw a figure moving through it. Perhaps this was the drug starting to take effect.

"Should we… do you want me to start driving again?" The silence had become awkward.

Much to Nash's dismay, Virtue's response consisted of "You do know that Katrina fucked Chad?"

Chad was Nash's boyfriend and had been since her junior year of high school. They had been voted class sweethearts their senior year. Chad had been her only boyfriend and she made most of her plans, and set most of her goals, with him in mind.

"When?" Nash felt as if the car were now in motion, cutting through the falling snow, wheels turning in time to the music. This was all in her head.

"Oh." Virtue slashed the air, dismissing the question, and her hand left a rainbow trail. "Too many times to narrow it down like that. Usually when you are at mock UN, or in class."

When Nash said nothing, Virtue continued, "I am the one who introduced them. Katrina is so much fun to play with. She is truly too easy." Virtue pulled a foot up onto her seat and wrapped a hand around her ankle. She rocked forward, running her other hand through her hair, her forehead coming very close to the dashboard, the heat pushing her bangs apart at the center and blowing them up into hirsute horns.

Nash reached for the bottle. "Can I have some more?" She was hoping to calm her heart which was beating frantically. She felt a familiar pull in her abdomen, as if she were going to have diarrhea. She knew the sickness wasn't because of the drugs or alcohol, but because the perfect protective casing of her world had melted away, leaving her bare and vulnerable and, potentially, alone.

"Chad had seemed so... lonely. The poor guy, he only knew

you, he has only known you. He needed to… expand his horizons, try new things. Just like we are doing now."

The temperature in the car was slowly increasing. Nash pictured a miniature weatherman standing on her dashboard, waving in a warm front despite the whitening of the world outside the window. This made her smile despite herself. Most people have those angels and devils that sit on their shoulders and ponder the big ethical dilemmas of life; Nash had the five o'clock news, reporting the obvious and not caring to interfere, even if she were to rush head-on into disaster.

And, at that moment, her broken heart was hungering for disaster.

"He said that he craved Katrina's smell. That she smelled different from you and that he was sick of you. He needed something strange and different." Virtue dug out some lip gloss and slowly applied it to her pursed, and already glossy, lips. The gloss smelled of cherries, but Nash saw it like gray fingerprints on the girl's mouth. Greasy drops seemed to appear on the girl's chin, as if she were drooling oil. Was this what it meant to "trip"? Nash had always heard about the colors, but she was now seeing things in black and white.

"But, why?" Nash's voice sounded sluggish and deep to her

own ears, like someone had slowed down a record. Virtue, on the other hand, sounded quick and sharp, like a small rodent. "What did you care? What would you gain?"

Virtue raised an eyebrow and dragged a finger through the dribbling oil beneath her lip. It was thick like blood but completely colorless. A part of Nash worried that there was some type of void or black hole forming inside the car and that it had attached itself to Virtue's face. Another part of Nash hoped that this nasty girl would get sucked right into a vortex of her own making. "I was bored. Everything I do I do because I am bored. Even asking you for a ride. Didn't you think I could have taken a train or something? As if I don't know *everyone*...I couldn't get a ride from anyone else? God! You are too funny."

Nash rolled down her window a crack and took a deep breath. The car was stifling.

Virtue began to laugh. "I mean, remember Courtney? God! Do you remember her?"

Nash nodded but kept looking out the window. Courtney had been a girl on their floor who had dropped out right before Thanksgiving break. She had been a shy girl who had never really made any friends.

"I was the one who told everyone they shouldn't talk to her. I told them she was from a residential, that she had severe mental problems. I said she was a habitual liar and would never tell the truth. I told them she was a klepto and convinced her roommates to move out once there was another free room." She was giggling hard, and the sound was getting caught in her throat. "I told them that it was for the best because she would not be tempted to steal if she were in a single. I even said that I had heard that her therapist recommended it." She wiped at her eyes, pulling tears that looked like ash across her face. "What can I say, I'm a giver," she snarked.

Nash's stomach began to hurt. What was happening to her? Was she having a bad trip? Was the acid burning her stomach? Why was it so hard to breathe?

"I was just bored, and I was glad that she left. What a douche. She deserved it. Anyone who wouldn't stand up for themselves deserves it."

There was a bad taste in Nash's mouth, and she felt like she needed some time to focus. This was too much information for her to absorb at once, and she was reeling over Chad. How could he have cheated on her when she had given herself so completely to him? All that she had done and wanted over the past two years had been for him—for his benefit. He had selected their prom colors, their graduation trip location, their college. He had decided when it had been time for her to give up her virginity. He oversaw her diet and exercise regimen. And yet, he grew tired of her *smell?* Well, she was tired of quite a bit, too. Of everything, in fact. She was tired of working for Chad's affection, of trying to appear as if she "had it all together." She was tired of trying to impress worthless, useless, oxygen drainers like Virtue Degloria. Why wouldn't Virtue stop talking? Her confessions were sucking the air right out of the car. It was almost as if Virtue were strangling Nash with her words.

That was exactly what was happening: Virtue was drowning Nash. Nash could see the words literally filling the car, burying them alive. The words were piling up, blocking the windows, and quickly taking up any and all available space.

"And Brett Coulstring... that kid that got—"

"—Yeah, Katrina's old boyfriend." Nash felt that she had to try to say something even though her tongue had grown lethargic. She had to prove to herself that her voice still worked, that she was still able to take in oxygen and run it over her vocal cords. The air in the car was now deadly, thanks to Virtue's poisoned processing.

"Yeah, him. I was bored, so I got Alexa to accuse him of date rape. It was brilliant." She shook her head and licked her fingers, removing the blackened slime from around her nails, and flicking away the words that had lazily fallen on her cheeks. "The counselors were so stupid. Those dykes are so willing to accept the worst about any man. They are just terrified of a penis. But that's the best part, isn't it Nash, the penis?"

Nash nodded and tried to take in some more air, but the car was too full of words. They were mostly small words, but that did not make them any less deadly.

"Just like those snowflakes, no two are alike." Virtue licked her lips, smearing more of the gloss around her face.

"It is all they are good for, right? God, if we had one right now, we wouldn't need them, would we? I mean if you or I had a dick. Girls could just go about their business. Girls like us, not old bull dykes like those counselors. They have cobwebs growing over their crotches." She shook her head and began laughing anew. "They will trust pussy over penis any day of the week. We didn't even have to give them any evidence. It was her word against his and that was all it took. It will always be *hers* over *his* in their world."

Nash's heart began to beat too hard inside her chest. It made her feel dizzy. She was afraid she was going to have a heart attack before getting around to choking on Virtue's words. A heart attack or suffocation? How had she arrived at this choice? And in addition to all the anxiety inside the car, something was moving outside her window. She could see it, in the cracks between the words. A shadow, slinking close to her door, brandishing bright yellow eyes that competed with the moon for luminance. She was sure of it; something was stalking the car. This was not a hallucination, but she couldn't concentrate and save them as long as Virtue kept prattling on.

"Then I got bored, and I convinced Chad to cheat on you." Virtue was back to digging in her purse. Her head was bent, and her hair had fallen forward, exposing the white skin on the back of her neck. This was skin that had not seen the sun in years, and it was flawless. Its perfection infuriated Nash for some inexplicable reason.

"It wasn't that hard; he wasn't that hard to convince. I don't think Katrina really even had to try. She certainly didn't have to ask twice!" The rustling in her purse sounded too loud and the occasional screeches of nails against mirror or compact assaulted Nash's ears.

Nash swore she saw a face outside her window: a man's face, and he was accompanied by large creatures.

"—And once they started, they were just like rabbits. At it every time they got the chance. It is nothing short of a miracle that she isn't pregnant—"

Nash grabbed the girl's throat. She wrapped her hands around that white neck and squeezed. The surprise attack gave her the advantage and she managed to weaken Virtue before the girl even realized what was happening.

Virtue's eyes grew wide, and she stared through the front window, seeming to see the figure that had grabbed Nash's attention earlier. She choked and gargled, coughing small black pebbles onto the dash. The pebbles dissolved and disappeared immediately, leading Nash to believe that they were simply spittle. Virtue raised her hands and began to claw at Nash, raking Nash's skin with her talons. As Nash squeezed, the words popped like bubbles and it became easier for Nash to breathe. Her head was clearing, and, while she was startled by this turn of events, she knew it was what she had to do to save herself.

The girl began to kick and buck in her seat, but Nash held on. The quiet was saving her, was saving them both. She just had to get Virtue to a point of calm that would melt the remaining words away. "Cheating," "Lies," "Manipulation," all these words had to disappear, then all would be right in the world, and it could return to its not-affecting-Nash-by-being-ugly-status.

The man's face was right outside the window. It appeared that he was only a head, without a body. Nash knew she had been right to assign their part of the woods to the haunting of a headless horseman. He was joined by a large animal, and then a few more. Soon, there was a group of figures, moving through the falling snow and coming closer to the car. Nash no longer feared them. Instead, she felt them cheering her on; she felt them taking the pain of Virtue's slashing nails so that she could press harder on the girl's neck. Nash's hands almost met somewhere in the center of the girl's throat, trying desperately to high five each other.

Virtue's eyes widened even further, threatening to leap from their sockets and run for freedom. Nash turned her head away from the girl, partly to avoid being scratched, but mostly to concentrate. She was focused on quieting her passenger, on gaining control over her sudden loss. She hadn't realized how much anger she had stored inside of her for so many years, nor how good it would feel when it was all spent. Anger over trivial injustices that had grown in mass in her memory. Rage over larger injustices that had found no resolution. This was the high Nash had been waiting for. She had been waiting most of her life for a feeling like this: like truly being alive. Despite replicating the murder scenario, Nash would have to wait another twenty years to feel it again, an emotion returned when her husband was stolen.

Virtue was no longer making gagging noises, but she was convulsing and shuddering. Her feet were kicking at the dashboard, and she slid down in the seat, trying to slip out of Nash's grasp. Her struggle was futile, and, after a few more minutes of struggle, Nash was left alone in the car, staring at the famished yellow eyes of the coyotes that had surrounded her vehicle.

Two weeks after school reconvened, Virtue, the queen of the scene, was a specter, and her memory barely registered on the social radar. It was almost as if her classmates and dorm-mates had digested her legacy, just as the coyotes had digested large parts of her flesh and bones.

Nash had benefited the most from this shift in peer caste. She had sold the drugs in Virtue's purse, gaining popularity and fattening her own purse enough to pay for her spring formal wear, where she had met her future husband, Derrick.

She had also found a small plasticware container outside her car door, after she had dragged Virtue's body into the woods. The container was a strange oblong shape, like an enlarged pill or vitamin and was sealed tight. It rested on a note which read:

When closed, all doors will be open to you

When opened, the final door will close

Nash kept the box closed and securely stowed away from

anyone who might open it. She kept it closed and amassed power and wealth and managed to get away with whatever she wished. It was as if she were a magician. People failed to see the crimes she pulled right in front of their eyes.

This story should end "happily ever after" yet we know, from reading her thoughts on the hospital table, that Nash's story ends with a stab to the throat.

Do not forget that women are mass murderers, too. Too often, they fail to kill all their victims, so they fall under the radar. For example, on Thanksgiving Day,

1980, Pricilla Joyce Ford ran down pedestrians in her Lincoln Continental. She had hoped to kill seventy-five people but was satisfied with a death toll of five. On January 29, 1979, Brenda Spencer opened fire on a school yard, killing the janitor and principal and wounding eight children. On October 30, 1985, Sylvia Seegrist opened fire on a mall. Three people died, eight were wounded. On May 20, 1988, Laurie Wasserman Dann began delivering food laced with arsenic to homes where she had been previously employed. She then started several fires before taking a .357 magnum to an elementary school. She killed one child and wounded six others. No one stopped her as she got into her car and drove to a stranger's house. She wounded the owner before taking her own life. On January 30, 2006, Jennifer San Marco killed seven people at a mail processing plant before killing herself.

Nash knew of two things: that she had to find Derrick, and that she had to get rid of the spiders. Doing so would put her back in control of her life and return her to the elevated status she experienced after killing Virtue but before misplacing her husband. Nash chalked the spiders up to Cape Cod's continuous cycle of irritants: seasonal vexations worse than the tourists. There were the noisy little birds that the government protected—harming a bird would have put Nash behind bars faster than all her prior felonies combined. Yet, the birds did nothing to alleviate the tiny green worms that managed to crawl into cars, hair, mouths, and nostrils. There was the aggressive sand that appeared one summer (Nash suspected P.P. had imported sand from some foreign galaxy but could never prove it) and took up residence on their peninsular road. It stuck to shoes and invaded homes despite outdoor showers and elaborately grated foot fountains. She saw these spiders as no different, yet their basic rhythm pointed to an organized power behind their appearance.

What force had caused Derrick's disappearance? Did her "winning him" by virtue of Virtue mean that they were eventually destined for tragedy? He had been the only person that she had viewed as truly belonging to her. The kids would eventually form their own families. Her parents, who she felt barely knew her, would grow old. But Derrick had been honestly possessed (as honestly as anything else in Nash's life, which held very little honesty). She shared more of herself with him than she did with anyone. Even though he knew little of her proclivities, he was still light years ahead of anyone else in terms of intimacy with her.

Winning Derrick had been the first in a long line of wins for Nash. She had moved to the second largest house by the sea (eclipsed only by super-frenemy P.P.), had given birth to two beautiful and healthy children, had lorded control over the women in her town and her social circle. She gave the best parties, owned the latest electronics, pimped and pushed the women around her until half were addicted to drugs, the other to deliverable food. Then, the piece de resistance: the Plasticware.

The Plasticware had come in waves, in flood-like proportions. Box after box marched into homes, drowning out any remaining air in the cabinets in a sea of synthetic product.

When the women opened their cupboards, their cabinets, spun

their Lazy Susans, they were whirled and twirled in an avalanche of artificial supplies. It had sent off a tsunami of nearly supernatural competition. The women wanted nothing more than to obtain set after set, and to rub each other's noses in their acquisitions. The Plasticware had been the most addictive substance Nash had ever peddled.

Not only had she hosted the Plasticware party, she had won the most special set when an elaborate, and fully rigged, contest had been staged. It was a scavenger hunt of sorts. Since the party was at her house, and she had made the scavenger hunt list, Nash was at an immediate advantage. The other women could not complain. Many were too narcotized to understand what had happened. The others were too afraid of Nash.

Except for friend Sylvie.

Sylvie had taken Nash's victory the hardest. Sylvie always had to win, in everything from flatware to childbirth. She actually lorded her multiples over the others, with their mediocre single births.

Sylvie had manipulated nature. She had cried wolf. She had told her doctor that she had been trying to conceive for ages, for so many cycles of the moon that she had run out of calendars with which to keep track of her conception days: the mucous-filled, pang filled, craving days.

She had lied.

And she had lied several times over, to several doctors. But this was not her crime, and not the crime for which she would be punished during the search for Derrick.

She lied and received treatments and pills until her ovaries were so stimulated that a final doctor warned her against sexual relations for at least a month. He told her it would be dangerous to attempt to conceive unless she were an animal and capable of producing a litter.

This was her crime: she went ahead and seduced her husband. So that she could have multiples, so that she could win. She was the only mother on the Cape with quintuplets and that garnered a great deal of attention. The Cape Quints were always on the front page, enjoying the fireworks, enjoying the Christmas stroll, enjoying everything that everyone else enjoyed only with far more publicity.

And Sylvie's sacrifice had been five-fold—that was why she would be punished. She had had to be bedridden for months of the pregnancy—this fact garnered a great deal of sympathy, so she repeated it like a prayer or mantra. And she had the best mother-of-all delivery stories as it involved incubators and ICU and residual occupational therapy and follow up visits that required the entire family to leave the Cape.

How Sylvie had hoarded and not sold the Plasticware. She had run up an unforgiveable tab with the bank of Nash. She had whined and groveled and said that she was desperate for additional Plasticware. She declared that no one could appreciate how hard it was to pack school snacks for the Quints, to keep their hair accessories organized, to simply function in the face of day-to-day tasks times five. She was, after all, the victim in the scenario. It was almost as if she had expected Nash to eat the loss.

Which would have happened over Nash's dead body.

Nash, seated in her sunroom, placed her coffee mug onto the table, and noticed a spider lurking on the opposite side, taking a ride on the ceramic. It peered at her quizzically. Without thought, she placed her thumb over the arachnid's many eyes and applied pressure, leaving a purplish blotch on her otherwise pristine mug. She stood and carried the mug to the dishwasher, trampling spiders as she walked, grinding them into the carpet, leaving stains that would challenge the cleaning lady when she arrived on Thursday. The spiders did not seem intimidated by Nash's return volleys. They continued their assault, trying to touch her, while she persisted to stain her house in her attempts to take them out one at a time. There were probably other, more systematic approaches to ridding the house of spiders, but it is often difficult, when you are accustomed to others doing so much for you, to recognize what you really need to do for yourself.

Once in the kitchen, Nash swept her hand along the counter, leveling the spiders that had aligned themselves with the window. Because she had survived Virtue's suffocating words all those moons prior, she did not fear the spiders in terms of their number. Because she had scratched and clawed her way to the top of the social caste on the Cape, she felt invincible toward these insects. She knew she could open the windows and usher some to freedom, but they did not seem deserving. She had rarely met anyone, human or insect, who merited leniency or compassion. For years, Nash had broken other's wrists and wills in order to protect her own. She had smashed the nose of the pretty bank teller who had screwed up her siphoning job. She had cut off the pinky finger of the Girl Scout troop leader when the woman had tried to keep part of the cookie sale kick back. Nash had destroyed marriages and lives. She had trampled those less fortunate than she with the same anger she had felt for herself in the days when she had had less than others. And when the sun set, and darkness crept over her house, she slept just as soundly—swathed in age-reducing serum—as the innocent.

Prior to amassing a Plasticware empire, Nash dabbled in Oxycontin, Ativan, Klonopin, and Percocet; in bookkeeping and gambling. The mother lode of money had come from hiring out escorts. After the wedding season, the same men whose vows Nash toasted and feted, paid for the attentions and company of women Nash procured. Prior to having what some would consider an obscene amount of wealth, Nash had learned how to put herself in places inhabited by the very rich. She haunted important charity functions, political parties, and film premiers. It did not require a great deal of effort; women have a much easier time slipping past security and cozying up to men of importance. Nash, for her part, had taken Virtue's "boredom" activity of unleashing girls on unsuspecting boyfriends one step further. Unlike Virtue, Nash profited monetarily as well as psychologically.

In her mind, Nash ran a catering service. She just happened to cater to people's vices and hidden darknesses, as opposed to their celebrations and milestones.

While Nash was the red-headed, wrinkle-free Godmother, there was one woman in town that she had never been able to get the goods on. There was one woman who simply appeared infallible and off limits. Nash could neither hurt nor coerce the

Porcelain Princess (P.P). P.P. had a real name, but the women by the sea had christened her the Porcelain Princess because she never had a spot or an imperfection. And she was so bloody cold.

P.P.'s perfection infuriated Nash for some inexplicable reason.

Once, Nash had turned one of her own men on P.P., asking for the woman's head on a silver platter, or a nice china plate. This man was more of a boy, but he was good at doing what Nash told him. *Was* good. *Had been.*

This incident had taken place prior to the Plasticware and long before the bracelet party:

There are times when one is so preoccupied with putting one foot in front of the other, with having soles touch concrete and souls remain embedded within bodies of the earth, that one completely ignores the anvil gunning for one's head, dropped from dozens of stories above.

This had been the case with Danen Hill when Nash had discovered him, circling trees in the town square. Thin and ropey, Danen was the poster-child for the need for sports programs in school. Greasy and acne-ed, he was an after-school-special about the obligation of personal hygiene. Lost, literally and spiritually, he was a predator's dream. She had watched him for nearly twenty minutes from the safety of her BMW S5, before she had approached him with her offer. In the past, when she had used him to run errands and do jobs for her, he had appeared more stable, more alert. More a part of this world.

Now, he had that look about him, the one that was simultaneously surprised and pleased about the cleanliness of a sidewalk or patch of grass when viewed from nearly six feet above it. This was the look of someone who was accustomed to sliding down onto the ground, hoping against hope that the puddle welcoming his flesh was that of his own saliva or bodily fluid, as opposed to that of a stranger.

Danen's family lived far away from the sea. It was not that they couldn't afford to be placed further from the houses that continuously displayed garbage on their front lawns—garbage spangled with hand lettered "for sale" signs, begging for anyone to see the beauty of the discarded relics. Danen's father, at one time, ran several successful businesses. The businesses dealt with either grass or concrete and, as everyone's landscaping required one or both, Danen's father did well.

Then Danen's mother ran off with a cult. Then she returned with two adopted children (who resembled her a great deal) to add to her brood of three. Then, she left again to "find herself," and, in that instance, lost her children to her husband who convinced a judge that she was unfit.

Next, he convinced others that *he* was no longer fit by squandering money on gifts and vacations for a variety of women. No one in their small community was sure if Danen or his four siblings had a parent at home at all, but apathy was the latest fashion, it was the new black, and Nash wore it better than most.

"Some mothers would have been better off not choosing life," Nash sniffed to herself as she watched Danen scratching at his sides like a page from Darwin's proposal.

Nash knew how to use Danen's needs to her benefit, and he knew how to use stainless steel tongs and salad forks on a human face, which was Nash's need. He had a detached interest in violence that matched Nash's detached interest in anyone but herself.

"Danen?" She had left her vehicle only after the foot traffic in the square was at an ebb. He was muttering to himself, forcing his fingertips into his tight pockets. He stared at his high-tops; his lips moving quickly on a peaked, sweaty face.

"Danen?" Nash moved close enough to touch him but didn't. Not without a tissue or some sort of protective barrier between them. He had a funny smell, like a car's ashtray on a blistering hot day. "Will you let me help you?"

She was able to pick up some of his mutterings in much the

same way that she understood some of the words on the menu at Sangre Bleu: she was a tourist in Danen's mind. What she understood was that he had seen a white squirrel chasing an albino peacock and that this sight had agitated him. She wanted to ask him why an albino peacock would have any value without its emerald encrusted tail, but she knew that that was not the path to clarity with this young man.

"Danen." She dug into her purse for something she could slip over her hand so that she could touch his shoulder and bring him into focus.

Her rustling paused his mania. He must have recognized his benefactor's Kate Spade.

"Good." She kept her hand inside her bag and his bloodshot eyes on the poppy-colored leather. "I need something from you and then I can help you."

She slipped him a few tablets of Oxycontin that she had secured from the pharmacy in exchange for a favor from the pharmacist's son's teacher that resulted in the son not having to go to summer school. She knew that Danen was after bigger game, but this would tide him over, at least until his job was done. There was something to be said for dangling large carrots.

"I have this, too." She pulled out a packet of papers and pointed to a blank line on the final sheet. "Remember, you need to sign this. It's for my taxes. It's a contract saying I paid you for some construction work on my house." As she handed Danen a pen, she remembered the work he had actually done and smiled. There had been far more gore than she had requested: he was a true artist.

She took the papers and pen back from him, wiping the pen before returning it to her bag. "Contracts really are quite beautiful, aren't they? Just simple paper but they mean so much to those IRS men."

Nash's life of crime had begun honestly. She had felt too smart and too rich for housework, but without chores, she had grown very bored. While crime was bad, boredom was worse. She had joined the ladies' clubs and country clubs and school boards. She had done "mommy and me" yoga and ballet. Finally, she had been enticed into selling *Cranberry Craving* products. These were all natural, organic, MSG-free meal complements meant to cleanse the pallet and reduce the need for calorie-laden desserts.

As Derrick had been blissfully unaware of this venture, any commission Nash earned had gone directly into her pocket and had been utilized to suit her needs. As her family and her role in the community grew, so had her needs. She had decided to move from commission to pure profit with the creation of *Kitchen Goddess* meal plans. Nash had created and cooked the meals, delivering them to women who were not willing to take the reins and limit their food intake themselves. The women in her social circle considered themselves too busy to cook, and their personal chefs too "continental" to serve anyone but the women's children. Nash would spice up the recipes with laxatives at first, allowing for the scales to herald success in numeric hallelujahs. Then, prior to the charity galas and wedding seasons, she upped the caloric and fat content, sending the customers into a spiral of shame and fear. Then "plan 2" would be introduced, at a higher price, and the cycle would begin anew.

It was process and demand 101.

But food bored Nash, until the Plasticware containers were introduced. That was when storing food and hoarding food created whirling dervishes of excitement. Before the Plasticware, food was boring, and food regimens were worse. Then Nash had remembered Virtue and her golden stash. And she had remembered Virtue and how smug that girl had been. And she had remembered strangling Virtue and how she had never really chalked that experience up as a victory. And so, she had traded her meal plan business in for something with a greater return on investment.

Here is a story that Nash would rather forget, but should tell, for the sake of providing background information. This story settles inside the Danen container, helping it to retain its shape and substance. She recalls this story as she sits in her sunroom, knowing that Danen was either carrying out her instructions, or failing miserably:

Nashville's intense dislike for the Porcelain Princess, as well as her desire to see her dead, was well founded. She had not only shamed Nash in ways that hearkened back to Virtue, but she had shamed Nash's son. Her second born. Everyone had attended a school social: the kind where kids were not invited, and the teaching staff moonlighted as the wait staff. Senior faculty were blessed with remaining in the coat-check room and keeping an eye on the guest's valuables (if the guests could trust the faculty with their children, they could certainly trust them with expensive outer garments). The newer teachers were forced to shuffle from table to table, bitterly serving the demanding parents of the high maintenance kids they wanted to eviscerate all day, every day.

Nash would call this scene *Heaven. Paradise. The way things ought to be.*

During the meal, P.P. tossed over her glass of wine in a way that was so elegant, it had to be premeditated. From prior "business," Nash recognized the school's behavior therapist as she was sent to clean the liquid, using one of those brick-like erasers as a sponge.

The Porcelain Princess recognized her, too. But she made a big production of making sure that everyone realized that she was *pretending* not to know her. That she was above her. She made sure that everyone saw through the charade and understood that unless the Princess wanted to recognize you, you were invisible.

Then it dawned on Nash: the Princess not only knew a staff member, she knew a *special needs* staff member. The humanity!

Nash practiced her most self-deprecating, yet sympathetic tone in her head, deducing the exact point of stress on each syllable in order to parry the greatest thrust.

"Princess." She leaned across the table and tapped her hand consolingly—for good measure—"You *actually* knew her, didn't you? Does that mean....?" She swallowed audibly and retracted her hand in the shape of a claw to demonstrate the primitive distress. "Is Garrett... you know... does he take those classes?"

Without missing a beat, the Porcelain Princess mirrored Nash's shock and added a pinch of disgust. "Oh no. No, no, no, no, no, no. Absolutely no! Garrett has been nothing but honors since day one. Why, he's the youngest student ever to be allowed into AP classes. We've even hired him out to others... less fortunate, intellectually… as a tutor. Well, *hire* is entirely wrong: it's charity, of course." Her eyes scanned the table, tallying entry and exit wounds of those whose children had just been labeled *less fortunate, intellectually*. Her eyes rested on Nash's as she finished off the round. "I am so lucky to have a child who does not need… *extras*… just to get by." She ticked off her bejeweled fingers. "Tutors, counseling, classes… *speech*."

Before Nash could prevent the tell-tale drop in her poker face, her mouth gaped enough to park a car on her tongue. Riley had been in speech therapy the summer after his braces had been installed to help with a sloppy "s" sound. Nash had told everyone that he had been selected for voice classes for stage and screen, but somehow, that bitch *knew*.

It was that exchange that painted a picture in Nash's mind of raking her nails down P.P.'s face and pulling large patches of her hair out at the roots. She imagined pummeling the woman's face with her fists, breaking that perfect nose, breaking those fake glasses (P.P. always wore cat's eyeglasses with gold rims. Not because she needed visual assistance, her eyesight was 20/20, naturally, but because she liked the way they accentuated her cheekbones). She pictured pulling off the lashes that had to be fake; the spider-like lashes that posed an insult to Nash, who had fought so hard to repress a fear of the creatures. Nash imagined smashing one of the wine glasses or coffee cups and shoving pieces into P.P's cheeks, carving the smooth, wrinkle-free skin until it hung in strips, dribbling blood down her neck and onto her Hermes scarf.

Blood stains never come out of silk.

It was this shaming that had led Nash to ask Danen to brutally murder P.P. Unfortunately, this task was a work in progress. Every time Danen got close to P.P, she either escaped, or invited him in for cookies or brownies or cake. The woman obviously never touched the stuff, but her house was a veritable bakery. A sugared Danen was almost as useless as a drugged Danen, and so, P.P. survived, to steal Nash's friends, to say terrible things about her in public, and to basically live as if she were better than everyone else.

It was as Nash remembered this regrettable failure that a few of the spiders lurking about her entered her brain. One or two crawled in through her ears. Another managed to scurry up her nose. When she gasped in surprise, one more catapulted into her open mouth.

Once she resumed control and recovered from the shock, Nash turned to her ever-present cell phone and called her gardener. He would know how to handle the spiders; she planned to focus on locating her husband.

Fortunately, or unfortunately, the spiders nestled inside of her were willing to provide her with clues.

✹

You should consider: Lady Macbeth went insane only after her husband began consorting with witches.

First things first, Nashville and Derrick had always been completely faithful to each other in the physical sense of the word. Nash had never interpreted fidelity to mean sharing every secret and every aspect of oneself. People needed to retain something for themselves or else the containers in one's closet would be shamefully bare.

Despite the lies and fabrications, her marriage was a happy one, and she made a silent vow to reinstate it to normalcy, as she watched her gardener traverse her circuitous driveway in his pick-up truck. The gardener was short and stocky and nondescript in Nash's eyes. He was accompanied by a woman who was all those things in an extended sense.

"You remember my mother?" Hector swept his arm graciously

toward the older woman, as if presenting something worth beholding.

"Is she helping you today?" Nash asked with absolutely no interest.

"No, Mrs. Nash, I was taking her on her errands, as I do, when you called and said it was an emergency."

"Mrs. Nash," the woman called cheerfully, "I brought you some flan!" She held out a container. Nash could see matching ones of differing sizes in the truck behind the woman.

"Where did you get those?" Nash pointed a manicured nail at the container, completely ignoring the flan inside.

"Mr. Derrick gave them to me." The woman gave a wide smile and shook her head as people do when astounded by the good luck that has fallen upon them. "Such a nice man. A nice, nice man." She winked. "And handsome, too, right?" Her smile managed to grow even wider.

Nash had thought that Derrick had never even noticed the Plasticware, much less knew where the main stash was contained.

"I had Hector bring him a pie, Tuesday," she announced proudly, "I hope you enjoyed some too?"

"Tuesday? Hector, you saw Mr. Derrick yesterday?"

Hector nodded. "I come Tuesdays and Fridays, Mrs. Nash."

"Of course I know that. I am the one who hired you, aren't I?"

Hector looked confused, as if he were trying to remember how he came to be employed by the DeCotas.

"What I meant was," Nash clarified, "You spoke to my husband yesterday?" She had thought Derrick had been in a work training the entire day. He had gone out of his way to remind her of the event and to specify that he would be late. She had fallen asleep before he came home and realized that she was not sure he had ever returned home. She had no clue as to when he had officially gone missing. "He was in the house, and you saw him?"

"Not in the house, Mrs. Nash, in the garage. I went in to get the…" He looked at his mother blankly and said something in Spanish.

"Sulfur," his mother said plainly, "Hector had to go into your garage to get the sulfur."

Hector nodded enthusiastically. "For the rose bushes in your garden. Because the soil around them had become too sweet. And Mr. Derrick was in the garage, with the eggs."

"Eggs?"

"Spider eggs. He said you had a mosquito problem. Mr. Derrick never likes for me to use chemicals, says the toxins could hurt the kids if they play in their bare feet, or don't wash their hands too good. So, he did the smart thing and was using spiders to get rid of the mosquitos." Hector shrugged. "But now you say the spiders are a problem."

"You saw the eggs yesterday, Hector. Would the spiders be hatched today?" Nash rolled her eyes condescendingly.

"Probably not. Some take a while. I am not an expert, and I don't know how… ripe… those eggs were." He blushed as if they were discussing human reproduction.

She could not imagine that the spiders that had assaulted her were the same that her husband had tended the day before. And why would they be? Why would he intentionally do anything to harm or scare her?

Then again, she thought they had agreed to a bat house to deal with mosquitos. They had never discussed spiders. She wasn't even sure that spiders actually ate mosquitos. Besides, Derrick had been aware of her fear. When they watched movies together, in the early days, they would snuggle on the couch in the darkened room and Derrick would tickle the back of her neck, laughing when he made her jump, as she always imagined a dangerous black widow or some other poisonous arachnid on her skin.

Hector brought a spot sprayer and bottle of liquid from the back of his truck. He smiled at Nash and nodded at the bottle.

"Peppermint, tea tree oil, citrus, dish soap, and vinegar. Spiders hate it and it has no toxins, like Mr. Derrick likes. This will keep them out of your house."

The spiders in Nash's brain scurried, causing a feeling that was more ticklish than uncomfortable. It felt like Derrick's light fingertips, trying to spook her, or simply arouse her. She could have sworn she heard one of the spiders talking, but that would have been ridiculous. And Nash lived a very serious life.

"Mrs. Nash?" Hector's mother peered around the open door of the truck. "There is a note in here for you." She held it up and Nash could see her name carefully typed on the outside of the origami-style folded note.

"Where did that come from?"

The woman shrugged. "It was in one of the empty containers. The lid slipped, and when I went to put it back on, I saw it."

Nash spoke very slowly, "Think carefully. Has anyone been near those containers?"

"That's what's weird… just me." She paused, thinking. "And Mr. Derrick, I guess. Before he gave them to me."

The note said:

The power of poison

The power of plastic

Precious time is wasting

The note was wrapped around a swatch of hair and the overabundance of the letter "P" did not escape Nash's notice.

The spiders grew angry. They grew agitated. They did not grow in size but in the complexity of their voices—which were now clearly voices.

It was Derrick's hair. She knew that it came from behind his right ear. She swore that it appeared sweaty, and she considered, for not the first time, that Derrick was under great duress.

First things first, Nashville DeCota was not a drug addict. Not in the sense that Danen was an addict, at least. Sure, she had sampled some of her products, when her products were of the pharmaceutical variety—prior to the Plasticware. Her adventure with Virtue had left her a little more open to experimentation. Secondly, it would have been difficult, even for a woman with Nash's drive and tenacity, to accomplish all that she had (and to have wreaked all the revenge that she had) without the assistance of non-prescription medical-grade enhancements.

The spiders were certainly not the result of drug inducement, or drug withdrawal. They were far too articulate to be a hallucination. At the moment, they were telling her to go back into her sunroom. They were going to help her devise a plan to find Derrick. She had hours before the kids came home from school, but time would soon be running out for her husband.

✳

Remember the myths. Remember that, in the beginning, there were two: the god of light and the Spider Woman. They created all life. Everyone loved the Spider Woman because she was radiant and because she sang them to life.

Plasticware does not hurt your arms and hands when it lands on you—no one has ever been stoned to death using pill containers, soup canisters, plastic jars, or tureens. No one has been stoned to death with anything but stones because plastic does not hurt you, even when so much of it falls on you.

More than the others, Nashville had enjoyed storing food in her new containers. She had no desire to acquire more, and her secret stash to sell held no temptation for her. The purple-rimmed Plasticware continued her eating protocol of abstinence and heralded her win over the others. As Nash stashed grains and pastas, sugar and flour, cereal and candy, (and, in a secret container, arsenic) she recalled Sylvie's fallen face when Nash had gone to claim her prize. She remembered P.P.'s put upon retrieval of checkbook from within the confines of her purse as she had to actually purchase (imagine! no free sample for the Princess!) her set with the mundane coral lids. She saw Wi Fi and Gwynnie passive aggressively passing the "better" lavender set between them, punctuating increasingly hostile thrusts with disclaimers:

"No, you take them... " "Oh, but they match your curtains... " "I'll take the next set... " "Please, I'd be happier if you had them... "

There is nothing inherently dangerous about Plasticware, but it does trap notes in rose gardens, and it does transport the wallet and hair clippings of a captive Derrick. And, it does promise to send body parts soon, if its demands are not met.

Nashville knew that she could not go to the police. They had been overly generous to her the many times she had been falsely accused of nefarious crimes. They had looked the other way when Dinah misbehaved. They agreed that the DeCota family was often on the receiving end of false accusations. Yet Nash knew that the true corruptions she tried to bury would resurface during any investigation of her home and family.

She also knew that she had to listen to the spiders' plan. Even when they introduced her to someone she did not want to meet.

Pray you remember Catherine Howard, the adolescent wife of Henry VIII. She died for her love of another man and was shrewd enough to request her own chopping block so that she could practice for her execution. One must look equally good with and without one's head. And remember Catherine's Lady in Waiting, Jane (Rochford) Boleyn, who wrongly accused her own husband of incest, sending him to the block. Karma's humor found Jane accused as an accessory to Catherine's adultery and cost her her head. Sometimes, we are our own worst enemies.

The second unique occurrence, for Nash, was the appearance of the man.

As she sat, frozen in her seat under the lecture of the spiders—grimacing over the ones that had managed to crawl into her brain—and reading ransom notes, a face appeared in the top corner of the sunroom. That a face appeared at all was a source of great amazement as the window was so far from the ground. That it appeared distinct, separate, severed—if you will—from a body, was also significant. But what struck Nash the most was that the face was recognizable, impossible to place, but strangely familiar. She had never had a talent for paying attention to faces or names, but she knew this face had factored importantly in her life.

This was not the first time that Nash had seen a severed head, but this head blinked and stared directly into her eyes. The prior severed head had been an intentional accident. It had been business. The piano teacher had enjoyed more Adderall than she had paid for. Much, much more. And her liberal supply had made Nash appear foolish.

At the time, Nash had tried to find *le mot juste* for her predicament. She had asked Derrick, "What is the female equivalent of 'emasculate'?" to which he had responded, "There is none. The nature of being female is emasculation." Then he had smirked and muttered, "You can't remove power where it doesn't exist in the first place."

Nash had been furious. Again, with his lack of understanding. They would not have their house at the end of the street if it weren't for her. Did he really think that the original owners had agreed to come down that far on their asking price? Did he really think that he garnished a salary that merited beach front property? There were those occasional nights where she prayed she could tell him the truth, where she could see his face when he recognized who the true general was on the war front. Most nights, she simply prayed that they were never audited.

She truly loved Derrick. At first, he had been a prize after the Virtue incident. She had showed him off on campus, delighting in the jealousy he inspired by being so handsome, and athletic, and sweet. And precisely because he had been all those things, she had fallen in love with him, had confided in him (about all save the murders, the drug deals, the prostitution, and the taxes), and had relished making love to him. In her estimation, they truly had a happy marriage. She was continuously grateful that she didn't come home to chaos, like Sylvie, or an empty relationship with a habitual cheater, like Melanie. For all appearances, her life was idyllic, save the drug deals, the prostitution, and the murders.

Which creates a full circle back to the piano teacher. This story doesn't even have its own container on Nash's mental shelf. It is part of her hidden life where she has lumped her crimes together and given them a variety of faux labels like "overhead" and "inventory." Even in the privacy of her own mind, she was covering her tracks from auditors.

The piano teacher was a classic case of displacement (and of a displaced head). The piano teacher's large tab with the pharmacy of Nash would not normally merit a death warrant, but, because

Derrick had called her powerless, Nash would make another woman quake.

There are things about Nashville DeCota—characteristics attributable to environment, not heredity, that would be surprising to some. Case in point, she can expertly hotwire a car, she can cut brakes, she can even plant bombs when the mood strikes. With the piano teacher, there would be a perfectly executed hit and run—really, more like a startle and swerve. The plan was to leave the woman severely injured, hooked on pain pills, ideally permanently disabled. If the hands that tickled the ivory were left unable to even itch a phantom scratch, then all the better.

Nash had waited for a night cloaked in mist and fog. A night so dark that even her red, red hair would be easily masked. Her Egyptian eyes had been given dark circles with shadow and the freckles the laser removal had missed had been covered with a deeply shaded concealer—all to make her less conspicuous. She had gone down the teacher's road earlier that day in order to compose a little symphony with the woman's steering wheel—one that would cause it to lock with the right provocation. She had also played a tune on the brake wires. In the night, in the dark, Nash had come at the teacher's car with her own, knowing the teacher always left her house after her last lesson—knowing that most of

Nash's friends and acquaintances finished their high-button-days by entering plunging neckline nights. Nash came at the teacher's car, causing her to swerve into a row of Cape pines.

Nash had meant only to hurt her, but the broken glass and shards of metal had other intentions. Nash had assumed that the woman would have her seatbelt fastened, as they tell you to do on commercials and billboards. She hadn't expected the woman to fly up into the windshield like a sheet that flaps on the wind as it dries on a clothesline. As Nash was squealing her get away, she had seen the piano teacher's head take leave of her body which was hanging out of the windshield. The head rolled down the hood of the car, diluting the paint with blood that beaded in the rain. The head rolled as if liberated via guillotine and Nash drove away, convinced the head would roll after her, nipping at her heels in retribution. Ironically, Nash's story began, but actually ended, with Nash dramatically considering herself nearly decapitated. When the bracelet party acted as a catalyst for catastrophe, it was Nash who nearly lost her head.

Now Nash watched this familiar but anonymous head move past her sun porch window and she felt the spiders rolling around in her own head and she knew that this was not the worst she would experience in the coming days.

Remember Lolita: the nearly-grown wolf in lamb's clothing.
Nabokov, a fan of Poe's, echoed the enchantment of the eloquent "Annabel
Lee." Its most important refrain in terms of our warnings: "In a kingdom
by the sea..."

The spiders seemed happy to be seated on the other side of the principal's desk, beside a blasé Dinah. Nash was not happy. She wanted to scream that her husband was missing. She was highly concerned that she had seen a disembodied head outside her house. She was tired of listening to the musings of spiders. Mostly, she was frustrated that her daughter did not recognize how much stress she was under. Instead, she had raised the stakes.

"Mrs. DeCota." Principal Doyle slowly laid his fingers out on his desk, signifying that everyone in the room should keep their tempers below the level of his palms. "You understand that we have Dinah's best interests at heart. We are not in the business of doling out punishments. We aim to provide learning opportunities—"

"By keeping her home?"

"For a few days. During that time, she will be expected to

reflect on what she has done and to keep a journal detailing her journey toward ownership over her actions."

Dinah synchronously scoffed with the spiders.

"And you are going to allow one woman's testimony to irrevocably mar the permanent record of a minor?" Despite life being far from normal at the moment, Nash reminded herself of who she was and how she normally handled these situations.

"It is more than Mrs. Holloway's statement. Others witnessed the abuse and also testified to the reason the Quints were removed from the Super Bowl float."

"I signed a waiver regarding that field trip."

Principal Doyle sighed and rubbed his forehead with one hand. "The waiver, Mrs. DeCota, is merely coverage for if Dinah, or any student, were to be injured on an outing away from the school campus. There is no coverage for if a student were to injure others."

Nash turned to Dinah and fixed her with any icy stare to no result.

"There are strict anti-bullying laws in this state. We are all fortunate that no criminal charges have been filed."

"But the pot part," Dinah interjected, "it's legal now."

Principal Doyle frowned. "Not for minors and especially not on school grounds."

"She threatened us." Nash both loved and was irritated by Dinah's inability to give up easily. "She said to 'flip a coin' or something and if it were heads she would handle it legally, tails…I don't know but it was threatening."

Nash was beginning to lose the threads of this conversation as the spiders were loudly and cruelly reminiscing about the costumes Sylvie had amassed for the Quints to wear on the Super Bowl float. They were to be four fingers and a thumb representing five rings that had been won. The spiders counted correctly that it was six rings. They also chuffed at the horrible costumes. Nash wondered how the spiders knew of this unfortunate information.

By the time the spiders quieted, she found herself walking out of the school with her suspended, but unremorseful daughter.

"I am going to get back at that incubator," Dinah sneered as they made their way to the car. The spiders thought that was a wonderful idea.

It is important to remember that suicide bombers can be women. It is important to recognize the grenades hidden beneath skirts.

Prior to leaving the house, Nash oversaw the lawn work, meal preparation, and house cleaning. She was extraordinary at delegation. No one questioned the squelched spiders. Just as no one ever wondered why a fresh lawn needed to be rolled over the sandy patches in front of her house in the fall, precisely when natural grass would be dying, or in the early spring, when snow was still a threat. There was nary a raised eyebrow at oddly, artificially colored roses that were required to be cultivated and killed in order to fill vases on a dining room table that serviced no one. Orders for elaborate meals were filled, even though most nights Dinah and Riley took sandwiches and snacks up to their rooms, and Derrick consumed more post-work martinis than food. And we already know about Nash's food predilections. Nash was rarely questioned about anything in her own home, or anywhere, for that matter. That was just how things were. *Nearly perfect.*

The disembodied head *had questioned* her. In their conversation, Nash had remembered the face that had watched her kill Virtue and wondered if they were not one and the same. The spiders had sided with the disembodied head instead of the fully bodied head that gave them shelter. The head and the spiders told her that she must stop obsessing over the Plasticware and host another party. When she had argued that the Plasticware had made her who she was, she had been told that she was only looking at a sliver of the moon. This new party would instigate so much more: it would be *everything*. She had been promised that this road would lead directly to Derrick, and her number one goal was to bring him home.

Nash, following orders, had ordered her social set of non-questioning minions to meet at Michaels, so she could introduce the idea of the bracelet party. Because they did not seem rapacious enough, she (and the severed head and the spiders) ordered a second meeting at Boomers. Boomers was not a place they normally frequented. In fact, it would be a safe bet that none of the ladies had ever darkened Boomers' door before.

Seated around the table were: Melanie, Gwynnie, Wi Fi, P.P., Sylvie, and Nash. Nash tried to move away from Sylvie, as the woman had taken to calling or texting her several times a day, usually about Plasticware. One text was about the Quints and the five elements they represent. The spiders had laughed at the Quint that had been linked to aether, or void. The spiders thought Sylvie was a horrible mother and suggested that someone take care of her soon.

"On my list," Nash had sighed, but the spiders were not known for being patient.

There were televisions in all corners of the room and several more above the bar. On a few sets, a commercial could be seen featuring a handsome man waxing poetic about protein bars. Nash rolled her eyes at the pathetic bun on the actor's head: she truly knew how to sport one.

The women were all vivacious and hungry for gossip, save for Melanie who was staring gape-mouthed at P.P. who was telling a story with her usual flourishes. While Nash could not discern if the stare was positive or negative, she hated for that woman to receive any kind of attention and she warned Melanie that she was about to catch a few flies (with the level of cleanliness in Boomers, this was not out of the question). The spiders groaned hungrily at the idea of flies.

It was difficult for Nash to separate the urgent whispers of the women from those of the spiders. Nash didn't know who she wished would shut up more.

Sylvie was loudly discussing her husband's position at the high school. He was doing some research while on sabbatical. P.P. was countering by discussing Allen's prior stint as artist in residence. The spiders were snarking about the fact that these women were competing over abstract, inflated stations at what was basically a public school—a wealthier district, but public nonetheless. Plus, the spiders had developed a vendetta against Principal Doyle. Nash took a deep breath before addressing her group.

"Maybe we could talk about why we are here," Nash used a louder voice than normal. She had to in order to be heard above Boomer's music and televisions, and in order to hear herself above the spiders.

"Let's talk about *why* we are here and why we are *here*." P.P. wrinkled her nose as if she smelled something rotten.

Because you are a filthy whore. You deserve to wallow in the mud, the spiders whispered about P.P. to Nash, who was impressed with their speedy and accurate diagnostic.

"Well, we are soaking up the local flavor, Princess."

P.P. glanced over at two men sulking beneath baseball caps in the corner. "Eclectic bunch," she muttered and took a tissue from her purse, so she could wipe the section of table in front of her.

You really should kill her, the spiders instructed.

"I know, I know." Nash rolled her eyes and realized she was speaking aloud, so she continued speaking in order to cover, "And we couldn't meet at my house... you know... construction."

"Ooh," Wi Fi leaned forward, her enhanced bosom tilting the table in her favor. "What are you having done?"

"A combination solarium/parlor," Nash said humbly.

"Why?" P.P., simulating boredom over Nash's life, examined the bottles of hot sauce and vinegar in the center of the table with visible repugnance. "You already have a sunroom…"

"Because a solarium/parlor is not the same thing as a sunroom, dear, dear Princess. This new room will be for Riley's music. The perfect acoustics for his violin. I mean…" She put on the face of a true martyr. "…we pay so much for his lessons… at the Conservatory…"

"The *Boston* Conservatory?" Sylvie asked mischievously.

Bitch. Kill her. The spiders understood.

"No," Nash responded patiently, "with lacrosse, fencing, and Latin after school, Riley just doesn't have the time to leave the Cape."

Melanie sighed audibly at the word *time* but Nash ignored her. "Regardless, we are not here to discuss the extension on my house—"

"Why, exactly are we here?" P.P. was not about to stop jabbing any sore spot she could find.

Kill her. Slash her. Slice her. Insufferable twat… If it were possible, the spiders seemed to hate P.P. even more than Nash did. This hatred fueled her suspicion that P.P. was behind Derrick's disappearance. Naturally, that woman would want to hurt Nash in the most obvious way possible. Considering herself a seductress, it only made sense that P.P. would put on the appearance of luring Nash's husband: of winning. If it wasn't P.P., who else could it be? Wi Fi, who was now presenting her ample assets and drawing unnecessary attention from the tables around her? Nash had sold a pregnant Wi Fi off to men of a much higher caliber than the present company. Men with a fetish, but of a certain social class. She knew Wi Fi held no ethical delusions when it came to dalliances with other people's husbands. But she did not have the intelligence to pull it off. If nothing else, P.P. was shrewd.

And then there was Melanie, who could barely dress herself in the morning. And Gwynie who was too tiny and naive to even think up such a plan. And Sylvie—there were always cameras on Sylvie and the Quints—she would never be able to get away with any crime.

"Oh, P.P., you hurt my feelings. I thought you simply enjoyed my company… I didn't realize we needed a reason to get together."

Gwynnie snorted happily. She loved when they turned on one another.

"It's just that…" P.P. continued to look around, as if she expected to be jumped. "This is like one of those really bad dramedies on TV…"

"I wouldn't know," Wi Fi interjected innocently, "I don't watch TV."

Liar. Lying right around her pillow lips.

The spiders were right: for a woman whose claim to fame was not watching plebian television, Wi Fi was always able to give a character summary or plot synopsis of shows on the major networks, as well as cable. Wi Fi claimed TV was too difficult for her with her hearing loss, but everyone had captions these days. Besides, her hearing seemed entirely selective.

"The reason we are here." Nash paused for effect, and to allow last minute instructions from the arachnids in her head. "Is we need to nail down the details of the bracelet party. This is not one of our typical parties. It's… bigger and better than the others… I guess you could say it is a party to end all parties."

The women, except for P.P., sighed appreciatively.

"It will be a big night. We can dress formally, if you want—"

"Husbands, too?" Gwynnie asked.

Ladies only.

"Ladies only," Nash directed.

"Oh, God. Not one of those… what do you call…" P.P. innocently feigned racking her brains. "Naughty Nightie things."

Sanctimonious cunt.

"I wouldn't know what those are, dear." Nash invoked her best schoolmarm tone. "Would you care to explain?"

Gwynnie, missing Nash's intention, chimed in, "It's where they sell …marital aids."

Who needs 'em?!

"Well, when you've got a man like Derrick." Nash grinned mischievously, fully secure that none of the women were privy to the current status of her marriage—with the exception of the kidnapper. Nash never confided in anyone, as she trusted no one. "He's just so attentive."

"No one really cares about your sex life, or lack thereof, Nashville." P.P. had taken to spinning a bottle of hot sauce on the table. "Get on with it."

Stab her. Eviscerate her.

"I don't want to give away too many…"

Surprises.

"…surprises, but I can promise that this one will be different."

"I am up for different," Gwynnie chirped mischievously.

"You need a second husband," Wi Fi chimed in.

Gwynnie laughed a fake, loud laugh that caused patrons at the bar to look in her direction. "Like brother husbands? What on earth would I do with two of them?"

"Seriously," Nash redirected them, "I am talking HUGE. Bigger than...what was the last party you hosted, Princess?"

P.P. scoffed.

"And there will be write ups in the society pages. In off-Cape papers."

"Ohh," the women exclaimed, sounding as if they were watching a fireworks display.

The bait is set, reel them in.

"There will be games and prizes."

"Ooh." Wi Fi wriggled her eyebrows at Gwynnie.

"And bragging rights."

P.P. turned her attention away from the bottles and back to Nash.

"All I will say is, come and have fun—"

Bring a friend.

"Bring a friend if you like..." She winked. "And your husband's checkbook."

The ladies chuckled, delighting the spiders.

Ladies only.

"But remember, it's ladies' night." Nash sat down and leaned forward, "One you'll never forget."

Here is what you need to know. In order to seduce a senior Caesar, Cleopatra Thea Neotera Philopater kai Philopatris was rolled into a sumptuous carpet. Cloaked within the wool and shag, she was carried to Caesar's chambers. How her heart must have thumped, encased in fringe and floral—her cocoon smelling of anticipation and hope. She was unfurled, naked, at his feet. It was almost as if she had rolled out of time, out of another, more perfect dimension. He had no option, this great commander, this powerful leader, then to succumb to the fresh beauty of a twenty-one-year-old. She was known as the conqueror of conquerors, and her womb met fresh victory by conceiving a son that very night. She survived the elder Caesar and lived to love again and again. You need to remember that she died by partnering with a snake. Eve may have been the first woman to foster her own destruction by collaborating with terrifying creatures, but, as history as taught us, she would not be the last.

Nash licked the cheese puff residue from her fingers before letting them re-invade her snack filled Plasticware container. She crunched the puffs loudly, not worrying about being offensive, as she was alone.

She was truly alone.

The spiders had an aversion to junk food. When she wanted to quiet them, she plied herself with candy and chips. It reminded Nash of when she had been pregnant, and she had stopped controlling everything she ate.

That had been a magical time. She had attended weddings and parties in ill-fitting clothing, reveling in the fact that she had a precious excuse for being so sloppy. Publicly, she had stuffed down hors d'oeuvres and crepes and tapas and dumplings. She had throated grilled filet mignon with garlic confit cloves and red wine reduction sauce. She had mouthed double-cut boar chops with a wild blueberry, balsamic, and sage sauce. She had sucked on sun dried tomato tilapia stuffed with rock lobster and asparagus. Privately, she had feasted on ice cream and cookies, brownies and cakes, bags upon bags of flavored pretzels and tortilla chips. She had crammed nachos and jalapeño poppers and greasy chicken wings into her mouth, licking her fingers with abandon and caressing her expanding waistline lovingly. With Dinah, she had relished the permanent link that the baby was creating between her and Derrick. Even if he were to leave her, and she knew he wouldn't, they would always be tied together by this little life. It was almost as if she owned him, and that was a very attractive idea.

With Riley, the aspect of giving Derrick a son had really upped Nash's game. She had given the man everything he could want. He would forever be beholden to her. She could seal off any anxiety she had over their relationship as easily as closing the lid of her Plasticware.

After giving birth, she forced herself to return to her eating regimen of denial. The Plasticware had added an element of satisfaction to her protocol, but it never stopped feeling like deprivation. Now, she had to eat in order to silence the spiders. She needed moments of silence to collect her thoughts, her own thoughts. There was no guilt with the food, as it was for the greater good.

But mostly, she needed to put food in her mouth so that she wouldn't scream.

It is important to remember that some of the most malevolent guards occupying Nazi concentration camps were women. Here are some instances that it would be wise to take note of: Irma Grese (1923–

1945) was dubbed "Beautiful Beast" for her predilection for perverse and violent acts. Grese's specialty was setting her half-starved pack of dogs on camp victims. She also enjoyed a good whip. Isle Koch (1906-1967) was lovingly nicknamed "the Bitch of Buckenwald." She had acquired a taste for souvenirs: taking the skin of victims and creating lampshades and other practical items. Maria "the Beast" Mandel (1912-1948) was reputed to have been directly responsible for ordering the deaths of 500,000 prisoners. Emma Zimmer (1888-1948) was renowned for her abuse of prisoners prior to sending them to the gas chambers. The same could be said for Elsa Erich (?-1948), Ruth Closius (1920-1948), Greta Bosel (1908-1947), Elisabeth Marschall (1886-1947), Margot Dreschel (1908-1945), Jenny Wanda Barkmann (1921-1946), Dorothea Binz (1920-1947), Juana "the weasel" Bormann (1903-1945), Therese Brandl (1902-1948), Ruth Elfriede Hildner (1919-1947), Wanda Klaff (1922-1946), Elisabeth Lupka (1902-1949), Ewa Paradies (1920-1946), Gerda Steinhoff (1922-1946), Elisabeth Volkenrath (1919-1945), among others.

All of these women died of hanging: only Ilse Koch's was self-inflicted.

The world is safer if you remember: when checking the closet for monsters, do not discriminate based upon the monster's gender.

Nash knew how to manage obsessions. The Plasticware had prepared her.

The Plasticware had both spurred and taken sides in a mini-war. Over possession of the containers hair was pulled, fingernails were enlisted, names were called, and uncultured four-letter words were introduced.

Regarding possession by the Plasticware, some fared worse than others. The dance instructor, for example, was found scorched on the floor of her dance studio. In the days before the Plasticware, she had taught ballet, jazz, and tap. In the many years before the Plasticware, she had performed other, more profitable styles of dancing that involved tabletops and steel poles. That had been before her marriage, before she had found a husband/patron to help pay her bills and allow her the luxury to only teach two nights a week.

The instructor had always had a fantastic body topped off with an acceptable face. Her body had been kept toned by coming to the studio prior to her classes for a lengthy independent warm up. Classes had run for the fully allotted time, with the instructor literally dancing circles around the teenaged students. Then, she would continue to dance long after they left, enjoying the electrifying feeling in her muscles and the smell of her own sweat.

Once she had obtained her Plasticware, the instructor ended classes early so that she could obsess over stashing items into her newly purchased mauve-lidded plastic containers. She carefully placed ribbons and elastics in the larger square tub, chocolates in the rectangle, and stickers and other rewards in the smallest circle. So busy was she with classifying and categorizing items, that she took no notice of the door opening. So enthralled was she with the satisfying snap of the lids that she did not notice the intruder's reflection in the wall of mirrors lining the studio. So mesmerized was she with the multipurpose containers that she did not hear the hiss of the MIG welding gun as it approached her skin.

Plastic can muffle screams. It can also contain a wedding band, previously worn by the receptionist from the pediatrician's office. This woman was not a friend of the country club set and she had made it a point to be curt to them regardless of if they were bringing children for routine office visits or severe illnesses. She had found her way to the Plasticware by means of an interest in accounting. She had caught some discrepancies in Nash's bill, some large funneling of medications, and she had wanted in.

The receptionist had always wanted to study marine engine repair, and to work on the boats that were so plentiful on the Cape. That had not panned out, but she had still tinkered, and had acquired some new tools and equipment courtesy of Nash's charitable donations. The receptionist's hands were duly calloused and bereft of almost all jewelry. There was a tell-tale pale line circling her ring finger, indicating that a band had normally been worn. Her nails were clipped short, to prevent germs from embedding themselves on the tips of her fingers, and her hands smelled of antibacterial gel. The focus on her hands is important, as they were found several yards away from her body. Her body was extremely difficult, even for professionals, to look at. The hands themselves did not lie on the ground but were nestled within a Plasticware container the size of a bread box. They were swaddled in a linen napkin that coordinated nicely with the orchid lid of the container.

A smaller container held the ring, but that was not found at the scene of the crime. That would be found later, in the possession of the woman who had both Derrick and his wedding band.

Also found later was a woman who had lived near the others. The neighbor's name was, had been, Shayna, and that was all that Nash, or the others had ever really learned about her.

What they did not know was that Shayna crossed three town lines four nights a week in order to cut and style hair. There were plenty of beauty parlors close to home, but it would have killed

Shayna to have the other mothers know that her family had trouble paying their bills. It would have killed her if anyone found out that her tips went directly to groceries and school clothing and that she hadn't bought herself a new dress in over five years. It would have killed her to have to set and style the hair of debutantes knowing that, short of an appearance from a fairy godmother, her own daughters would have to settle for mom as a stylist during prom season.

No one had found out, so that wasn't what had killed her. What had killed her during a routine power outage was the cat o'nine tails, followed by demonic teeth, followed by a sound stabbing. Long after the lights returned, she would be found clutching the lid of a Plasticware cake caddy as if it were a shield.

First things first, Nash was not responsible for any of these murders, but someone in her social circle was.

Nash had not hosted a "for profit" party since her Cranberry Craving days. Arguably, Nash was not the actual host of the party she was planning, and the profit, for once, would not go into her pocket. Yet, she retained her type-A approach. She would make sure that the color scheme of the decorations inspired envy. That the hors d'oeuvres were the talk of the town. That the drinks were inspirational.

And that the bracelets on display, and for sale, were to die for.

There were parts of her brain that worked on autopilot. She created evites and a buffet menu. She bought plates, disposable tumblers, and plastic utensils at a store specializing in the unique. She sent the evites to everyone in her email contact list, even to those she had tortured in the past, even to the teachers at the kids' schools. She completed all these tasks without any sense of accomplishment, as she no longer had awareness of her actions.

The spiders were not a fantasy. They were real, and they were instructing her to hold the party soon, in the dying days of winter when the branches on trees were bleeding with icicles and navigable roads were a thing of distant memories. Fall was when the crone aged and raged, without the benefits of Botox. Winter was her demise, and spring was when the young mistress replaced her. This was what the ancestors knew.

Nash's mind was on Derrick and on finding him before he received any harm. She also hoped to find him before he found out any of her secrets. It was entirely possible that the kidnapper knew things, things that Nash would want to tell Derrick herself. She made a silent promise to any and all gods that she would confess to her husband if she could only be granted the chance to see him again.

Something told Nash that long awaited plans were being set into motion. There would be an epic culmination. This plan tried to suppress its true intentions, but the subliminal spiders whispered of major conflicts for Nash's frenemies. They also pledged the demise of P.P.

Lest you think the spiders were intrusive, or lest you accuse poor Nash of harboring a fear of them, there was some relief in having these parasites direct her. She did not have to labor on details, as she did with business or taxes. She did not have to plot and set traps. Such as loosening all the shelves in the Recess Monitor's china cabinet, so she would be badly cut and bruised by the free-falling dinner ware. (Riley had never been forced to submit to a recess suspension again). Or, rerouting the gas line in the postal worker's stove so she would be unable to report the suspicious packages that came addressed to the attention of Nashville DeCota. Or, drizzling peanut oil into the bank's coffee pot, knowing that the teller she feared knew too much was deathly allergic.

There had been no twelve-step program for that stressful addiction. In this, she was like the green worms and black beetles who returned every spring to the Cape. She was doomed to live her days in the same way. Not happily ever after, simply forevermore.

She would be a slave to her habits until she died. Then, she would be reborn to begin the cycle anew. That is what Nash had learned from watching *The Lion King* with her children: the circle of life is really a shackle.

A shackle that resembled a bracelet that would bring Derrick back to her.

Scientists have learned to record the "earworms" or hallucinatory music that people hear inside their heads. The music comes from several brain regions: those that process melody, memory, and images. Though scientifically explained, the earworms can still drive one insane.

Nash did not need help, but she was tired of working alone, so she went to get Danen. Or, the spiders insisted she use Danen. As she lay on the cold, steel operating table of her external container, Nash would not be able to tell which was true. And, with the spiders pulling the puppet strings, it no longer mattered.

She remembered he had signed another contract and that that contract resided in a container in her closet along with some unmentionable items. The contract had been scrubbed of anything illegal and simply allowed for a business transaction to be understood. It reported mileage and other items of deduction.

It was a way of covering the non-existent ass of Danen and the lifted and molded ass of Nash. As she lay on the cold, steel table, she realized that contracts couldn't help either of them anymore.

When she had realized she needed him, she went directly to his home. Nash pushed open the door to Danen's room and was immediately greeted with a scent that described adventures with french fries, incense, Vicks vapor rub, and pot. Danen was stretched out on his small bed in the corpse pose, his booted feet hanging off the end like an afterthought. Without an invitation, Nash entered the room and seated herself on the edge of the bed closest to the door. Danen did not flinch, his eyes did not move. He was already an expert at playing dead.

His head was now shaved. He had earrings crawling up the tops of his ears and ear stretchers hanging in his lobes like babies in a sling. Nash wondered how Danen would look as an old man, with the wind whistling through his saggy, hole-filled ear lobes, tufts of ear hair cascading over what was once cool, but later simply tragic. Something in her gut (or the spiders whispering in her brain) told her that Danen would not have to worry with old age.

Nor could she afford to worry about Danen. Her head was

beginning to feel as if it were on fire with pain. She could imagine spiders crawling over her brain, but these arachnids were not ticklish, they were wearing steel tipped cleats, or stripper stilettos. Sharp needles seemed to enter her at irregular intervals so that she could not prepare herself for their onslaught. A mentally weaker woman would have succumbed instantly.

Nash glanced to the ceiling where there were a few small stains. She remembered her husband telling her that, as a youth, he would spit while lying on his back and try to hit the ceiling in a test of marksmanship. If that was the source of these stains, this particular young man was a regular William Tell.

Nash had never had time for adolescent foolishness. Whereas time was a ravenous animal to Melanie, it had been a commodity to Nash as soon as she was old enough to understand the power of money. Her early childhood had been downright laborious. Once the training wheels had left her bike, Nash had been continuously employed. She had babysat, mowed lawns, delivered newspapers, walked dogs. Then, at age fifteen, she had begun working thirty-five hours a week—stashing money in a bank shaped like a southern bell in a hoop skirt so she could go somewhere *better*. Her only break had come when she had inherited Virtue's purse, but that windfall had been short lived.

Despite her parents' adoration of plantations and cotillions, Nashville had not been raised in luxury. Not like P.P. and some of the others, yet she could never let them find this out. It would be the equivalent of falling off your horse during battle. It would mean exposing a weakness.

"Danen, I need your help." Nash was rubbing her forehead, trying to squash some of the insects inside. "I need you to help me bring boxes from the warehouse off Cape."

He remained silent, staring at the ceiling. Now, he had become irritating. Didn't he know how much pain she was in? Or had evolution truly rendered the males of the species emotionally illiterate?

"You know that place just beyond the bridge? It won't take long, and I'll make sure you are... compensated."

Danen rolled his eyes, blonde lashes flapping, cueing Nash to the fact that he was alive and listening.

"This will be a little different," she continued, "but probably easier than anything I've ever asked you to do. Just load up my car."

The spiders' activity increased. She pictured them spilling out of her ears like ice skaters tumbling off a frozen pond.

"We just have to grab all of the Plasticware."

"Jesus," Danen managed, "Plastic."

"Yes," Nash confirmed, "Christ and Plastic." She was planning to repurpose some of the smaller containers as jewelry boxes for the bracelets that the disembodied head (and the spiders) wanted her to sell. She would move as much of her merchandise as she could and then retire from the game completely. The thought had startled her at first, but the more she mulled it over, the more attractive it became. She could dote on her husband and children more. She could help Dinah with her personal demons. She would no longer have to hide her activities from Derrick. She could devote herself to him completely.

Danen sighed and crossed his arms over his chest. "Wouldn't it be great," he mused, "if we could all be honest?"

Nash looked at him, really looked at him, and saw how young and hopeful he should look in comparison to the image in front of her. "No," she answered softly, "stories are always better than reality. Reality disappoints. It's always better to hide from the truth."

He rolled his eyes, but, apparently, not at Nash. He was disillusioned with something that she could not see. "I thought adults knew everything, had it all together. I thought adults had answers," he continued, more to himself than to Nash, "but adults are just as fucked up as kids… maybe more."

"Definitely more," Nash agreed.

"I mean, my parents were seriously in love with each other. Completely in love with each other." She could see tears filling his eyes. "At one point, they were so into each other. Then it all went completely to shit."

She nodded, wondering if she and Derrick were completely in love with each other, or with the idea of each other. She felt she truly loved him, in the way that nearly two decades of waking up next to each other provided. She knew everything about him and did not judge anything she saw. She wondered if he would grant her clemency if he knew everything about her, too. Soon, when she was free of her business, she would no longer have this worry.

"So, why bother?" Danen mumbled, "I mean, if it is all fucked up anyway, if it's all going to go to shit eventually, what's the point?"

A small part of Nash wanted to give true consideration to his question. A small part of her recognized the importance of the inquiry. However, the spiders won. They always won. "Look, Danen. Someday you can go to college and wax philosophical all you want. Right now, we have a job to do, and it is very important."

He nodded. "But then, this is it," he told her, "I am getting too fucking old for this shit."

She both knew what he meant and was completely lost for his meaning at the same time.

They met later that night and drove over one of the two bridges that provided an escape from the Cape. Nash used to wonder how they would all evacuate if the bridges were destroyed. She pictured families and pets piling onto boats and kayaks and canoes. She pictured rafts full of refugees fighting the massive current of the canal. Those images rang quaint to her now, now that she was obeying arachnids and loading hundreds of Plasticware containers into her BMW S5.

Together, they drove back to Nash's house and loaded the Plasticware into Nash's garage. Danen had begun to shake, from a combination of hunger and withdrawal. She gave him his supplies and sent him away, anxious to be alone with the glistening Plasticware that she had been sent to retrieve, and alone with the spiders. Her family had seemed to abandon her, then she realized that Riley was on a camping outing for scouts and Dinah was staying at a friend's house to finish a big project for school. Dinah had cleared out the apples from the fridge and left the house for the first time since her suspension. Nash had been trying to keep them away so that they wouldn't notice their father's absence, but, she had recently lost the ability to keep track of them or much else.

The garage was filled with the scent of acrylic. The smell reminded Nash of nail polish remover. Or of the filler at the plastic surgeon's office. As with any strong scent, Nash became convinced that she could taste it, that the odor was riding down her throat and into her body. But how could anything else penetrate her at this point? She was so full of spiders and plans as to be fully sated. Even in the days of delayed gratification, she felt like a glutton. She did not know that the body-free head of before was now watching her through the window in the garage door. The head was taking inventory of more than the Plasticware.

Nash remained blissfully unaware of everything until she cracked open the bottom of the electric door to let in fresh air. As the motor worked to divorce the paneled slats from pavement, she saw something slithering in the shadows along the ground. At first, she thought it was a snake or wayward ocean critter, but, as her eyes adjusted to the darkness, she was able to make out a long tail with serrated spikes glamorizing its tip.

The spiders in her brain danced in recognition, and Nash clutched the plastic like a shield, praying to anyone that would listen that this would all end soon.

✷

Remember: it was the notorious Egyptian serial killers Raya and Sakina who proved that women did not deserve leniency from the court of law. These two killed nearly 20 women in the early part of the 20th century. For our purposes, they also proved how much more powerful women are when working together instead of competing against each other.

The Porcelain Princess, P.P., who knew herself by another name, busily tidied the storage nook off her attic. Even in the early morning hours, it was easily ten degrees warmer than the rest of her house in the equilateral space. The sun hung directly across from the room's one small window, baking the alcove. Yet, P.P. did not sweat, nor did she rush through her chore. This was a secret room, a place the maid was not allowed to touch, as it housed P.P.'s most cherished memories. She took her time filing Garrett's old report cards and academic papers into properly labeled boxes. She carefully stacked photo albums in chronological order with strategically marked bindings displayed. She straightened and dusted, even though no one ever ventured into the space except for herself.

She moved through more boxes. There were six stacked along the longest wall. Each holding thirty-six files: three for every month of the year, containing bank statements, receipts, repairs, and itemizations. She would have never guessed that she and Nashville shared an obsession about taxes and auditing. P.P. compulsively filed away facets of her family's personal life. There was no reason for this; she never fantasized about a future anthropologist finding her day-to-day expenditures. It simply made her life neat and tidy and her memories accessible.

From the small sunlit window, she had full view of Nash's front yard and garage. The garage door was open, and Nash was inside, moving things around, much like P.P. herself was moving things around. She knew that Nash slept sporadically, but it appeared as if the woman had not been to bed at all. She was fully dressed, in rumpled clothing, and her hair was falling frenetically out of a bun. In contrast, P.P. was in her matching yoga pants and Under Armour, so she could jog later. Also, in contrast, P.P. was not standing in a place where anyone could see her. Recently, Nash had provided many spectacles. She had been spotted (by P.P.) stomping around in her sunroom, and apparently talking to herself. The other day, P.P. had taken her yoga practice to the beach, when she had noticed the side of Nashville's house swarming with spiders. P.P. had found it only fitting that that evil witch was branded by something as malevolent as spiders. It was as if the universe were warning the others to guard themselves from her.

"The Tooth Snatcher," P.P. whispered, as she lowered the lid onto a box of old auto insurance vouchers. "The Island Impaler." It made her shiver in the same way that "Bloody Mary" had when P.P. had whispered that phantom's name in front of mirrors as a little girl. Not that P.P. had ever believed the rumors about Nashville, but many of the women in their circle insisted it was true. Not that that had ever stopped them from inviting Nashville to every event, or from attending hers. Those luncheons and charities were business, after all, and sometimes it was necessary to dance with the devil.

"And what a devil," P.P. continued with her thoughts, alone in the airless attic. P.P. was very aware that Nashville had tried to thwart her at every turn. The woman consistently tried to outshine her, as if that were possible. P.P. had always been *that girl*. She had been Home Coming Queen, Prom Queen, County Fair Queen, and her wedding had been the biggest and most expensive in Cape history. Nashville DeCota had gotten the house at the end of the street, but P.P. knew that hers was grander. Everything P.P.

had was better. She was the woman with everything. And when Nashville tried to sic her minion on P.P.—that dazed boy—P.P. was able to deflect him with a social power that bordered on supernatural.

And now Nash had usurped her via a bracelet party. At first, P.P. had thought it would be some arts and crafts fiasco, with the requisite impoverished artist hawking wares that did not deserve a good hawk. But this party had required several planning meetings and had showcased Nashville looking more and more obsessed with each phase. Anything this tantalizing to the Cape Capo merited a level of seriousness from the others.

P.P. thought of her friends and how they needed her guidance. If Nash was coming completely unhinged, it was up to P.P. to act as a role model. She was honestly the most important person in their town. Without P.P, who would run the majority of the events? Who would manage the allocation of school and town funds? Who would keep all the pointless ninnies updated on fashion and culture?

P.P. slid a box of medical records to the right and saw a small radio that had once belonged to Garrett. His iPhone had rendered every other mode of entertainment obsolete. There was something so innocent about the radio and its knobs and antenna. She turned it on and was surprised to find that the batteries had retained some juice. A man's voice was heard first. It was difficult to decipher around static, but he was asking someone not to cut his hair. He asked someone where his ring went. He asked when he could go home.

P.P. held the radio up to her ear. It did not sound like a program, but like someone talking. It sounded unrehearsed, impromptu. She remembered how sometimes baby monitors could pick up conversations in other houses, on cell phones and things, and she wondered if that was what was happening.

Another voice was heard. This was a woman's voice. She was talking about containers and competition. P.P., hating alliteration as much as metaphor, felt assaulted by this voice. The woman sounded familiar, and she clearly said Derrick, but the voice did not belong to Nash.

Poor Nashville, plagued with spiders and a carousing husband.

P.P. shook the radio a bit and played with the knobs, searching for music or NPR. She did not really pay attention to NPR but liked to tell others that she was a regular listener.

No matter how the knobs were twisted or turned, only one station could be heard. No matter how she shook and abused the radio, the now synchronous voices prevailed, with the woman speaking on top of the man's words.

The woman was yelling at this Derrick, and P.P. knew it was Nash's husband. She looked out the window, looked to see if the mentally wounded wife were still in her garage, and what she saw caused her to gasp.

The garage door had been closed halfway, like a tired eye lid. On the inside of the garage, P.P. could see Nash's torso, standing and looking as rumpled and disheveled as before. What had caused her to gasp was what was standing outside the garage door: another Nashville DeCota.

But what is most important, the take home lesson, the grand-daddy memory, parable, or story —the inner-most-container-morsel-of truth...: Pandora opened a box.

Just as Pandora opened her magical vase, so was the Plasticware opened, unleashing the whirlwind and so were the bracelets opened, threatening to end it all.

Just as Eve had to take the red, shiny apple, the women had to own, possess, capture, caress, the enchanted beaded bracelets.

This is what it has been leading up to. You might want to take notes.

The party was held right when Nash feared she would lose her mind if her husband were not returned promptly. This was the event that was the catalyst that would send Melanie's Time Between Time in motion, and cause P.P. to fall from her throne. The party itself, its setup and overt agenda, was not unusual in the women's neighborhood. They often invited product representatives to demonstrate the latest and greatest in conveniences. The spiders, and the severed head, promised that this would be the greatest product party of all.

It would not be like the Plasticware, which had been so adaptable. With the Plasticware, some pieces were round, others were square and yet one lid could safely and effectively seal off each piece. Separately the containers had been mundane, but together, as a set, they were magical. Each set had its own tinted lid. Every shade and hue of red, pink, or purple imaginable was available. Each unique. Each color especially matched to its owner by way of demonic Feng Shui.

The Plasticware party had changed everything. It had upped the competition to nefarious levels. The Plasticware had driven the women from their closeted and cloistered lives, like herds migrating in anticipation of an ice age. It had been survival of the fittest, with interlocking, dishwasher-safe lids.

While the women tried continuously to not eat, the containers would provide witness. They would display, in their transparent way, the food that remained.

The Plasticware had an energy when touched. It sparked the fingers like Briar Rose touching the spindle. Instead of putting the women to sleep for a hundred years, it breathed life, energy, alertness, and a rebirth.

They had played games to win the Plasticware. In the first game, Wi Fi, who appeared dazzled, won the red set. She had to tell the most scandalous secret in the room. She had told them that she wanted to work, to write, and to support her family with her writing. She told them she was tired of asking her husband for money and of depending on him.

Melanie won the lilac set for having "moved the least/changed the least/lived the least" of anyone in the room. Nash joked that time stood still for dear Melanie as she presented the containers.

It was the purple containers that everyone wanted. For these, Nash handed out a scavenger hunt list to all but Melanie and Wi Fi (who were instructed not to help the others, even though that prospect was unthinkable). The list was intentionally vague and open to creativity:

A. Something of Value

B. Something from History

C. Something with Integrity

D. Something Shocking

The women were allowed to return home to retrieve the items, which gave Nash the home field advantage, just as she had planned.

Sylvie was the first to return with:

A. A credit card

B. An heirloom quilt

C. A picture of the actress Gwyneth Paltrow

D. Her vibrator

Gwynnie brought:

A. A picture of her clan of adopted children

B. The Family Bible

C. Girl Scout Cookies

D. The results of a drug test taken in college

P.P. brought:

A. The keys to her Porsche

B. Her Grandmother's diamond necklace

C. A copy of *Joined at the Heart: The Transformation of the American Family* by Al and Tipper Gore

D. Her facial crème with secret revitalizing ingredients (the shock being that her youthful appearance is not *au naturelle*).

Nash brought:

A. A locked box filled with gold fillings, baby teeth, and a loaded Smith and Wesson

B. Her hoopskirt bank

C. A cat o' nine tails whip

D. A taser

Wi Fi and Melanie were told to vote. The competitors glanced nervously at each other, licking their lips, and desiring the containers more for the fact that they could keep them from each other than from an actual need for Plasticware. Fear forced the judges to crown Nash the winner.

Nash knew P.P. would lose her mind over her acquisition of the superior purple containers. She also knew that she would use the containers at every event graced with P.P.'s presence. Nash would hold them right under P.P.'s nose. She would rinse them in P.P.'s porcelain Italian sink and she would use P.P.'s specially tatted guest towels to dry them.

That had been a party. But this bracelet party was already proving to be bigger and better. And it promised the return of Derrick.

When everyone settled, and Nash commandeered a proper amount of attention, a man came to the door, exactly as the spiders had promised. This man triggered a memory in Nash. His was the face on the dissevered head that had looked in Nash's window. What she didn't know was that his was also the face of the mangy, leech infested figure blocking Melanie's road. His was the face of a certain Marsh Person, and of a man who stood outside her car while she had killed Virtue. His was a face that could launch a thousand ships, and the women all felt it. Somewhere inside of them, they felt a desire to touch this man, to be with him. Little did they realize that he was not yet substantial. He was like a hologram. If they knew, little would they care. Whatever he was selling, they were buying.

Nash glanced at the crates on his dolly and then to the mountains of Plasticware stacked around her house like diamonds twinkling in a mine. How did this connect to Derrick? Did she really need to relinquish her Plasticware in order to save her marriage? She hated herself for wondering if the sacrifice were really worth it.

The man began to speak to the rapt audience. He told them that he had something they could buy. His pitch was simple: he promised them ownership and independence.

The ladies listened gravely. Nash; however, wanted to scoff. What were these bracelets compared to her arsenal of secrets?

She wanted to scoff but found she couldn't. Her voice was caught somewhere mid-throat. As the man continued to speak, he looked at Nash, securing an ever-deepening eye contact. As he spoke, she found gum forming inside of her mouth, as if his words had a consistency that filled her like jelly filled a doughnut, seeking every crevice. She stuck a finger between her lips and pulled out a large hunk of the gum. It was purple and thick and cottony. As she discarded the wad onto her saucer, another, larger supply appeared inside her mouth, gagging her. Again, her finger was inserted, fishing out a cotton ball of sugar, and again, a larger deposit took its place. Eventually, she stopped fighting the gum, fearing she would choke, and decided to chew and breathe around it. She knew it was dangerous to lose one's voice—or to let others speak for you—that was when bad things happened.

They played a game, but Nash's heart wasn't into it. Melanie won a special bracelet, and after the fanfare, Nash held her breath. And held her breath. And exhaled and held it again.

Where was Derrick? She had done as the head and the spiders had asked. She had hosted the party; she had set the bracelet bait. Whoever had Derrick had no intention of returning him.

The man circled the room. He was stopped by P.P., who was fawning over a metallic bracelet. The man clumsily stepped on

Sylvie's clutch, then bent over and straightened it.

The ladies disbanded, with Sylvie leading the charge, claiming her sitter had some sort of naturalization process in the morning. She was rushing, clutching her handbag to her chest and rubbing it as if it were a relic—just as she had rubbed her sacred belly when it had housed five fetuses.

P.P. lingered, draping herself on the bracelet man, and Nash swore they were whispering about Derrick to each other. She texted Danen and asked him to follow P.P., while she would follow the man who wore the dissevered head as his own. These actions were met with crucial failure on both ends. While Nash lost sight of the man, Danen lost far more.

Don't forget, mothers take children from watery wombs and send them to watery graves. Hundreds of children in the U.S. are killed each year by their mothers. Half of those murders are altruistic: those mothers go beyond bandaging boo-boos to spare their children the pain of life. Susan Smith strapped her two young sons into their car seats and allowed the family vehicle to cascade into the John D. Long Lake. She stood on the bank, in darkness, as it took a full six minutes for the car to submerge itself. Andrea Yates drowned her five children in the household bathtub. She drowned them and then laid them on a bed, draping their arms across each other. Yvette Yallico drowned her small daughter in the bathtub after believing that the soap and shampoo commanded her to do so.

Nash returned home. More out of habit than from an actual hope that Derrick had returned. Her house was empty, yet there were damp footprints on the kitchen tile. Her Plasticware was gone. Not one piece amongst her set remained. A few days before, this would have bothered her immensely. Now, she wanted her husband back more than she wanted to laud her possessions over others. She wanted her family back. She realized she had gotten into the most trouble—she had done things to ire the law and the tax man—once the kids were in school all day and no longer in need of her service. This is why many of her crimes focused on teachers, on the people molding her children, on the people they looked to with respect.

She had always been so competitive.

She wanted to go back to the days before the plotting and planning against the other mothers. She longed to take naps with the small Dinah and the small Riley again. The three of them in her bed, Dinah's tiny fingers clutching Nash's arm, reassuring herself of her mother's presence even in her sleep. Riley, sleeping on his back, his puffy tummy peeking between his pants and shirt, his breath sweet and sticky.

The spiders did not tell her any of this and she was neither relieved nor disappointed at her remaining ability for solitary thought. The spiders had been quieter since the bracelet party; they had gotten what they wanted. And the headless man had disappeared.

Don't forget that the followers of the boyishly armored Joan of Arc claimed to have seen her rise from the dead.

There is nothing familiar about a dead body.

Whether chopped or burned or crushed or killed from the inside out, bodies no longer look as they did when breath filled them. Faces are not distinguished, or full, or beautiful. Eyes no longer contain nor reflect life; they see nothing of this world. Nostrils and cheeks sink. Skin becomes filled with cement instead of blood. Jaws fall slack and tongues crawl like cowards into the backs of throats. Maybe choking screams. Maybe choking down a chorus of hallelujahs.

Maybe nothing, nothing at all.

There is nothing familiar about a dead body, no smell or laughter, no squeezed hand or hugged waist, no cocked eyebrow or half-smile, no wink. Maybe that is why it took an entire day for an identity to attach itself to the dead and mutilated body of Danen Hill.

Nash found Danen, strung up by hooks strategically placed through the flesh of his shoulders, stretching the skin to give the appearance of wings. His feet had been cut off. His eyes had been gouged out. He was an Icarus who had seen too much, an Icarus whose crime had only been flying too low, aiming for the dark crevices, eyeing the basement instead of the cathedral ceiling. Or perhaps he had only been searching for that honesty he had craved.

Hanging like that, he looked very young. He was a painting entitled, "The Wasted Life." The footholds provided by the universe had always been slippery, yet they had existed. Danen had scaled his own path far away from support and full force into quandary. His mouth was open in a small o, as if he were slightly, but not completely, surprised by his predicament. There were strange carvings on his chest: spider shaped scratches that belted his ribs.

There was also a Plasticware container in close proximity to the corpse. The container held the gauges that had once been in his ears. Nash realized she had been right, the saggy holes looked ludicrous, even when the body they belonged to was in such a serious state.

Because Nash felt partially responsible, she had called the police as soon as she reached a public telephone several towns over, so that Danen's body could be found in a timely manner.

When she returned to her car, her own phone was ringing.

"I'd never guess that you would always be a few steps behind me," an obviously altered voice said. It was difficult to hear the voice between the waves and the incessant piping plovers. This difficulty gave away the location of the caller.

Tennessee Williams rightly said, "We all live in a house on fire." This idea certainly spoke to Nashville DeCota's gentility and predilections. If all houses were on fire, then one might as well burn in the largest house beside the sea. P.P.'s house did not smolder as much as it threatened to collapse on itself like a cosmic black hole. Yet, the stained glass in the doorway and the crystal chandelier in the foyer blazed like adjacent suns and filled Nash with jealousy, even though her mind should have been on Derrick.

Nashville would not have been standing on P.P.'s doorstep had she not heard the ocean and piping plovers when Sylvie had called. Handing Nash her location proved that Sylvie was not in her same adversarial league.

More important than the phone call was the fact that Sylvie had missed her own interview with the local news station regarding a follow-up to the bullying at the high school. Sylvie had been something of a local hero for blowing the whistle on some girls—Dinah in particular. Sylvie was never one to relinquish the opportunity for free publicity, even if the Quints were not featured. But Sylvie had avoided the interview; she had not appeared on the news as had been promised. This meant that she was in hiding and she was hiding something big.

"About six feet, one hundred and eighty-five pounds," Nash thought, and the spiders ended their silence to agree.

Sylvie was genuinely surprised to see Nash in the foyer. "You don't belong here," she said meekly.

"Neither do you, unless the Princess is renting rooms now." Nash lowered her eyes at Sylvie. "I know the economy is bad, but I never thought it would touch P.P."

"She's been gone, for a few days, to Marrakesh or some place." Sylvie sniffed with resignation. "This seemed like a good place... to end it."

"Or a good place to hide behind someone else."

Sylvie rolled her eyes. "I can't do anything at my house. My kids' stuff is everywhere. Besides, you would never agree to come to me."

"Correct. Now, give me my husband and I might go easy on you."

Sylvie honestly looked as if she had tears in her eyes. "Since when have you ever gone easy on anyone, Nash? Especially me? You know, I used to feel sorry for myself, feeling like I never made it to the inner circle. I felt like I was never really your friend. But now, I feel sorry for you, because you have no friends."

The spiders chuckled, and Nash was irritated that Sylvie went off topic. "Am I to learn a lesson here? Am I going to realize what a horrible person I truly am, and then we hug, and everything rights itself? I am here for my husband, nothing more. You don't deserve any more of my time, and you certainly don't deserve my leniency."

Sylvie sighed. "What I deserve... what I wanted... the containers..."

Now the spiders were really excited. This had become entertaining for them. "You have containers, Sylvie, you have plenty of containers. You don't take someone's husband for more containers. That is not playing by the rules." Sylvie was rubbing her sides as if harboring aches and pains. Nash had no more time for this woman now than she ever did before. "Tell me, where is Derrick?"

"Rules? Who are you to talk of rules? I am just doing what I was told. They told me I could have whatever I wanted if I got your set."

"You can't have whatever you want, Sylvie. No one can."

"You seem to."

Nash chuckled, remembering the current stress in her home and remembering that taxes were due soon. "So, you decided to ruin my life, by taking Derrick."

"That was not why, They told me—"

As much as Nash was focused on Derrick's predicament, this statement stopped her. "Who is *they*?"

Sylvie blushed and looked down at her Alexandra McQueen heels. The shoes were not conducive to chasing quints, but no choice in Sylvie's life was ever made with practicality or being a mother in mind, despite what she told the newspapers and local

TV stations. "The leeches... they told me."

"Leeches?" The woman with spiders in her brains figuratively clutched her pearls.

"From the marsh." Sylvie's eyes darted around the room and Nash feared she would try to escape. "Didn't you look at the business card the bracelet man gave you? He gave me one, too, slipped it in my purse—"

"—Sylvie, what are you talking about?"

"His *address* is the marsh."

Nash had read the card, of course she had read it. Hers had said nothing of the marsh. It had listed the man as being from some small, unfortunate town to the west of the bridge. A part of her was angry that he had shared more of himself with Sylvie than with her.

Finish her, the spiders ordered. Nash wondered whose side they were on. The spiders had not led her to Derrick, she had done that on her own. The spiders seemed to be making everything in her life much, much worse. Did the bracelet man control the spiders and the leeches? Was he forcing a show down between the women? Or did he simply want his secrets to remain hidden?

It was secrets that had brought Nash to where she was now. The secret of killing Virtue, the secrets in her various businesses and dealings, and whatever secret was stashed in that small container that she never opened. While she cherished her marriage and her children, she couldn't help but wonder how different her relationships would have been if they had been built on honesty. She might not have spent most of her nights sneaking forbidden food from containers, alone.

She couldn't help but feel sorry for Sylvie. She had always found the woman to be pathetic, but she knew what it was like to be plagued by orders from invading forces. "Are the voices gone now?"

Sylvie shook her head. "They wanted me to do things… and I did things… because of their promises. But they never stopped talking. It's maddening."

"Did you try eating? Junk food keeps them quiet for a while."

"What? Are you talking about carbs? How would you—"

"Nash?" The voice came from a different part of the house, and it definitely belonged to Derrick.

Nash turned her back on Sylvie and ran down the hallway to where she thought the voice was coming from. She knew that the rooms on this floor consisted of the laundry, pantry, kitchen, dining room, and sitting room. All rooms were secluded behind locked doors: there was no free-flowing design to this house, reflecting the rigid nature of its owner.

Locked doors had never stopped Nash before and she found Derrick in the laundry room, tied to a chair. He looked gaunt and tired, but he looked more handsome than she remembered.

"Honey?" He blinked at her. "I thought I heard you." His smile appeared within his patchy beard growth. "I knew you would find me."

"First things first, you are getting a shave," Nash instructed as she untied him. "I didn't marry a Viking." She wondered where Sylvie was, expecting her to bust into the room with some haphazard weaponry.

"And then we will talk," Derrick stated flatly. "We have been hiding and pretending for too long."

Nash batted her long lashes, knowing that usually had an effect on him. "I don't know what you are talking about."

"I am talking about everything. Everything about our lives, about our house, about the way things are, Nash." He rubbed his newly freed hands before placing them on either side of her face. "I know everything."

Nash was stunned. "Everything? Derrick, I highly doubt that."

"Everything. You are not as good at concealing things as you think you are."

She thought of the containers, especially the tiny one she carried with her everywhere, and frowned, "Then why are you still with me?"

"Because, despite it all, I love you. I love our family… and the perks can't be overlooked."

Sylvie appeared in the doorway behind them, snorting. "How precious…"

"You know… you know where the money comes from?" Nash had had dreams where the skeletons in her closet were revealed, but those dreams had been more like nightmares.

"Yes, I do." Derrick tried to stand, but his legs had stiffened from being seated for so long. "Nash, you did some horrible things. I hate what you have done, but I still love you. I promise, we can work through this, together."

"I don't believe this. I can't believe you're still here." The room had grown quiet, but in a good way.

"I wouldn't be anywhere else." Derrick smiled and it reminded her of how he used to smile at her when they first dated. "I mean, not in this house, but…you know…"

"Everything is back to normal," Nash exclaimed, touching her head. The spiders were silent. Moreover, they were gone. No more scurrying about in her head, no more directing her moves. The freedom was a sweet relief. "Everything is quiet."

Sylvie, clutching her head, got an idea. "I am the Island

Impaler. I only wanted the containers…" She was twitching, trying to shake the leeches from her. "I tried to get the dance teacher's set, and that fat receptionist. I got them, but it wasn't enough. And I pinned it on you, Nash. Those women who died, I set it up to look like you had done it. Then, I killed the kid, the one who knew about the warehouse." She pointed to Derrick. "I tried to sleep with him, to get the Plasticware, but he wouldn't budge."

Nash had always known that Derrick was not a cheater like Chad, but this confirmation was welcome.

"I did so many things. I did everything they told me to. I used the weapons they told me to, and I killed people that didn't even deserve it."

Nash was becoming angry. Not because Sylvie had tried to ruin her reputation, but because the woman would not stop talking and she wanted to enjoy the spider-free silence. Furthermore, Sylvie's words were filling the room, suffocating them. Her words were purple and puffy, like the invading gum that had nearly choked Nash at the bracelet party. Nash could see the confession flooding all free space; it was deadly. Sylvie had to be stopped. Nash leapt and wrapped her hands around the woman's throat, squeezing.

Sylvie's dress fell open, exposing a body that was far too thin to belong to the mother of the Cape Quints. Even more disturbing was that her body was infested with leeches. The creatures were throbbing with each suck they committed on Sylvie. But she was not Sylvie anymore.

Nash pulled her hands away and Sylvie laughed, showing her mouth which looked like a steel trap, and her long leech-like tongue.

"Your husband may forgive you, but no one else will." Sylvie's voice was low and raspy; her eyes were large and glazed and mostly pupil. "Everyone still thinks you're guilty. They never really liked you; never really trusted you. You never noticed but the women stopped trying to impress you long ago. And…" Sylvie snapped her jaw a few times as if testing it out, biting through the purple bubble words that remained. "Everyone thinks your new solarium sucks. It's too ostentatious and so 2018. They will continue to make fun of you and think you are guilty." A few leeches dropped from the Sylvie-creature's body, fat and fully sated. "I even doctored receipts."

This would have sent the old Nash over the edge. How dare someone mess with her taxes. But then she remembered Dinah, and the gun, and how much her family needed her, and realized that none of this mattered.

"Do your worst," she said calmly to the creature. "I never really cared what anyone thought of me. I was simply bored. Everything I do, I do because I am bored." She lifted the special container from her purse. "And because I am protected."

This was where Nash was wrong. This was her fatal mistake. She took the risks she took believing she was infallible due to a mystical container. She knew she was wrong when the Sylvie-creature attacked her with the bracelet that had been slipped into Sylvie's handbag at the party. The bracelet concealed a switch blade which she dragged across Nash's throat. Warm blood quickly coated the front of Nash's dress and fell onto the hungry leeches still hanging from Sylvie's body.

Nash felt the pain shoot through her, and it was stunning. Yet, she still had enough strength to open the container from Virtue's murder scene before falling to the ground. The container blazed with a light that rivaled the chandelier in P.P.'s house. The light flashed several times before the container split open, bursting as it finally displayed all that was within. Appearing from the tiny space was a bag of pills, the disembodied head, and the image of an urn.

The pills were the ones she had taken from Virtue and sold. They had sold easily and quickly and had been the impetus for all that had occurred after. Nash remembered she had sold them to a boy, a boy with a very familiar face. That same face was on the disembodied head that had influenced so much of her life and now shared the room with them. The spiders crawled out of Nash and scurried toward the head. Nash felt her energy leaving with them. Her own internal container was emptying. The head looked at her and smiled. She had spent her life doing its bidding and it would give her one final reward.

The head floated around the room, in search of something, until it came to rest beside the Sylvie-creature. The head's jaw opened, unhinging so that it opened wider than possible, and consumed the leach filled monster. It started in on Sylvie headfirst, so that the last thing seen were her Alexander McQueen's. The head then spun in dizzying circles, before disintegrating.

Where the head once was, lights could be seen. Flashing lights. Red and white. Nash thought she heard a siren above the bloody roar inside her head.

"Hold on, sweetie." Derrick was bending over her, his face lit up in alternating red and white. "Help is here."

The urn floated behind his shoulder. Nash realized that this was her final container.

She could not move. She was struggling to breathe. She tried to tell him what was needed for Dinah and Riley. She tried to tell him about passwords for accounts and how to handle the household budget. She tried to tell him about the taxes.

Instead, Nashville DeCota fainted into the lights, confident that her husband knew everything. She was confident that he knew her.

Attempt 3: Hazing

The most heinous and destructive words fell from the mouth of a child.

"Is there a baby in there?" she asked, pointing to my lower abdomen. Admittedly, it was a bit swollen as carbs had found their way down my throat, but it was not *that* swollen and this particular child—who was really a teen—knew better.

That was exactly why she asked, pointedly, in front of all the women. Only one looked appropriately horrified for me. The others resembled the notorious cat who swallowed the canary to such an extent that I could practically see the feathers sticking out of the corners of their plumped and painted mouths.

The accuser, Dinah DeCota, batted her eyes innocently, awaiting a response, as if she deserved one.

"Of course not, dear." I forced sweetness through my clenched jaw and turned to walk toward the bar that was lined with fake roses and tassels. Every party contains several attacks; it is customary. I simply was not expecting that the girls were now engaging in warfare for their mothers. Although I suspected Dinah, in this case, operated as a social soldier of fortune.

As I reached for my wine, I realized that Dinah had followed me. "Would you know the father?" she asked quietly, but I was reading her lips. "I mean, if there were a baby in there?"

This conversation took place in the very middle of a whirlwind year. It also confirmed my suspicions: Dinah was no less treacherous and possibly just as dangerous as her mother.

$$\bullet$$

I began the stories like this:

Prior to Melanie Voss's first experience with Time Between Time, she had been well acquainted with the phrase "be careful what you wish for."

And

Nashville DeCota lay chilled and dying on the operating table.

I had sold the narratives as if they were fiction. I tweaked the main players and their agendas so that I could distance myself from the tragedy and turbulence. The story is, to me, truly unbelievable, and the hazy film of fiction tenderly obscures access to the truth.

I also committed the sin of omission to protect myself and those I love.

It is a miracle there were any survivors in the situation that I was contracted to write about. The writing brought me a level of recognition on Cape Cod and the surrounding areas. I would go to a store or to a restaurant, and a stranger would approach me and say, "I know you!" and I would think, "You don't. You know very little. Because of me. Because I didn't always write the truth."

What was not reported, what had really happened would have sold far more copies. The story had momentum, but the repercussions would have been staggering had I recorded the facts. For reasons that are both obvious and beyond my understanding, I felt a need to preserve an innocence that was long gone. An innocence desecrated by the very person I wanted to protect.

The following is the truth.

A contract is a thing of beauty.

It is binding, legal. There is nothing passive aggressive about a contract. It doesn't talk about you behind your back. Even though the women called me "Wi Fi" because they thought I was the biggest gossip, I only spread news. I spoke of events coming up, who was attending, what they were wearing or what they wore, and I recapped the occasion. The others spread maliciousness as if spreading jam on toast. They speculated and invented and attributed atrocities to people that they deemed deserving. Reality had no role in their use of language.

Then I received the contract. I never had one before. I never had anything to hold up to the ladies at lunch, to make me special, to make me the center of attention.

Before the contract, which very few of them lived to see, they had laughed at me for wanting to be a writer.

"Everyone thinks they are a writer," P.P. had said, "But very few have a story to tell. Allen was just saying the other day, after lecturing at Emerson, that he would kill, simply kill, to see some real talent out there—"

"—You need experience before you can write," Nash interjected. "What is it that you know about?"

"—Allen finished another play, a historical drama about the lost colony of Roanoke. It has mystery and romance. It's very astute and only for the literary minded." P.P. pushed her superfluous cat's eyeglasses further up her perfectly sculpted nose. "Allen is an intellectual as well as an artist. You can't be a writer when your only intellectual pursuit is shopping."

"Glen's research—" Sylvie tried to speak, but no one allowed her psychic space at the table.

"How can you find the time to write?" Melanie asked. "You have the children…"

"And don't even dream of making any money at it," Nash offered. "The publishing industry is long dead."

"And Nashville knows where the body is buried," P.P. quipped, but she laughed alone.

That conversation had taken place a long time ago, and the publishing industry is still alive and kicking, unlike many of the women who had lunched that day.

I was accustomed to their verbal assault. They continuously forgot that I had a secret weapon: my hearing aids, which I routinely switched off as a psychic shield.

Someone once said, "the best revenge is living well." For these ladies, the best revenge is living, at all. I also have the revenge of being paid to write; I had been approached to document the mysterious circumstances surrounding my social circle. I was first writing about the Island Impaler and the Tooth Snatcher. While crafting those stories, friends died and disappeared and became diseased. I had been commissioned to capture the competition and misery of the women around me but had become ambushed by the bigger story: the girls.

It started at the Cards and Stars charity event. The "cards" part was self-explanatory. There would be charity poker and blackjack and even a bingo table (for the affluent women of the senior's center who had been affectionately nicknamed "steel magnolias" and who, by virtue of outliving their looks and interest, had escaped the mystery that was soon to come). The "stars" part alluded to the famous, reclusive author who was rumored to have been drawn out of hiding courtesy of a large loan with the bank of Nash, and who had been put to work signing copies of his latest manifesto—and donating half of his evening's take back to Nash.

The author had also promised, mostly likely on promise of future pharmaceutical favors, to bring along a surprise guest. This guest hailed from the set of the author's novel-turned-film, and it was obvious that the women had all hoped it was the leading actor who had a penchant for "real" women: waitresses, hostesses, and soccer moms. While none of them qualified as such, they would certainly fare better than if the author brought the actor whose name appeared under the title and who only dated Victoria's Secret models.

While Nash was architect and engineer of the party, P.P. took it upon herself to grab a microphone so she could begin asking everyone to find a seat. This action was easier requested than done. While the men complacently sat anywhere, the women jockeyed for seats closest to the stage where the writer and actor would appear. They also strategically placed themselves between the friends that they thought were the least attractive, thereby raising their beauty ratio exponentially.

"If I could have your attention…?" P.P. quietly implored. She never raised her voice because she was *that* girl. She was the one who always held court, who was always the center of attention. She was the one that men gravitated to at clubs and parties. She would always be listened to, even when she had nothing of importance to say—which was most of the time.

"Your attention, please," she insisted, sounding demur and hostile simultaneously. She ran her fingers through her hair and waited for silence.

After P.P. introduced the author, he, in turn, introduced the actor. The actor's dimples gleamed and danced. He was tall and well-built with deep, dark eyes that made most women forget about everything that had come before. Even in the brightly lit ballroom, surrounded by card players and candelabras, the actor shone.

The actor motioned for P.P. to pass the microphone. She reluctantly did because everyone knows that Hollywood trumps the East Coast bourgeoisie.

"If I can direct your attention to the piece of paper taped beneath your chairs," the actor began, and most of the women, stunned by his presence, needed their dates or escorts to direct their hands and find the slip of paper. "I was given a number." He made a great show of digging into the front pocket of his tight jeans and coming up with a piece of paper. "If it matches your number, then I will be obliged…" He smiled devilishly. "…to share an afternoon with you… In whatever way you'd like. Could be lunch. Fellas, it could be golf." He displayed his dimples. "Could be up to you."

Nash reached for the number under the seat she had hastily stumbled into, looking as if she regretted not being more selective. P.P. grabbed the last vacant chair, beside Melanie, and snatched her slip with gusto.

"The lucky winner is…." He dramatically unfolded the paper. "Number 12!"

Melanie gasped and raised her hand holding the coveted number. Before the spotlight could find her, P.P. motioned to give an air kiss and shake the winner's hand—the hand holding the paper. Violently. She violated Melanie's fist and snatched the slip away, bounding towards the small stage and large actor.

I was in shock. That number had been Melanie's. Had anyone else seen P.P. steal it? I could not believe that woman's audacity, to stand there with her arm around the actor's slim waist, as if he were rightfully hers.

I felt guilty for having stolen Melanie's breast pump years before. I don't really know why I did it. I had no desire to ever nurse again; my new breasts cost a fortune and my priority was to protect them. I know when I wrote Mel's story I mentioned "Wi Fi" being demented over an emergency hysterectomy. The truth is I had my tubes tied. This would not have been a popular choice in my social circle, so I kept it hidden. Amongst the ladies, more children meant you were not struggling financially. More children meant more photo ops and more chances to show off at school and sports functions. More children proved you were still young and fertile which held equal importance to wealth. But I had enough children. I felt like I had too many. Not that I would trade any of them for anything in the world. I had a special relationship with each of them. And with my stepchildren. I just wasn't in a marriage that needed any more of a commitment. Honestly, I fantasized about a day when I would be free of children. I looked forward to pursuing my passions. Alone. So, I don't know why I stole from Melanie. It was just that the pump, with its little motor engaged, was very relaxing.

Melanie deserved better treatment, which was why I allowed her to escape via The Bracelet. In telling her story, I wanted to grant her some respite. The truth is none of us treated her kindly. That was the missing ingredient amongst any of our exchanges with each other: kindness. We all deserved kindness.

Most of us did, anyway.

It was difficult to wish Nash or P.P. well as both had caused irrevocable harm. I got my revenge on Nash by no longer allowing her to profit off me.

I got my revenge on P.P. in other ways. Basically, I took her prize from her in an even more degrading way than she had with Melanie. I could be accused of stealing much more than a breast pump.

Later, while sipping our final drinks of the evening, P.P.'s husband waved me over as he spoke to the writer. There were some introductions, and the writer asked me a few questions about P.P. and Nash and the relationship that the women had with each other. He seemed very interested in our "lunch group" (Nash would have died to have heard us labelled anything so pedestrian. Her actual death would have been just as embarrassing to her).

"There is a story here," the writer said, and it was obvious that he was already trying to write it in his mind.

🍎

"I have been having weird dreams about a watery cave," Allen told me. "I wonder if I am supposed to write about it?"

I shrugged. "According to Freud, boys usually dream of tunnels…"

I had met Allen long before the Cards and Stars party. Our relationship had begun with casual betrayal: he had slipped his hand down the back of my skirt in the coat room at the Country Club following the art auction to benefit family and marriage counseling sessions for the nearly indigenous Cape Codders who had settled so deeply on the peninsula that they could not make it across the bridges to benefit from the therapy offered closer to the city. Lest his clumsily obvious intentions be misconstrued, he informed me that his wife would be away for eleven days, touring Marrakesh with her book club. The higher end book clubs never managed to read anything, they simply used the moniker as an excuse to get together, cause turmoil, and plan exotic trips. I had visited him on each of those eleven days, not because I had needed or wanted the sex, but because he said he found me remarkable.

"I could write an entire play about your deafness," he had said, handling my breasts with a roughness I did not care for.

"My muse," he sighed, "my Rubenesque bodied, lip reading muse." I knew very well who Rubens was and I am a far cry from one of his models. I am a size 4, and only because of the implants that Allen admired, and that his own wife refused to have inserted into her body. I am down to 1250 calories a day and am a regular at spin class.

Allen could be very ignorant for a genius.

"I feel sorry for hearing people," I sniffed. "It must be unnerving to live in a world where everything makes a sound."

I had spent eleven days with him, coming home in shorter and shorter spurts only to find my absence had barely been noted. The nannies had tended to the little ones and the teens and tweens were losing interest in me with each passing day. I was most hurt by the neglect delivered by my oldest, Kristianne. I had been a young mother with her. I always felt we had raised each other. We had been close, speaking a "secret language" (AKA sign language; thus, not a secret but not widely used). I want to take all responsibility for my choices, but I can't help but wonder if my children's lack of needing me drove me to Allen.

The relationship with Allen was feast or famine. We could go months without seeing each other, then just when I would suspect the affair was over, he would text, and we would spend days sneaking enjoyment from each other.

"What about tomorrow?" he asked, as I searched for my clothing in his home office. His wife was at her "MIG weld a creature" class, followed by her anti-gravity fitness class.

"I have a PTO meeting at the middle school, and I need to run errands before that," I lied. I didn't want him to take me for granted. Besides, I needed a break from the sex.

Allen snorted. "I like the middle school, I really do. I am just lucky Garrison goes to private and won't be in that high school."

I had long grown tired with the beach-dwelling residents' collective snobbery toward the public schools. They received the king's ransom in funding and had more equipment, fields, and technology than most colleges. "What's wrong with the high school?"

He ran his fingers through his hair, stalling for the right words. "The girls run it. Bad girls. Not like the ones I went to school with."

"I'm sure you knew some bad girls," I chided, "nostalgia has a way of coating our memories with sugar."

"No. I am not a victim of 'the good old days' syndrome. Sure, I knew girls who drank and did coke. Plenty of girls got pregnant before graduation. These girls are... different... scary... even worse than their mothers."

He was pulling up a chair to his desk, mumbling, "When I was there, as artist in residence" —I hated his humble brags— "I observed a lot of...disturbing behavior. But I heard the worst behavior happens where I couldn't observe, in the locker room."

I remembered Nash and Gwynnie bragging about their girls' prowess on the lacrosse team. Everything was a competition, even skills that they contributed nothing to beyond a ride to and from meets.

"They tortured one girl so badly, she had to be placed in a residential. Not even a private school, a *residential*," he stressed. "And another girl, we don't really know what happened, but the rumor was that they pushed her to it. She was found dead—"

"—yes, I remember her." In fact, Kristianne had known the girl. At the time, I had tried to get Kristianne to open up about her feelings, but she was never big on words. I used to blame myself for that. I believed that my deafness thrust her into a world of silence and communication via facial expressions and finger spelling. Her siblings had each other to speak to; she had spent her formative years responding to and speaking to me in sign language.

"But the girls get punished for some of this stuff, right? I mean, when they are caught." I knew the answer to my own question but asked it anyway. The girls were just as bad as their mothers. They hazed and bullied and inhaled each other's humiliation as if it were an exotic fragrance. And they were rarely caught.

"Not in this town." He lowered his eyes. "The Cape Capo. The Tooth Snatcher. Nothing gets past her." He shook his head. "She should get into politics."

"Your wife would have a fit."

"Jackie? Nah, she is over Nash."

Sometimes I forgot P.P. had a real name.

"If you want to hang around." He nodded to the love seat beside his desk. "I will let you read what I am working on."

I politely peeked over his shoulder while slipping on a heel.

It was hubris that tattooed the girl's face, as she chanted: *'When old age shall this generation waste.'* Ironically, the tattoos that lined her body predicted a mockery of old age. She, like the other girls, was completely vain in believing that all was well in their world…

"Did you write that? It's familiar…"

"Not that line." He pointed to the italicized words. "But all the rest. It's an homage."

I kissed him on the cheek and walked out the door. If he continued talking, I would be pleasantly unaware.

On a day with thickening clouds, I went to the boutique that is sandwiched between the café and the religious paraphernalia store. I expected the shop to be empty, as it was a Tuesday afternoon, yet I spotted the girls lingering amongst the handbags and sunhats. I had come for earrings, but was compelled to watch the girls, as it was the only way I could eavesdrop on their conversation.

Undeniably it is wrong to invade people's privacy, even teenagers, but these girls were not like anyone else. They were a unique combination of gender and crime. As far as I know, they were the first girls anywhere to hold this level of rage and they had every right to be angry. Every public humiliation by their mothers was a psychic murder.

It was Gwynnie's daughter, Talia, that caught my attention

first. Her face was sweaty, as if she had been running—which was something this particular group did, but Talia excelled at. It quickly became apparent that she was showing the effects of something other than exercise.

"You said that if I made her cry..." she was saying to Dinah DeCota.

"Did she? Did she cry?" Dinah looked eerily like her mother as she leaned over Talia.

"Yes."

"Did you give her the apple?"

Talia nodded.

"I don't understand," a boxy girl named Leah said sweetly. Leah was all sharp edges and shoulders and owned her anger over cruel genetics. "You are alone. Where's Kristianne?"

My heart stopped. As far as I knew, my daughter was singular in her name.

"I couldn't get her to come."

"She wouldn't come? She knows about tonight..."

Talia became very nervous. "I think she is on to us."

Dinah sighed. "That doesn't really help us, does it? We are kind of...useless... unless we have Kristianne."

Talia nodded sadly, while Leah edged closer, looming largely.

"We will go tonight anyway we have plenty of things to use." Dinah decided.

"Does it have to be the marsh?" Talia seemed to whisper, as the words pushed through her lips on little bursts of air.

"Yes," Marjorie Voss intoned, "It has to be the marsh."

I noticed that Dinah had slipped some earrings into her pocket before the girls glided out of the store.

I went to yet another school meeting before heading out to see what the girls were up to. They had mentioned my daughter's name. While I was always cautious of Allen's love of hyperbole and histrionics, I was haunted by his words. It is one thing to discuss girls that were only names from the newspaper, or daughters of acquaintances, it was entirely another to suspect that your own daughter was next on the list.

My youngest, Clemmie, was happily ensconced at the children's snack table, while the pre-K mothers made plans for the graduation ceremony to be held in June. Her twin was in a separate pre-K class, per school rules. They wanted them to develop independence. I had explained to the superintendent that we made separate play dates for them and often hired two sitters so they could have individual activities, but she was not sympathetic to my desire to make my life easier by having them in the same class.

"The girls will wear white, the boys blue," instructed the mom in charge of the tiny caps and gowns the recent toddlers would wear for all of four minutes. I was thinking of two separate ceremonies followed by two separate celebrations. What was the point of having twins?

"Uhm," the mother who insisted on gluten-free snacks raised her hand, even though we were all free to speak. "That is insensitive to any gender neutrality."

The only dad in the group, who was bored or hateful or both, interjected, "They are babies. They don't know anything about sex yet."

"Gender. Sex is biological, whereas gender is a social construct. And research has shown—"

"The girls will wear white," the mom in charge began again. I turned away to watch Clemmie and lost the rest of the adult conversation.

Clemmie was shoving her snack dish away. Her baby lips were forming the word "diet." She had picked up a crayon and was drawing on her leg. Her three favorite dolls at home were covered with "tattoos." Clemmie thought they were beautiful, but the other moms gave me odd looks when she dragged them to the playground.

The marks she was making on her beautifully chubby thigh looked different, though. Usually, her tattoos were a majesty of swirls and curves: a Rorschach of rounded hills and shapely clouds. These marks were strident x's: the visceral negation of flesh. Whereas her babies wear celebratory tribal art, my baby was covering herself with visual warnings.

On the way home, I asked Clemmie why she didn't eat her snack.

"I'm a good girl," she said, banging her hands on her car seat to the rhythm of her words.

I had been reading her lips in the rearview, surprised at her assessment. "Good girls don't eat snacks?"

She shook her head. "Nuh uh. Snacks make you fat. Fat Nancy, fat Nancy, fat Nancy."

When I was able to look at her again, I asked, "Who is Nancy, honey?"

"Big girls don't like her. She fat. Kissy told me to be careful and not be fat."

"Kristianne told you to worry about your weight?"

Clemmie was pumping her legs rhythmically in her car seat.

"Good girls eat apples, apples, apples," she sang.

When we got home, I cornered Kristianne.

"Are you talking to your baby sister about her weight?"

She rolled her eyes. "Someone has to."

"She is not fat, and she is just a child." I felt like pulling my hair out, which is how I had consistently felt in recent months when talking to Kristianne. "What is going on with you anyway? You seem so... miserable."

She signed, "You talking about me or you?"

I signed back, "I am well, everything is well, but when you are here the house feels... stressed."

"Wow. You really make me feel wanted."

"Kris, baby, it's just that I wish you would talk to me. We used to be so close, we used to tell each other everything."

"Are you telling me everything?" Her arched eyebrow was so sharp she could have cut paper with it.

"Of course I am. I have nothing to hide."

She grabbed her backpack and pushed by me.

"Where are you going?" I asked.

"Out with the girls," she over-enunciated so I could see the words on her lips.

The girls being precisely the last words I wanted to see.

I could see seven girls seated in a circle, wreathing a small fire made of twigs and pinecones. They had a rickety altar consisting of an overturned wooden box which held items, including a shiny red apple. They were tucked into a grove along the marsh. I could smell marijuana above the tangy, salty smell of the seaweed laden sand. I recognized all the girls, my relationship with most dated back to the days of diapers. They had been a part of a "snack pack." We mothers gave birth to a ritualized socialization, wanting our daughters to seek friendships with the "right kind of girls."

Obviously, we failed in our attempt.

Kristianne had lied: she was not with the others. I was relieved, as I felt they were definitely a danger to her but wondered why she lied about her whereabouts.

I made sure to position myself so I could see the main players in their clique and read their lips.

Dinah was silent, fire dancing in her eyes as she sipped from an old wine bottle. Leah was pontificating about a random girl stealing a lacrosse girl's boyfriend and how they would make the trifling offender pay. They talked about a big dance and how "basic" the other girls in school were about it. They also talked about us.

"She freaked on me again, about nothing," Dinah said, passing the bottle around.

"My mom kind of did, too. I wish she could get a life and stay out of mine," Marjorie said, digging a snack-sized bag of pot from her pocket.

Kayleigh, the sister of that boy who is always mooning around Nash, was wearing an oversized black rain poncho with a hood. She resembled a witch wearing a cloak during Sabbat. Her red ringlets were tinted with jet black streaks and twined with velvet ribbon. She held an ancient book between hands clad in poison rings.

"Hemla, pneumna, vexen," Kayleigh chanted. She lifted the book above her head and closed her eyes. Her eyelids were covered with the same sparkling eyeshadow that the girls had to wear at dance recitals in pre-school and the makeup caused me to immediately go back there, to the front row of the school auditorium. I remember my heart pounding; I remember praying that Kristianne remembered her cue. She was only three, new to the school scene, yet already immensely influenced by her peers and the girls a year or two older. I, too, was new to the school scene. I simply wanted everything to be better and easier for her than it had been for me. Then again, in high school I had thought that the mean girls simply evaporated at graduation. How wrong I had been.

I had left her backstage, sitting on Dinah's lap, both girls having their hair and makeup done as if they were on a movie set, instead of preparing to spin and tumble to one song that would last all of two minutes and twenty-eight seconds.

Two minutes and twenty-eight seconds can be unbearably long when a mother's heart is in her throat, waiting for her daughter's soul to be crushed by a missed step.

Dinah had always shown an interest in Kristianne. She had taken her under her wing, even though I would have preferred to keep a distance between the girls. Especially after I realized what Nash had done to me during my pregnancies with the little ones.

I cleared my head and focused on the girls, who were no longer little and are knocking on the door of womanhood. They no longer took organized dance, but they were swaying and gyrating in time to the leaping flames. I didn't see any phones alit and playing music, so I believed they were moving to the beat of their chanting.

Talia pulled out a small box and placed it near the fire. It was a piece of a Plasticware set. When she lifted the lid, I saw tiny pearl-like teeth.

"A moment of silence for those girls," Kayleigh commanded.

"We had nothing to do with them," Marjorie interjected.

I noticed a few girls looking pointedly at Dinah and I didn't know if that had anything to do with the statement about the victims of the Tooth Snatcher, or because she was still holding the blunt instead of passing it along.

The book was opened, and the girls began chanting: "Pastu paladin virecta anima mea." A few looked around while some stared intently at the fire.

"Why isn't it working?" Talia asked impatiently. "It's supposed to—"

"Don't question," Dinah corrected, "You are never supposed to question."

Kayleigh lowered her head and gazed up at them, her hood shadowing her face. "Maybe that is the problem… one of you is a nonbeliever…"

"Or maybe someone is afraid." Dinah cocked an eyebrow at them.

The girls shook their heads somberly, denying any fear.

Kayleigh grabbed the apple and sunk her teeth into it, taking a large bite as she passed it to Talia. "We almost forgot. Points off—"

"Mr. Holloway would never know." Talia rolled her eyes, and

I could tell they were not taking this solemn ceremony seriously. I wondered what any of this had to do with Glen Holloway, Sylvie's husband. I knew he was doing a project at the school, but I had never truly paid attention when Sylvie had detailed it. I had always chalked it up to a competition between Sylvie and P.P. They were forever trying to claim the most creative, most intelligent husband. I knew Allen well, but had little interaction with Glen, so I could only speculate that P.P. was not fighting above her matrimonial weight class.

Marjorie handed Dinah a bedazzled seashell. "I almost forgot... I found this when I was going through a drawer in my room. Remember when we used to make these?"

Dinah's face clouded over. "Remember *who* we made these with?"

"The Quints." Marjorie sighed. "I kind of miss those little jerks. Too bad their mom—"

"Don't worry about her." Dinah had regained composure. "She is being taken care of."

Marjorie smiled. "Is your mom going to get her?"

"No, not Mom. We can talk about it after we finish this."

"I am getting cold," Talia complained. "Do we have enough for the assignment?"

"No, we don't," Dinah snapped. "Repeat..." She stood and took the small container Talia had presented. One at a time, she tossed the teeth into the marsh. She had turned away from me, so I don't know if she accompanied the ceremony with any words.

"Mr. Holloway didn't say anything about teeth, just the apples..." Talia was shivering and looking very uncomfortable.

A final box was opened. It housed a charm bracelet. I recognized the bracelet; it had belonged to Kaitlin, the girl who had killed herself after someone had posted naked pictures of her online. I don't know how the girls had come to possess the bracelet. I didn't think they were friends with the deceased.

Kaitlin had spent the night at our house, once, about a year before the suicide. Kristianne had a habit of rotating through friends. My husband joked that she "wore people out." I always try to make small talk with my children's friends. I had complimented Kaitlin's bracelet and she had cautiously explained each charm to me, glancing at Kristianne for approval.

The girls returned to their chant, and I tried to wipe the debris and sand from my Jimmy Choos. I could never understand why Mel loves the marsh so much. The smells assault you. The air feels heavier and the ground harder than anywhere else on the Cape. And the sharp reeds are murder on calves and ankles. Then again,

I hate the beach, too. I can't wear my hearing aids there due to the water, salty air, and blowing sand, and it makes me feel incredibly vulnerable to leave my defunct ears bare.

My woes and my shoes were forgotten when a few sharp screams came from the girls' area. They were high pitched enough that even I could hear, or more truthfully, feel them. Squeals of that timbre carry an electricity that vibrates in the bones.

"It's a leech." Talia was pointing at Dinah and the tube-shaped creature dangling from her shirt. The leech sucked and writhed, pulling in the area of Dinah's nipple in a bastardized impression of nursing.

"Looks like a dick," Marjorie said, turning her head sideways to get a better view.

"It's obvious you've never seen one," Kayleigh retorted. A few other girls were speaking, throwing their hands around, but I couldn't understand them. Dinah remained eerily calm, gazing down at the leech as if this were a normal occurrence.

What was not normal was the outcome when Dinah walked to the water's edge and flicked the leech from her chest. The creature fell with barely a splash, yet the water began to ripple with concentric circles. The circles grew larger, their disruption of the surface extending aggressively. The girls backed away from the water, while Dinah leaned over, peering closely.

I had not been sleeping well recently, and I had been taking sedatives to help me relax. At the time, I blamed what happened next on the pills. Now I know better.

There was a man in the water where there had only been ripples before. I gasped and quickly covered my mouth, not wanting the girls to hear. They were too engrossed with what they were seeing to take note of any distractions. Part of me wanted to grab the girls and run. I had no idea who this man was or what he wanted. What type of man simply appears out of the marsh? I was quickly trying to compose an explanation for my presence so that I could reach out to the girls, when the man began walking slowly toward them. Drops of water glistened in the moonlight on the man's skin. He was perfect, and his skin appeared warm despite the chill in the air. He began to move very slowly through the water, holding Dinah's eyes.

Dinah reached toward the water, with arms open, seeming to request an embrace.

"What the actual fuck?" Leah asked, tearing her eyes away from the man and looking at Kayleigh. "What's she doing?"

"We have to go," Kayleigh responded, her eyes large and frightened.

The others obeyed, cleaning up their knives, candles, and wine bottle, yet Dinah stayed rooted at the edge of the water.

Marjorie was facing me, and I could read on her lips the words, "It worked." She looked perplexed, as if success had never been on the agenda. Talia nodded before grabbing Dinah and dragging her back to the car.

Once the girls were gone, I could no longer see the man.

Hesitantly, I stepped closer to the water, but the moon had darted behind a cloud, and I was left peering into the darkness. I could tell the water was very still. The entire marsh was very still: I was completely alone.

I walked back to my car, brushing sand from my shoes and sticky seedlings from my legs as I went. As I pulled away from the marsh, I spotted our small Toyota, the one Kristianne uses. It was partially hidden by the bushes and brush and the car appeared to be empty. I waited for as long as I could for her to return, but I had to get home to my other babies. She had disabled the "find my people" ability from my phone, so I was unable to virtually locate her. Due to a much needed sleeping pill, I have no idea when she returned home that night.

***

I had been excited to go to Nash's house, as she had invited only P.P and myself. I was still shaken from what I had seen at the marsh and was doubting whether I had dreamt it or imagined it or was completely losing my mind. Perhaps my guilt over Allen was causing me to be trauma reactive. He was encouraging me to journal. He thought it would help to break my insomnia. He told me that creativity requires courage, and it would be good exercise for my psyche. He said that his wife lacked the introspection to be a good writer. He said that I was very observant, and my deafness would lend uniqueness to the descriptive nuances I could employ. I knew he meant well, but I didn't want his advice or his concern. Our relationship did not need emotional intimacy. If it were a relationship at all.

I knew that an afternoon at Nash's would be a distraction, even though I had just witnessed her child playing wet nurse to a leech-man. P.P.'s presence was an added bonus. It was like I had a front row seat to a gladiator show, only I wasn't sure which one was the lion.

After Nash engaged me in a competition over whose daughter eats the least, and P.P. bashed Sylvie's welding skills in the artsy course they shared, P.P. moved to a deadly topic.

"I know these… containers are your new drug of choice, Nashville," P.P. condescended, "but I have to admit that I have been maligned in my 'score.' " The woman curled her taloned fingers into air quotation marks. P.P. went on to say it was like purchasing cocaine cut with baby powder. This woman had the audacity to claim this inside Nash's sunroom, in full view of the sea and me as witness.

"Honestly, Nashville." P.P. had the unnerving habit of always addressing Nash by her full name. "I am simply not happy with these… little plastic caskets." She frowned and pulled from her oversized purse a piece of her coral lidded set, which was small and oddly shaped, and mostly useless. The funny thing is that I don't remember them appearing that way the night of the Plasticware party. I wondered what the Princess was up to.

"Didn't we mention there was a no return policy?" Nash smiled sweetly. "It is obvious they have been used and… after all, you are not the most meticulous person when it comes to doing dishes."

P.P. sniffed. "I haven't washed a dish in a decade, Nashville. And Irma is a fantastic domestic."

Nash sighed. "What are you suggesting, Princess? An exchange? Another set?"

"I want yours," P.P. said candidly.

I couldn't help but gasp.

"While it is natural that you should want my hand-medowns…" Nash shot her a side-eyed look. "And only befitting, I cannot accommodate you on that."

P.P. chuckled. "Oh, Nashville, is that what you thought I meant? I simply meant I want a set that is not… deranged. A few of these actually look… melted. Remember how you looked after that one collagen session…?"

P.P. paused for a moment, allowing her words to take effect. If I had not been sitting directly across from her, I would have sworn that I misread her lips. "That is how they look. All lumpy and misshapen. It is only fair that I get my money's worth. I mean you didn't have to pay for yours!" P.P. squinted with mock sympathy. "It is certainly only fair that Melanie won hers… we can't expect her to keep up with us in terms of our spending, can we?"

I wondered if they thought it was fair that I had won my set.

"No." Nash frowned. Her eyes moved upward, as if listening to something from far away. "We can't… Okay, P.P., let me see what I can do. It may take a while; you know I am so busy—"

"Oh, I know, I know. It has absolutely been the same for me. It has just been so busy, busy, busy, busy," P.P. moaned. "You know, Allen's written another play…"

I couldn't help another sharp intake of breath. It wasn't Allen's writing that was taking all of his time.

"No, no I didn't." Nash unabashedly looked at the clock.

"It's a historical drama. About the lost colony of Roanoke. There is mystery and romance, but it is very astute and not for the everyday crowd. Allen is an intellectual as well as an artist."

Nash sighed but gave no other response. I realized that P.P. was talking about something Allen had written long ago and wondered when they had last spoken to each other.

"Many big names are interested in taking roles."

I knew this to be a lie. The play was shelved, and Allen was working on something else. Something about a man feeling trapped with all his job and duties and family and wanting to find a secret portal so he could sneak away and have extra time to do the things he wanted to do._

"Which will probably take him away from the Cape for a while, to the Great White Way..."

Or, to the hotel he and I frequent...

Nash perked up. "Oh, P.P. I had forgotten...I mean, I was so consumed with hearing about Allen's poetry—"

"—Play."

"Right. I have something for you. This will make you forget all about those containers. Wait right here."

When she had left, I reminded P.P. of the bracelet party and that she would need to be cautious about any further merchandise she procured from Nash.

"I can make up my own mind about what is good and what is not *Fiona*." P.P. had a talent of making everyone's name sound like a curse. She crinkled her nose as if smelling something bad. "I get what I want. Just ask your little friend, Melanie." She smiled mischievously.

Nash returned to her sunroom and held a pair of boots aloft in front of P.P.

"I had these specially designed for me by a man in London. A master cobbler—"

"—Cordwainer."

"Huh?"

"A cobbler repairs shoes, a cordwainer designs and styles them."

Nash nodded frantically, suspiciously pushing the boots on P.P. "Thank you, that is the word I was looking for. Anyway, this is a man who works for Kate Middleton and Kate Winslet and Kate Moss. All the Kates—"

"The idea of working for a Nashville must have astounded him," P.P. interjected bitterly.

"Of course." Nash could never refrain. "Your humor was certainly missed at the Public Works ball the other night."

"What ball?"

"The one at the museum." I knew that there had been no ball, but apparently Nash needed P.P. to squirm a bit.

"Oh, right, that one… as I said, I have been so busy, busy, busy. I had RSVP'd that I couldn't attend. I'm sure they told you—"

"—No. In fact, no one mentioned you at all. *I* was the only one who missed you." Nash consulted the boots again, as if changing her mind. "But what is most important right now is that I had these boots custom crafted so there is not another pair like them anywhere in the world. When I finally got them, I realized that they were too tight. I was *crushed*."

"Oh, dear." P.P.'s concern was a phony as her tortoise shell glasses.

"Really. I could just curl up and die." She twisted her wrists, turning the boots to showcase each side and back. P.P. followed their every move like a dog watching its master holding a juicy bone. And they were wonderful boots. Anyone would have been glad to have them, which made me wonder what Nash's ulterior motive was.

"They are too snug, so I asked myself, 'Who do I know with truly dainty feet?'"

P.P.'s desire to greedily grab them showed on her face and was exasperated by the added compliment.

"Are you sure your feet aren't just swollen? You do bloat up every month." P.P.'s eyes never left the shoes. "One time, everyone thought you were pregnant, but I simply told them, 'water baby.' Obviously, I was right. You should lay off the salt. Do you eat a lot of chips?"

"I could give them to one of the girls… Melanie could certainly put them to use."

That was the last straw. P.P. reached out and grabbed the boots, making sure to put a faint look of disgust on her face as she handled them.

"Are they leather? Recently, I have had my doubts about leather. Especially with the winters we have been having. I mean, there is less salt in fast food french fries than on the streets anymore. *You* should stay off the street, dear Nashville, you'll bloat up even more…"

Nash raised an eyebrow. "Why don't you try them on? I'd love to see them on you."

"Put them on?"

Nash nodded eagerly. "Yes, see if they are a good fit. You have had experience modeling, right?"

My neck was getting tired from the back and forth between

these two, but I could tell we were headed in an explosive direction.

P.P. chuckled. "Nashville, I know my shoe size, and I know if shoes will fit me or not on sight alone. These will obviously fit, it's simply a matter of if I would want them or not."

As she twisted and turned the boots, I could see inside. There were *things* inside. Crawling things.

I hadn't noticed Dinah enter the room, as I couldn't hear her approach. When she saw me, her eyes took stock of my clothing, hair, shoes, and basic existence. Her face registered disapproval but it was mixed with something else. Guilt? Fear?

P.P. turned to look at the girl and smiled. "You know, it is so difficult to evaluate what shoes look like on my own feet." Her eyes trailed down to the girl's Fear of God military high tops, calculating size behind her unessential glasses. "Dinah, dear, do you think you could slip these on so I can see how they look?"

"She can't... she has an infection, athlete's foot." Nash reached over and snatched the boots from P.P.

"Mom! Gross!" Dinah's face turned red, but she remained in the room. "I just wanted to remind you, Mom, of the bracelets. You know, 'ladies night'?"

"Yes, yes, of course." Nash was shooing the girl with one hand while a spider crawled from the boot and onto her other.

I gasped and recoiled, yet the other ladies seemed nonplussed.

"You know, Nashville, I have noticed that you have a problem with an…infestation," P.P. commented, "I wish I could recommend someone, but I have never had problems with… pests…"

Nash looked at the spider and frowned.

"But I would certainly never take anything of yours until you get it under control."

The spider looked like one of the species they warn you about, like a black widow, although it is hard to tell. There was a red splotch on its back. Nash was peering into the boots, her lips moving subtly, as if she were talking to someone secretively.

"Nash?" I began politely, "Can you swat that spider away? I'm afraid it might bite you." Despite my disgust, the spider and Dinah's nagging of her mother gave me plenty of fodder for when I told Nash's story.

Nash smiled sweetly at me. "Don't worry, I am immune." P.P. stared at Nash's arm which now hosted three of the black spiders.

Just as she had been at the marsh, Dinah remained stonily calm in the presence of something that would normally send the bravest of us screaming or swatting, or at the very least, leaving the room. "Mom," Dinah said insistently.

"I heard you. The bracelets." Nash touched her temples and

squinted. She gently pushed the spiders back into the boots and looked at them sadly.

Dinah stepped closer to her mother. Even though they were the same height, the girl appeared to loom over the woman. "Ladies only. They can bring a friend, but it's better if it is kept a secret." I could tell that this was meant to be heard only by her mother, but people often forget that I am a lip reader.

"I know," Nash said, "A ladies' night they'll never forget." Nash continued to rub her temples as Dinah stomped from the room.

❦

I have very keen eyesight, due to my hearing loss, so I had no trouble making out the video on Dinah's oversized iPhone. It was a girl, a naked girl, with marks and lines drawn on her body. The marks seemed to denote imperfections, the way a plastic surgeon may draw on the areas that need reconstruction. They reminded me of the marks that Clemmie had made on her pudgy baby leg. This girl was covered with them, even though her body seemed nearly perfect with its youthful, tight skin and lack of cellulite. Her high round breasts were marked the most, as were her firm buttocks.

She was walking down the aisle of a school bus and the seated and clothed girls were spanking her and slapping her and jabbing any available flesh. The accosters were all wearing matching lacrosse uniforms. Patriots' memorabilia were scattered around. The school had joined the celebratory Duck Boat parade for yet another Super Bowl win.

I knew what this was, it was called "running the gauntlet." I had thought it was an urban legend, like the Tooth Snatcher or the Marsh People. As the girl reached the end of the bus, she was turned around to run the gauntlet again. Dinah was at the head of the bus, seemingly to make sure that the girl did her laps. The cheerleaders were at the front, and I tried to remember if Kristianne had gone along. The screen was focused on the naked girl, so most of the passengers were cut off, but I could see a hand holding the sharpie that had desecrated the girl's skin. The hand was writing a sign that was held up for the camera once the girl reached her.

"Hi boys," it said.

I walked closer to where Dinah sat. She was unaware of my presence, thoroughly engrossed in what she was doing, and what she was doing was crafting an email with the video embedded. She was sending it to the football team. The subject was "Fat Nancy," and the message displayed a screen shot of the hand and the sign.

The hand was wearing Kristianne's class ring.

I both hated and loved these parties. I especially loved the ones that Nash gave, as I was eagerly awaiting the moment she would fall on her own sword. I had been waiting for over a decade, since I had been pregnant with Miranda, and Nash had profited from my condition. I had never heard of that particular fetish before and had not realized how little of the profits would find their way into the knockoff Birkin bag Nash had used to woo me. I had thought I would maximize my profits via Nash by trading up from husband number one to husband number two, but that result had been just as counterfeit as the purse.

This party itself, its setup and overt agenda, was not unusual in our neighborhood. We often invited product representatives to demonstrate the latest and greatest in conveniences. I was fine with it when it was local artists and salespeople. I was less comfortable when the display included parents from the school—the mothers who had to earn and were paid for their disgrace.

These parties were a ritual. Everyone vied to arrive with

the newest bag, the most fashionable shoes, the latest 'do, the thinnest waist. Everyone prepared stories of their husbands' and children's successes. We purchased more of what we did not need or registered for classes we had no intention of attending. Then we would return home and silently hate each other until the next party.

But, according to Nash, this jewelry party would be different. It was not yoga on paddle boards, or the hookah fad—The bracelets were beautiful: affordable, yet priceless. Something to collect. The mommy version of trading cards. The bracelets were crafted of special metal and contained beads in every shade and hue of red, pink, or purple imaginable. Each unique. Each color especially matched to its owner by some sort of personality, Myers-Briggs type test.

Nash greeted each of us individually and insincerely and seated us in the cleared-out room beside her sunroom. The two rooms combined felt like one large room, rivaling any ballroom found in any palace anywhere in the world. All of us wore silk and sequins, except for Melanie who wore a green-ribbed turtle-neck sweater accompanied by a brown suede skirt and matching boots. She was appropriately dressed for the weather, but not for the event.

"Not even last year's outfit," I said to Gwynnie, trying to bait her.

She was after bigger game. "It *is* nearly impossible to keep these older style windows clean," she said loudly enough for Nash to hear.

I couldn't help but be pleased when Nash's eyes narrowed with anger at the comment.

"Ladies." Nash held up her palms, as if psychically pushing us away from her. Her hair was in yet another tight bun, tighter than her lifted and treated face. Even in the bun, her hair looked greasy, unwashed. That was highly unusual for Nash, especially when she was playing hostess. She would normally unveil a new hairstyle—one she had seen on a runway or on the head of some Hollywood star. Her hairdressers knew to keep their eyes out and to look for anything that seemed European or *haute couture*. As I remember this event, I realize that it was the beginning of her end. The mystery around her death would remain, but it was certain that Nash's mental health played a large part in the circumstances. "Ladies, I want to thank you all for coming." She smiled at the room, the decency of her smile raining down on her guests. "I am always so…comforted… when we have our little get-togethers." She emphasized the word *little* as if making some cute joke. "While in the past we have attended community building benefits, this soiree intends to benefit us all, personally." She looked at each of us, and I could tell she was mimicking the concept of warmth. "Please make sure that you have enough to eat. And let's begin." After clapping her hands together, her front door blew open and I saw a man at the threshold, pushing a dolly loaded with boxes upon boxes of jewelry. I felt as if I had seen him before. I wasn't sure where, but his face was so familiar. Familiar, and very, very handsome. He had shocking blue eyes and pouty lips. I couldn't help but wonder what it would be like to feel those lips all over my body. Whatever he was selling, I was buying.

I also felt oddly fog-brained. There was something I was meant to remember, something important. If my tubes were not tied, I would have worried it was pregnancy brain.

The man began to tell us he had something special. His pitch was simple: he promised ownership and independence. We were free to keep whatever profits we made from selling the bracelets. If he hadn't had my attention before, he had it now. He went on to say that we wouldn't have to tell our husbands.

It would be a secret.

Better if it were a secret.

Part of what I loved about being with Allen was the secret. It was invigorating to know something that no one else knows.

Which is why I listen to gossip: to take that thrill of holding a secret away from others.

"What I recommend… my best advice to you, ladies, is tonight you treat yourselves. This jewelry makes anything possible." I could see the rise and fall of the chests of the women around me as they sighed with pleasure.

He then had us play a game, which was always popular at these parties as we loved to compete.

He had us write down our wishes on a piece of paper. I wished to publish something, anything. There was nothing I wanted more than to see my name on the cover of a book.

Melanie won, and this time P.P. was not able to come between her and her prize. Melanie's win was the impetus for including an enchanted bracelet in her story. Her story would not end happily, either in fiction or in real life, but I liked the idea of giving her a little magic. I noticed, though, that P.P. was after a prize of a different sort. She was hanging all over the bracelet man. Oddly, he seemed immune to her enchantments.

As he was brushing off her advancements, I was able to place where I had seen him. He had been in a national commercial a few years prior. At that time, he had sported a man bun and scruffy beard. He had been cast as an all-natural, hiking aficionado who had a great enthusiasm for protein bars. The eyes were unmistakable.

And then I realized that he looked remarkably like the Marsh Man who had appeared during the girls' ceremony. I tried to approach him, but he was making a beeline for the exit, and away from P.P. I started to follow him, only to be blocked by Sylvie who wanted to ask something about Kristianne making it home the other night.

"What? What night?"

Sylvie blushed and looked down at her shoes. "She had been working on a project and Glen was helping her. It was just so late when she left…"

I had lost sight of the man and could not find Nash to get his information. I was also never interested in anything Sylvie had to say, so I excused myself and headed for the door.

When I left the party, something moved within the darkness of the bushes and caught my eye. It was the girls, or, at least, a few of them. It was hard to discern their shapes and numbers amongst the topiary in Nash's yard. I couldn't mistake Kayleigh, as her red hair stood out against the black night. She was holding the same book that I had seen at the Marsh. When I began walking the pavement toward the driveway, they scurried away, heading toward the beach. I am convinced they had been spying on the party but have no idea why it would be of interest to them.

I got into my car and secured my seat belt. Before I was able to turn on the ignition, I felt something push against the driver's side door. It wasn't a push, exactly, more like a pressure. I turned on the flashlight of my phone, but nothing was there. When I got home, I saw that there were lengthy scratch marks running along the door of my car. There were four perfectly spaced lines in the acrylic; they were smooth and unbroken. I thought of the legend of the Marsh People who had nails like fishhooks, as this was exactly how it looked, as if someone had run his or her obscene claws over the car.

I shivered and went inside.

Kristianne was seated on a kitchen bar stool. Her face was flushed, as if she had been running. She had a book in front of her, but it was placed so that the text was upside down.

"Reading?" I pointed to the book.

"Just doing homework." I always knew when she was lying because tell-tale dimples would appear at the corners of her mouth. "What bracelet did you get?"

"How did you know about that?"

"All the mothers have been talking about it all week. When

I was watching the Quints—"

"That's weird Sylvie mentioned something about you being at her house, working on a project or something. I thought you had a falling out with her—"

"Mr. Holloway asked me to watch them. There was no project, only babysitting. That woman is insane." She plucked an apple from the basket on the counter.

The apple reminded me of the one I had seen on the altar at the marsh—at the ceremony my daughter had been expected to attend.

"Is everything okay at school, Kris? You'd tell me, you know, if anything were going on?" I finished with the sign for suspect.

She signed that everything was fine. Only everything wasn't. Those lie dimples had made a spectacular reappearance.

"Everything is ok with your friends? You haven't had anyone over in a while."

"I just get tired of them, Mom, of those girls. We have all been together forever. Sometimes I need some space." She shrugged. "I have to do some work on my college portfolio. Mr. Holloway is supervising me. He thinks I have a lot of good material."

"Is he staying at the school long enough to help you? I thought he was only there a month. That is what Sylvie said." I actually had no idea what Sylvie said, I just wanted to keep my daughter talking in the hopes of learning something about her now secretive existence.

Kristianne's eyes narrowed. "He will help me for as long as it takes. It is kind of like *our* thing."

I nodded. "I am sure he is a wonderful mentor. Don't forget to mention your fluency in sign language in your portfolio."

Kristianne frowned. "I am trying to move away from that."

"It's not like it is anything to be ashamed of."

"I didn't say I was ashamed, *mother*. I simply said I am moving away from it. If I say I am fluent, then they will want me to befriend every deaf kid that comes along. And I really don't want to do that."

"I am so glad I raised such a compassionate child." I rolled my eyes. "You know, sometimes I just want to do something for me. College is my chance to get away from here." She shot me a biting look. "Away from you."

I was shocked. I had no idea she felt such animosity toward me. Or was this simply teen angst?

Kristianne's face softened. "Mom... it's just... I have a lot on my mind right now. I am working hard. I just don't need anyone riding me, telling me what I should and should not be doing. I want to figure it out for myself."

"I understand. But understand that I will always worry. It's a mother's prerogative."

It was her turn to roll her eyes and I noticed the dark bags beneath them.

"It's getting late, why don't you get some sleep?"

She sighed. "I'll try. It's just not so easy anymore."

I tried to win her over. "If you don't tell your father, I can let you have one of my sleeping pills."

"That's okay. I don't like taking things. I am kind of straight edge."

"Good girl," I signed.

She paused for a moment. "Good night," she signed back.

The following day, I left Allen's to find my middle daughter, Miranda, gnawing away at an apple.

"Since when are you a healthy snacker?" I asked.

"Since Talia told me it would make my tooth come out."

"That's helpful advice."

"They've told all the girls that. Even—" she stopped herself.

"Even who?"

"Christie," she said quietly. Christie had been one of the victims of the Tooth Snatcher. Miranda had been particularly upset about Christie. They had been part of a jump rope group at school. She put the apple down on the counter and touched her tooth tentatively.

"You want me to wiggle it, honey? See how loose it is?"

Her eyes grew wide with traces of tears. "He won't get me will he? The Tooth Snatcher?"

"Of course not Randy," I put my arms around her, wondering how often these girls spoke of apples and what the obsession was. I wanted to tell Miranda that the Tooth Snatcher was a she, not a he, and that she needed to be most careful of the adults she thought she knew well.

"What is the deal with apples lately?" I said aloud, and Miranda assumed I was asking her.

"They use them for pictures."

"Who does?"

"The bigger girls. They post pictures. They give girls apples and then post pictures of them." She looked at me hopefully, wanting me to bridge the gap between her innocent mind and that of the girls. Unfortunately, I was equally confused.

"What do you mean? They take pictures with apples? Of like, girls holding apples?" Maybe this was some new fetish. I had learned about some strange ones through Nash and her internet incorporation.

"Not really." She had a habit of looking up to the ceiling when trying to find the right words, and it was still adorable in the tween years. "I am not sure I really understand. They give the girls apples and then they take pictures of them. Skyler said that Marjorie was talking about it. It has something to do with Mr. Holloway." She scrunched her face up and rolled her eyes some more. "And…something… the gauntlet or something…"

The awards assembly honored a student from each grade, starting with grade 6 and ending with grade 12. Six students should take a half hour tops, figuring five minutes each. But that was not how these things went. The entire ceremony could last two hours; longer if the parents kept interrupting for photos.

Glen Holloway gave the opening remarks. He smugly took a few jabs at the school and its student body, making sure that we all knew he was fighting well below his weight class. He then went into a speech that was lost among most of us. I believe I understand it now:

"Apples have come to represent knowledge, temptation, and sin." Behind him, an image of Rosetti's *Venus Verticordia* was shown, the apple in her hand appearing fragile, as if it could be squeezed so that its juices would spill over her bare breasts.

A few adults tittered nervously at this transition. Most wanted to pretend that they understood where this was going; the rest wanted to act as if they were above it. There was something about Glen Holloway that made the adults uncomfortable. He was not friendly with any of the other fathers, and he was not as involved in the Quint events as one would think he would be. Beyond what Sylvie reported about him, he was secretive. The girls seemed to have a different take and they watched his presentation rapturously.

Glen pointed at the overly ripe image and explained that the term apple was originally synonymous with all fruit, and not with a specific type. He then pontificated further: "The protruding Adam's apple found on men is meant to serve as a reminder. It is the visualization of a piece of the sinful fruit lodged in the first man's throat, a constant reminder of man's transgression. Moreover, apples are a distraction to the female of the species. First Eve, then Atalanta, and even Snow White who could not resist biting into an obviously poisoned one." I was seated close enough to understand all the words of this presentation and was vexed at why apples were appearing so often in conversations around me. "Paris of Troy began the Trojan War by chiming in on the goddess' battle with an apple." He paused to smile smugly. Unfortunately, none of us were picking up what he was laying down. His own wife was strangely absent, so there was no one there to faint and flutter over his genius.

Except the girls.

Especially my daughter, who blushed as if caught *in flagrante delicto.*

"Apples are knowledge. We gift our most knowledgeable, our teachers…" He gestured to the faculty who looked both bored and annoyed. "…with the fruit. Interestingly, coffins were originally carved from apple wood, furthering the linkage between the apple and the final knowledge of all.

"And the most illustrious type of apple." A new slide appeared, an aerial view of all the high school students standing in the school yard. It appeared to have been taken by a drone, which, according to the handbook, was not allowed on school property. "The apple of *your* eye." Glen smiled with mock warmth. "Tonight is about them." He started the applause himself before moving to the left of the stage.

Marjorie Voss won for grade 12. She had created a slide show of inappropriate gifts brought back from conferences by her father. The images documented shot glasses, lighters, pocketknives, and trail mix. The slideshow ended with her cat, Captain Von Waffles, wearing the "I *heart* San Francisco" t-shirt that her father had bought on his most recent sojourn. The image needed no tag; the fact that the shirt was snug on a cat demonstrated a genuine lack of forethought in the purchase.

The audience chuckled. Graham was absent and thus alleviated of any embarrassment. Melanie was in attendance but had spent most of her time looking at her watch.

Dinah won "the shining senior award," which was simply a way for the school to appease Nash by giving her daughter an award but not forcing her to share with Marjorie. The English teacher read select passages from Dinah's paper: "Failure to Thrive." It documented her tragic origin being born a week early and subtly hinted at some neglect during her formative years. It also contained the word *rife* which I recognized as a word that Allen uses often.

Nash was purplish and apoplectic over this public shaming, while I was deeply concerned by the fact that this paper had my lover's influence throughout. I was also relieved that

Kristianne's artwork received an award without the requisite family embarrassment. Her portfolio that she was working on with Glen Holloway was not included in the ceremony and when I questioned her after she informed me that the project was not complete.

"It has a lot to do with what he was discussing tonight."

"Apples? What is the deal with that? Miranda said something about girls taking pictures with apples…" I was hoping to lead her into a discussion of running the gauntlet.

Kristianne snorted. "What does Randy know? She is in the Middle School."

"I guess Skyler said… it doesn't matter. What matters is that I want to know what is going on."

"You wouldn't understand."

"Try me."

"Mom." She groaned. "There is just stuff that… you wouldn't get it, all right? You and Dad are just so…"

"So what?"

She made a face similar to the one that Miranda uses, but this face wasn't cute to me at all. It was aggravating. "Straight. You are so straight. You do the same things; you have done the same things for years. You hang out with the same people, in the same places. You just aren't open minded enough—"

"That is enough, young lady. I am plenty open minded. Why just the other night—"

"—Oh no, are you going to tell me something scandalous about the stupid bracelet party?" She was turning red, as she had in the audience of the awards ceremony. "You do know that party was just a joke, right? Dinah and I—" she prevented herself from continuing.

"You and Dinah what?" I moved to try to block her exit from the room.

"Nothing. It's nothing. You wouldn't understand," she said for maybe the millionth time in the past year and slid past me.

🍎

"She is a child, Fi, that is just gross," he stated defensively, even though I had not suggested anything sexual between them.

"Then why the special tutoring? It had your imprint all over it."

"You can't make that accusation—"

"You make me read your writing—"

"—make you?"

I sighed. "Allen, she compared her plight as an infant to that of Virginia Dare. Are you telling me that Dinah pays that much attention to history to know that name?"

His face dropped. "She knows. About us. She threatened to expose us if I didn't help her. Don't worry, I didn't spend time with her. I wrote it without her."

I could feel my eyebrows fly to the top of my forehead. "You wrote it for her?"

"Fi, honestly, we are going to talk about academic honesty right now? When we are both marital cheaters?"

He had a point. He also had the beginnings of an erection. Although the timing was odd, I allowed him to have his way with me in the bed he shared with his wife. His energy was intense, like he couldn't get enough of my body. Even after he was finished, he continued to fumble with my breasts, squeezing my nipples, and basically doing nothing for me in the process.

I was pushing Allen's hands away, trying to get dressed when he pantomimed the universal signal for quiet. My confusion led him to point out the window, and he leaned his head in that direction, listening.

That was the only thing I hated about not hearing: not being able to listen in. That was when the hearing world felt like a secret society, that and when people put on a delighted smile and pointed to the ceiling tiles in a store or restaurant, marveling over a song being piped in that took them down memory lane.

"What is it?" I whispered.

"Dinah and Nash."

We crawled to the bedroom window and peeked through the curtain, spotting Dinah in the backyard, rinsing her sneakers with a hose. A dark item lay on the ground in front of her.

Nash's heels made an appearance, along with her braceleted wrist that reached to pick up a gun.

Allen recounted their words after they had gone inside.

"Dinah kept saying it was no big deal and she 'had to do it.' Then Nash said something like 'Not again,' and 'I can't keep covering for you.'"

"Was that blood she was washing off?" I asked incredulously. Even after what I had seen of the treatment of the girl on the bus, the weird activities at the marsh, and the rumor of being connected to a suicide, I still could not wrap my mind around the girls being violent beyond sorority hijinks. Then again, in the case of Dinah, her behavior may have been honestly inherited.

"I think so." Allen shook his head. "Garrison better stay far away from those girls. They are nuts." He made a face as if smelling something rotten. "She said something about the Marsh People."

I knew that she was not talking about the fabled creatures, but about whatever had happened that night at the marsh when the man had appeared in the water. The same man who sold bracelets and acted on television commercials.

"You ok?" Allen asked. "You look lost in a thought. A big one."

I didn't want to tell him of the things I had seen, at least not until I had unraveled them in a way that made sense. I still held hope that my daughter was uninvolved.

As I was leaving, I saw animal control pull up to Nash's house.

Marjorie Voss should have been more careful of what she posted on Instagram. In another time and place, she would have been shrewder, and I wouldn't have been given the information I needed. In another time and place, Marjorie wouldn't have been so desperately lonely.

The girl loved to serve up key points of her life in visual form. There was a picture of a dining room table, five empty chairs and one plate with a sandwich and snack pack of potato chips. She had tagged this "the new normal." There were some odd entries. One was a car radio. The hashtag #thevoicesneverstop accompanied it. What was unusual was that several of the girls replied with comments about hearing voices through their car radios, too.

I scrolled through some old pictures, finding a few with my daughter. There were images of their trip into Boston. The girls were clad in the shortest of shorts, even though it had not been particularly warm that day. One picture was taken from an angle that focused on their tight rear ends and was captioned "Behind the Esplanade." I assumed the *behind* was more about their derrieres than about their location. Another was of the girls circling the Joseph Hooker statue. Dinah had her index finger posed so it looked as if it were going up the horse's rear. The caption was the obvious "Hooker(s)."

There were also some pictures of them at the beach, at the County Fair, and shopping.

What caught my eye was a picture of the marsh. There were no visible girls; the still life was of the infamous Plasticware containers. They had been filled with thick mud or wet clay and were labelled #plasticslippers. The containers were mine, were my color, the ones I had won.

One container was filled with what looked like blood and intestines. What had Dinah done to some poor creature that had caused animal control to show up at her door? That girl needed serious help and she would never get it from her mother. I suspected that the two were equally violent, and neither would curb the other. And I certainly wouldn't want my containers back after this.

My pantry confirmed that some of my set was indeed gone.

I ran up to Kristianne's room, to confront her. Instead, I found Miranda snooping in her sister's underwear drawer.

"What do you think you're doing?" I had caught her red-handed and she was still young enough to fear discipline.

"I was just looking for…" Her face paled, and it looked as if she were deciding if she should throw in a few tears on top.

"You know you aren't supposed to go through your sister's things." I pulled her hands away from the drawer and shut it. "She has told you many, many times."

"I know. It's just that Riley and I were looking for something."

"Riley DeCota?"

She nodded. "He heard Dinah talking. She is in trouble, mom. She says that Krissy could help her. Krissy is keeping secrets." She sighed. "I know it's hard to believe, but Riley said he has never seen Dinah like this." She locked me with her most intense gaze. "He believes her."

"Honey." I put a hand on her shoulder, and I tried to turn

her away from Kristianne's things. "I know that Dinah is in trouble. And sometimes when people are in trouble, they try to turn the blame on someone else. She and Kris have had a bit of a falling out lately, so it only makes sense—"

"—it makes sense that you will never believe that your favorite child does anything wrong."

"Parents don't have favorites, lovey."

"The two of you speak a secret language."

"We sign. You did too, for a while. If you want, I could teach you to sign again."

She shook her head. "Maybe spend a little more time finding out where Kris goes. Some of the kids have been talking."

"Then you should be sticking up for your sister."

She sighed. "When can I go back to dance?"

"The studio is still closed, honey. Ms.—"

"—I know. I know what happened to her."

"Do you?"

She nodded. "She was burned, very badly. Someone did that to her. Someone killed her." Her eyes were filling with tears, but there was no agenda behind this batch.

"I wish you didn't know that."

"Riley told me. He said bad things were happening all over and we should watch out." She frowned. "He said… he said Kristianne is to blame."

Allen was taking me from behind, quite aggressively, when a notification flashed on my phone. The phone was perched on the bedside table in his room and it vibrated and flashed lights, as audio notifications do nothing for me. I peered over my shoulder and confirmed that his eyes were closed before snatching the phone and putting it in front of me.

There was a video embedded in my messenger app, but I did not recognize the sender. The video was of a small car, stopped at a red light. The camera had a bird's eye view, as if it were a traffic control camera to capture offenders who run the lights. It was nighttime, but I could see that the car was red as it was in the range of one of the very few streetlights on Cape Cod. Before the light changed, another car came from the right of the screen and smashed into the front end of the red one, pushing it onto the narrow shoulder. Before I could see the make of the attacking car, it reversed and sped away.

The red car sat, smoking and crumpled, and a thin pale arm

hung from the driver's side window. Soon after, another car approached. This car was much larger than the hit and run car and it lacked any noticeable dents. The new car pulled over behind the red one and I could see P.P exiting the driver's side door. She trotted on her high heels to the red car and pulled the jewelry from the hand and arm of its driver before running back to her own automobile and speeding away.

I gasped, and Allen mistook this for a moan of pleasure. He pulled my hips up higher and drove himself furiously inside of me. I ground my teeth until he was finished, and I was able to return to my thoughts.

What had P.P. been doing? I recalled Marjorie having been in an accident and assumed that this was one and the same.

I had tucked the phone beneath a pillow and thought I had gotten away with it, until it began to vibrate again as Allen and I lay side by side. He was enjoying the afterglow, but I was still in shock.

He propped himself up on an elbow and looked at me exasperatedly, "Really? Your phone is in our bed?"

"It's your bed," I started, trying to sound playful as a way of derailing his anger. But I was overwhelmed, and I was tired of sorting through all this confusion and fear alone. "Allen, I think

I saw something very bad." I clicked on the video and handed him the phone. He watched the entire thing, including the part that compromised his wife.

"Fuck, Fi. Is this real?"

"I think so. I think it's from when Melanie's daughter had that accident, just a few days ago." I took a deep breath. "Where does she keep her jewelry?"

"You've got to be kidding me—"

"I just want to see. I need to know if she took Marjorie's stuff."

"Why would she take a kid's jewelry? She has really good, really expensive—"

"Let's see what it was and then we might know why."

He sighed and pointed to a painting of a flowerpot that hung on the wall across from us. "Her good stuff is in the safe behind that painting. Other stuff is in that box on her dresser."

I decided to take the easiest route first and went to the cherry wood box on her dresser. The box was probably something she had had as a young girl, as it seemed out of place atop her ornate set of drawers. I dug around for only a few seconds before I held up a beaded bracelet and Marjorie's class ring.

"What is wrong with you women?" Allen groaned.

"She didn't even try to hide them." I sorted though the other trinkets until my fingers came across something cold and hard. I brushed aside a small handkerchief and I uncovered dead leeches.

Allen had gotten up and was now leaning over my shoulder. "What the hell is that?"

"Leeches. I think they are from the marsh."

"Why would she have..." He groaned. "Oh God. What do we do? What do we do now? Do we tell the police?"

"And say what? We saw your wife stealing from a kid?"

"No… no. But we saw an accident. We could send them the part with the hit and run. We could say we witnessed it. Somehow, we saw it." He rubbed the stubble on his chin. "How did we see that? Who had that tape? Did someone send it to you?"

"Yes, I mean, it looks like it came from a surveillance camera, but someone sent it to me. I just don't know who."

He grabbed my phone and began downloading an App. "There are ways to find these things out." He copied a few links from my messenger and began entering them into the app.

His face dropped. "It's from Dinah."

This begins the hardest part to write. Because this is not

fiction, nothing can be left out.

I had been called into the principal's office. Several girls were being placed on suspension, and my daughter had been accused of some vague yet serious activity. The reason I was not clear about the violation was that Principal Doyle had barely begun to speak to me when someone knocked on his office door.

Glen Holloway was a bit out of breath, but he managed to put on his most charming smile. "Excuse the interruption, but if I might have a word with you?" He crooked a finger at Principal Doyle, and they left the room. Fortunately for me, they stood on the other side of the door, and I could see them through the panes of glass. Everyone always forgets that I am a lip reader.

"Under the circumstances, we won't be pressing charges against any of the girls," Glen was saying as he ran a hand over his wavy hair. "With Sylvie missing." He put the same hand up to his mouth, as if stifling a cry, but his face did not change expression. "The focus right now is on the Quints. Obviously, Sylvie was under a great amount of stress. That was why she left…" Principal Doyle put a consoling hand on Glen's shoulder. "Please do let us know if there is anything we can do for you during this time. I know the PTO has already been in touch about helping with childcare—"

"It was just so sudden, you know? But she had been under such stress. I know that now when I look back on things. She was saying really strange things and behaving oddly. She was not herself. I honestly don't know if the girls really did anything to provoke her—"

"There was a history there, as I am sure you are aware, Glen."

Glen nodded very slowly. "Yes, I know, it's just…" He sighed. "I wouldn't say that my wife was completely innocent in all of it, or that she was the sole victim. I think there was some jealousy and some back and forth and I just can't help myself… I believe she was looking for revenge."

I had heard that Sylvie had gone missing. Rumor was that she left Glen and the kids to stay in some silent nunnery in Calcutta. It was a crazy rumor, and I am sorry to admit that I helped to spread it. In fact, I may have offered the Calcutta part. I had enjoyed the image of a silenced and meditative Sylvie. No one really knew where she was or what happened to her. All we knew was that Glen did not appear overly distressed or worried; he simply looked sad and a bit overwhelmed at having to deal with the Quints on his own.

Principal Doyle shifted so that his back was now to the door. I could not figure out what he was saying, but Glen was nodding solemnly and would occasionally interject, "thank you."

Principal Doyle reentered his office and told me that he would follow up with me later. "Something has come up," he said, but he seemed disappointed that I was getting off the hook so easily.

I went to the field to get Kristianne from cheerleading practice. She was nowhere to be found.

None of the girls knew where she was. I waited for quite some time, but then had to get home to meet Miranda who had taken the late bus after art classes.

As the night wore on and Kristianne still did not come home, I became riddled with worry. I took one lorazepam, but that was all, as I wanted to be thinking clearly in case she or someone else called.

It is with great effort that I write of all the things I came to know to be true following my daughter's disappearance.

Allen tried to mentor me. He suggested I write it in the third person, to remove myself and my bias. He also recommended I write it as a screenplay or script: all action and fact, without judgement and analysis. He said to write it as if the Id were speaking; he said to write it so a child could understand it.

I tried the third person narrative in both *Wishes* and *Death and Taxes*. I added supernatural elements as a metaphor for how surreal my life felt. I tortured Nash with spiders, and I tried to make amends with Mel.

But there was no way to separate myself from the pain and the shock of not knowing where my daughter was. In the other stories, I had been able to hide behind a creative smoke screen: I had escaped in flights of fancy. Time Between Time was something I truly wished for and something Allen had suggested in some of his writing. I needed a day, or two, to simply pull the covers over my head and catch my breath. But there are no days like that when you have a family to care for. I even would have been grateful for spiders to dictate my next moves. Anything to prevent me from having to think. Moreover, from having to understand. In the other stories, I had hidden my responsibility behind bracelets and Plasticware. I could not do that with this part of the story.

"Who would she normally go to? Who is her best friend?" Allen asked, and I realized that he was truly trying to help. His eyes were concerned, and he was no longer pawing at me.

I was stumped. "I really don't know. These girls… they bounce from one to the other. She brings home different friends all the time."

"Does she have a boyfriend?"

My stomach sunk. These are things I should know, but she

had been so secretive lately. "No. No, she is very independent and says that boys her age are too immature." At least, that is what she used to say when she and I would have mother-daughter talks. It felt like so long ago that we had spent any type of quality time together. It was my fault as much as hers. Probably more, as I was the adult in the scenario.

Allen sighed and ran his fingers through his hair. "How about this... I will start at the school and head to the ice cream shack and then the movies and see if anyone has seen or heard from her. You can try the beach, the Commons—"

"—The marsh."

He looked at me quizzically. "If you say so."

As I started to leave, I thought of something. "Won't it look weird, you asking people about Kristianne?"

He smiled in a way that truly melted my heart. He looked so tired and so completely exasperated with me. "I don't care."

When I got to the marsh, I saw several sets of plasticware filled with wet sand. They looked like cement blocks and, when I went to lift one, were just as heavy. This was not my set from Marjorie's snapchat: this set belonged to Nash, confirming that Dinah had stopped fearing her mother long ago. It had just made sense, in Nash's story, to blame the missing set on Sylvie. It had also felt good as I would come to accuse Sylvie of being an active participant in my heartache.

I saw a basket of apples. They were the honeycrisp kind that all of us had tried to secret into lunch boxes. Those same apples would return home that afternoon untouched.

These apples had been touched. At the bottom of the basket lay a hypodermic needle. I carefully picked it up and smelled it but could not detect an odor. There were pinprick marks in the apples' shiny red skin that were beginning to brown. I stuffed the needle in my purse along with one of the apples, intent on figuring out what had been injected in the fruit.

One of the many drawbacks of deafness is not being able to hear someone approaching from behind. By the time I noticed the shadows, it was too late. I turned to find Talia and Leah. Talia looked nervous while Leah, as usual, seemed angry.

"Mrs. Walker, what are you doing here?"

I shifted so they could not see the evidence I had stowed in my purse. "I was looking for Kristianne. Have either of you seen her?"

The girls exchanged a look. "No," Leah said, taking a step closer to me. She was nearing my personal space. "We haven't seen her, but we will tell her to call or text you if we do." She took another step. "We just need to get our things." She pointed to the containers and the apples.

"Oh, that? What is that?"

This was met with another exchange of looks.

"It's part of our project. With Mr. Holloway."

"Is that the one that Kris is working on?'

"Kris is working with Mr. Holloway?" Talia looked genuinely surprised. "I thought she—"

"—We don't know anything about that," Leah interrupted, "She isn't a part of this… anymore." She pushed past me to grab the basket.

Talia put a hand on my shoulder. "I will keep looking for her, Mrs. Walker. I am sure she will turn up soon."

"Those containers look heavy. Do you need help?"

Leah's square shoulders dropped. My presence was not welcome, and I had obviously mentioned something I was not supposed to see. "We're fine, thanks. Seriously, Kris is not here but maybe try the *Snack Shack*. You should try there."

"I will. And girls, be careful."

They looked surprised, but quickly shrugged it off.

"Good luck," Talia said sadly and turned her back on me.

When I met up with Allen again, he was agitated. His face was pale, and he appeared to be out of breath.

"Oh my God, what happened?" I feared the worst, but my idea of *the worst* was not what we would face later.

He took a deep breath, but his hands continued shaking as he held his phone out to me. "Sit down. There is something you need to see. Something is really wrong."

I asked him if there was any sound with the video and he shook his head no, saying, "just noises, everything is sort of jumbled together and it's hard to make out what anyone is saying."

When I started the video, I realized that the confusion was due to it being homecoming, when the marching band was playing full blast and announcements were shouted over loud speakers. Combine that with the rumbles of hundreds of people talking simultaneously and it would be difficult to separate out any important conversations.

The girls were in the video. One of them must have been filming. I could see Dinah talking to Kayleigh and also to Kayleigh's "secret weapon": her boyfriend, Billy. Billy was never William, never Bill—and rumor had it that his birth certificate and driver's license also read Billy. Billy had been sent to a special school for juvenile offenders. This special school was merely marking the days until he turned eighteen and could be sent to a legitimate prison as an authentic convict. By all appearances, Kayleigh and Billy were a perfect match and sincerely in love, they simply could not control their own impulses for idiotic and criminal behavior.

Billy was leaning against the backside of the bleachers, sucking on a joint, while the girls were talking. Marjorie and Talia occasionally appeared in the frame, but the image was centered on Billy. At one point, he looked at the camera and winked and the image bounced, as if a shrug or a sigh was given in exchange.

Suddenly, Sylvie appeared in the frame, pointing her finger in a schoolmarmish way at the kids. The kids laughed, and Sylvie brazenly took a picture of them, in possession of marijuana, before turning away.

"That was what she showed the principal," I said, "that was the catalyst. After this happened the girls went after Sylvie and—"

"—And got the Quints kicked off the Super Bowl float."

The person filming the video stealthily followed Sylvie. There was a break in the film, while the auteur went to the parking lot. The video resumed with the lens focused on Sylvie's car parked outside of the dance studio.

Sylvie exited the car and entered the artisan welding studio that is beside the dance studio. She was seen pulling a small MIG welding rig with her. The image of her struggling to pull the equipment over gravel and into the dance studio while keeping the extension cord straight was comical at the time. It lost its humor when I learned the outcome.

I paused the video. "If someone has this, why didn't they show the police? Should I tell the police?"

Allen gave the universal sign for "roll tape," while saying, "Keep watching."

I pushed play and saw the flaming torch moving in the poorly lit room before the heavy door to the studio shut on the orange extension cord. The director backed away, framing the door in the darkness, until the screen went completely dark. It remained dark, then lit up once the camera holder opened a car door and slid into the lit interior. The camera swung around the car, as the driver climbed into the seat. Before the camera shut off, I could see that the car was our old Toyota, the one that Kristianne regularly used, and I caught her face in the rearview.

I didn't have any words for what I had just seen. This was record of the murder of the dance teacher, but it also involved my daughter.

"How did you get this?" I had almost forgotten Allen was

there, even though he was seated very close to me.

He put his arm around me and pulled me close. "Marjorie Voss. She is scared. She is afraid they will be blamed for Sylvie's disappearance." He placed a gentle hand on my head and lowered it to his shoulder. His smell was comforting, and it must have always been so, but I had been too busy trying to ignore any emotional ties to this man. I began to cry. I was upset about my daughter and her complicity in some very bad, very dark things. I was tired of the secrecy and the complicated relationships in my life. And I just realized that I loved Allen, and that was something I had sworn would never happen.

❦

I tried making a list of all the things that were different about Kristianne. She was not eating, not sleeping, and incredibly moody. But wasn't that true of most teenage girls? I still had the syringe but was unsure of what to do with it. Until I knew the extent of my daughter's involvement, I did not want to turn anything over to the police. That included the videos and images I had collected.

I decided to see if I could talk to Marjorie Voss. I went to the house by the marsh and was met by a pack of barking dogs. I wouldn't classify them as mangy, but they did not have the same look as the "show dog" styled canines who lived by the sea.

Melanie must have heard the dogs, as she appeared at the front door. She looked disheveled as always. In comparison to her appearance, the dogs really did not look unkept at all. She was holding a gerbil or hamster or small rodent of some sort. The animal was calm, despite the barking around him. Melanie told me Marjorie was not home. She barely raised her voice despite the dogs, and she did not seem surprised that I wanted to see her daughter.

As she came closer, I could have sworn I smelled pot, but Melanie was far too anxious to have imbibed.

"Marjorie is acting strangely, Fi. More withdrawn and… *emo*… is that even a word? You know what I mean, she is more emo than usual. This started even before the accident. She is always on her laptop. I have no idea what she does on it. Such a waste of time." She looked down at the hamster-gerbil-thing and sighed. "If she only knew she were wasting time. If she only knew that she had more freedom and flexibility now than she might ever have. Then again, no one could have told us anything at their age, right?"

I shrugged. I had really hoped to talk to Marjorie about the videos. As much sympathy as I was starting to feel for Melanie, she was becoming a time waster for me.

"It's just weird, her love for this computer. I mean, when she was little, she loved *Finding Nemo* but even then she would barely watch the whole thing. She would be outside or playing with Sky. Now, she is always in her room. And it seems like she is up and on the laptop all hours of the night."

The dogs finally quieted and walked off to lie beneath an awning that seemed to serve no purpose at the very edge of the property.

"I haven't been sleeping much either, so I have caught her on her laptop at strange times. I can see the light from the screen as I go past her door."

"Have you talked to her about it? About what she does on her computer?"

"No. No we haven't talked. It's been a long time since we have."

"Melanie, Kristianne is missing. I haven't been able to find her. No one has seen her. Do you think Marjorie might know anything?"

Melanie's face dropped. "I am so sorry, Fi. That is horrible. What can I do? How can I help?"

Part of me wanted to scream at her and part of me wanted

to laugh. What could she do? The only help would be some intel from Marjorie, but she seemed incapable of providing that. "I am not sure. I wish I knew. We have been looking..."

"You know, sometimes people are right under your noses, and you don't even see them," Melanie said cryptically. Maybe she *was* toking. "As mothers, we miss a lot. Things happen right in front of our eyes, but we don't see it."

"Are you saying she might actually be home, Mel? I think I would know—"

"Yes, yes, of course. Forgive me. I haven't been myself lately." She rubbed her abdomen with the rodent-free hand. "Please let me know if you think of anything I can do to help. And I will have Marjorie get in touch with you when I see her."

I told her I appreciated that and turned to leave. As I did, I thought I saw a curtain part in a window in Marjorie's room.

At first, Nash, who appeared at my door with a casserole that was reminiscent from her days selling packaged meals, seemed to be of no more use than Melanie. Nash bragged that Dinah, too, was eating less and skipping meals as Kristianne had. Nash felt this showed restraint, especially with the March Madness dance right around the corner.

After a hug that offered no consolation, Nash made a face, as if struggling to open the psychic Plasticware container that housed her secrets. "I saw Kris in Glen Holloway's car the other day. Dinah told me they were working together. A lot of the girls have been doing projects with him… for grades or for their college portfolios. Not sure how the school got so lucky to get him." She rolled her eyes.

"I take it you're not a fan." The casserole was becoming heavy in my hands, but I was not about to make the tragic error of inviting the queen of judgement into my home. She once called my six bedroom/four full bathroom house "cottagey." I was not about to repeat that mistake, not in the mood I was in.

"It just seems that he… I don't know… has this effect on the girls. He snares them in his web." She touched her coiffed auburn crown, a sneaky smile appearing on her lips. "No boys, though, huh? He only works with the girls. That seems… funny."

I didn't like where this was going, especially after hearing that my daughter had been in the man's car. "What are you suggesting, Nash?"

"I am suggesting that you do not overlook him. As you are

thinking about Kristianne, don't forget Glen. He has come to me in the past for pharmaceutical assistance and I am not overly thrilled with what I ended up supplying for him."

"What is that?"

"Roofies. And bath salts. White Knight."

I was incensed. "And you are just mentioning this now?"

"Client privilege. I can't run a business by gossiping about the people who support that business now can I? It's not for me to spill the tea, Fi." She frowned. "It's a good thing you live a clean life. Someone would maybe want revenge for your gossiping."

This was why I infested her with spiders in her story.

"It is just creepy, is all I am saying. Him spending so much time with young girls. Outside of school. Alone."

I wanted to remind her that the person she is seen most often with outside of our social circle is a very young man, but I was too irritated to continue any conversation with her.

I am not proud of what I did next, but in an effort to continue with an honest narrative, I will admit that I went into my house, slammed the casserole on the counter and took one—or a few— sleeping pills. I just couldn't deal with reality any longer and the nannies would make sure the kids were fed.

My favorite thing, the best feeling, is to fight the sleeping pill.

I love to try to outrun it. No wonder small children wage war against bedtime. It feels good to engage in some sort of combat; it makes you feel momentarily strong when the entire world is crumbling around you. I thought I would try to call Allen, but my hand would not reach for my phone.

I began to lose the battle. There was nowhere to run and no power to move at all. The only retreat was to fall into emptiness. In the emptiness my daughter was not missing, and I didn't hurt anymore.

I was fortunate that the high school secretary harbored a crush on Allen. She also harbored $8,568 dollars of grant money that was meant for tribal students; she was in no position to cast stones. Nor did she seem to think anything untoward was transpiring when Allen asked for some student logins. He pretended he was going to play a prank on Glen and switch in some items in students' portfolios. He promised he would make a copy and only "infect" the copies. With no consideration of the students' privacy, he was given access. The secretary thought this was all in great fun and Allen told me that she should consider investing some of her newly found grant money on a perfume that did not smell like a snickerdoodle factory.

He snuck off copies of the girls' projects and of Kristianne's on his nondescript, utilitarian USB and we met up to go through them. Leah's portfolio consisted of her application to Slippery Rock University along with her field hockey stats. She had one letter of recommendation from the phys. ed. teacher, and a hand-written essay on post-concussion syndrome that had been photographed and uploaded.

The portfolio of Marjorie Voss was more of the same ennui-via-photography diversified by a few collages and one very impressive monotype on glass that showcased an elongated leech curling around its mandala abdomen to swallow its own tail.

Dinah DeCota's portfolio was empty.

"Not to worry," Allen said, "her mother will buy or steal her diploma for her."

Then we got to Kristianne's virtual blog and project. She was wearing her cheerleading uniform and someone else was filming her. "Hate is not a part of this," she said, but it sounded calculated as if she had rehearsed, "I never hated anyone that I knew or lived with. Actually, I did hate Mrs. Rothsback, my math teacher in 8th grade. She was only ever nice to the boys, and it was so unfair.

She made fun of my hair once, after I got it cut. Teachers are not supposed to do that." She looked at the person behind the camera for confirmation. "I hated my brownie troop leader. And I hated that my father never wanted to spend time with any of us. But none of that made me want to kill."

"I am doing this because I am bored. Everything I do, I do because I am bored." She took a deep inhale, pushing her chest forward and looking down at the letter emblazoned on its front. "Just bored."

"The truth is it is simply *time*. When things reach a boiling point, you can cook or take the pot off the stove." She studied her pompoms in what was meant to appear as a thoughtful gesture, but I could tell she was nervous. "It is time."

There seemed to be an edit in the film. When Kristianne appeared again, the sun had moved, and the room was darker.

She continued, "My rage is because of countless holidays and birthdays where cheer and good will were as artificial as the meals my mother microwaved, and deceit was the only item seen beneath the gilded wrapping paper." This did not sound like my daughter. Had Allen been writing for another student? I glanced at him, but he looked just as perplexed as I felt.

"I am not bad. None of my friends are truly bad. We were

nursed on competition and weaned on jealousy. Our education was packaged in shoe boxes and garment bags. If one raised a lamb among lions, it would have carnivorous tendencies. Unless it were resilient." She dropped the pompoms, picked up an apple from somewhere off screen, and took a bite. "And human nature is never that resilient. By the time you find this…" Her eyes moved to a space above the camera, and it appeared that someone was talking to her. There was a large man-sized shadow on the wall behind her, beside her smaller one. She looked back to the camera and signed "suspect." I remembered our conversation when I had told her to ask for help and I knew this was a message for me.

The blog stopped.

"By the time you find this, what?" Allen was pale. "What does she mean? She said her anger never made her feel like she wanted to kill. Does that mean she feels that way now? I just don't feel we are any closer, or have gotten anywhere…" He looked at this watch. "Isn't the dance tonight?"

I was stunned. Why was my daughter talking about hate? I know my divorce when she was little had affected her, but we had gone to therapy for that. Her father did want to spend time with her; he simply had a heavy workload. That was why I wasn't involving him now; I would wait until we had more answers.

Right now, I had none. And then Allen mentions something as normal and mundane as a dance. "I had forgotten. Kris hadn't been all that interested—"

"—Yes, but someone there may have seen her. It's a great opportunity with such a large crowd gathered."

I was again amazed by this man's compassion. He truly wanted to help for the sake of helping. His intentions were good. I can count on one hand the number of times I have encountered someone who did not have a hidden agenda, so this was a novelty.

The shock must have registered on my face, as he gently took my elbow and led me to his car.

❦

By the time we got there, it was over. Not the dance, but the event, the horrible thing that was meant to happen.

Principal Doyle was reviewing the film from the security cameras, and he thought I should take a look. Later, Allen told me that the music in the gymnasium was generic and safe. The dancing was not. We could see Kristianne cutting through configurations of grinding bodies, careless about the gun at her side. No one seemed to mind a not-so-gentle poking by a hardened shaft. The lights were lower than the necklines on the gowns which glittered in time to the pulsating music and in the reflection of the mirrored disco ball. Most of the girls were clad in pastels, mainly pinks and lilacs. These hues were in direct defiance of the weather. The girls had selected their gowns in preparation of prom season: everyone knew that the March Madness court simply *became* the Prom court and that the king and queen of one ball merely exchanged crowns at the other.

Kris wound her way to the locker room where the yet-to-be-announced Queen's court were primping and preparing. She was met at the locker room door by Leah, who was pulling a wagon loaded with the mud filled Plasticware. The wagon had been festooned with apple blossoms. The video stopped and Principal Doyle gestured to a police officer who brought over a phone. The story continued on a video made by one of the girls. Allen helped me fill in the blanks when I couldn't understand what was being said. There were six nominated girls, each with the requisite best friend to help with lipstick application, push-up bra position, smuggled shot of schnapps production, and birth control of the evening decision. The gun toting girls were only a party of five, but the guns gave the impression of outnumbering the unarmed twelve.

Before announcing their presence, the girls made short work of a flask Glen had given them. Kris later said the liquid made her feel warm, as if she had mainlined the sun. It also made her feel confident, yet drowsy; boisterous, yet lazy. At times she even forgot where she was or what she was doing.

Marjorie raised her gun and pointed it at a queen-to-be's head. The gun shook and she seemed to have a hard time keeping it still. "You, girlie." She wobbled a bit on her feet. From behind the camera, Dinah snickered. Marjorie whirled around, turning on Dinah, and nearly fell over.

Kayleigh had a steadier grip on her gun, and she ordered the girls in the court to march outside to the fest float. The float had been nicknamed "The Hope Float" as so many of the girls in the court were named Hope. I remembered Dinah's joke that when the girls shared a bong, they were the "high Hopes." At the time I had found the joke to be in poor taste. Compared to what I was now seeing, it seemed very innocent. A homemade stockade had been stowed away in the locker room the day before and the princesses had ignored it, assuming it to be yet another tribute to their impending reign.

"Now is when we play Cinderella," Dinah told the girls as she, too, leveled her gun. "You slip these on." She tilted her head and the camera toward the mud filled containers on the wagon. "And before you know it, you'll be dancing with the Marsh People."

Gwynnie's oldest Asian child, who was not a Hope, but an Annabelle, sighed beneath her tiara. "Marsh People. What are we, babies?"

"No." Dinah shoved her gun toward the girl's waist. "Not babies, dead girls."

"C'mere," Marjorie ordered the tallest and blondest girl in the court to climb the float, "sit in this chair, your *throne*, your highness." The other murderesses giggled as the bejeweled and gowned girl numbly took a seat. Marjorie stood in front of her and put the barrel of the gun to her lips. "Suck it like you mean it, sweetheart, like you did Neil Cottle's sweet, sweet dick."

Again, the girls giggled, mostly to cover the discomfort of the crime they were committing and the effects of the flask.

With her gun, Kayleigh broke a Hope's nose and the camera caught the blood geysering to the ceiling. Marjorie took her San Francisco souvenir knife and stabbed Annabelle in the center of her palm.

Leah turned greenish. "You are getting blood all over the floor…I thought we were just supposed to take pictures of them. Mr. Holloway said…"

The girls of the court did not appear frightened. Maybe they truly were the "high Hopes" of Dinah's imagination. Or maybe they were so intent on letting nothing interfere with a day that had been planned their entire lives that they would not allow the fear to register.

Kayleigh was beginning to sway. "Let's... just... do the shoes."

Marjorie began to shake and sweat. The locker room appeared steamy even though the showers were off. Just as a low-level drone of "it's hot, I'm tired," began, a booming voice came over the loudspeaker announcing a code red. Steel doors slammed shut and the dancing princesses hit the ground, seeking shelter beneath benches and behind the flowered float. Two of the armed girls collapsed, saliva frothing on their pink lips. There were maiden bodies everywhere, like a collection of *Grimm's Fairy Tales* exploded.

Glen Holloway is suddenly seen in the frame of the cell phone. His appearance caused the high Hopes to shriek, even though they had been largely unreactive to the guns and violence. I couldn't help but wonder what that says about our girls that a grown man is the most frightening thing they could encounter?

"What are you doing?" He asks the gun-toting girls that are still alert.

Leah suddenly looks sober. "We were only supposed to put them in the stock and throw apples at them. Like you said, but she—" she pointed at Kristianne.

Glen rubbed his temples. "That is not what we discussed." His face changed. "Dinah, you need to put that fucking phone away now. No more videos." He grabbed Kristianne around the waist and pulled her away from the scene. Dinah chased after with cell camera rolling.

"She takes it too far," Dinah yelled after them, as Glen was shoving Kris into her car and pointing to the road as if instructing her to drive. "Remember the dog?"

That is where the video ends, as, apparently, Dinah stopped filming to get into her own car.

The police asked me to come with them to answer some questions. They had officers patrolling, trying to find the girls. Allen went home to the unexpected.

To be fair, *he* had not been expected. He was supposed to be in New York meeting with a publisher. That had been an alibi. While his wife was on some unspecified jaunt—we would later learn she had a deadly run-in with Melanie who had found P.P.'s panties in her laundry—Allen and I were supposed to rendezvous at the *Cuddle and Bubble* (famous for its hot tubs). The Kristianne drama had put that idea to a close and Allen had gone home to find his house was occupied. Garret was in Nantucket with his grandparents, so Allen had been surprised to encounter voices, and bodies, in his sitting room. The stained glass in the doorway and the crystal chandelier in the foyer blazed like adjacent suns, putting the players in the neighboring room in shadows. There was a man, the same man I had recognized from the protein bar commercial and from our bracelet party and from the marsh with the girls. Behind him, bound and gagged in a chair, was my daughter. In front of them stood Dinah and she was livid.

Allen witnessed the following as he hid himself in the foyer and debated between calling the police and calling me:

"The bracelet was for her." Dinah pointed at Kris who Allen reported was completely calm.

"You mean to give to her or *meant* for her?" the man asked.

"I don't know. God, we fucked up. We just wanted to stop her."

Allen texted me and decided to make himself known. I had just finished with the police, and he instructed me to go back and notify them, if that is what I wanted. I rushed to Allen's house, having 9-1-1 at the ready, but needing to see what was really going on before my daughter got into any more trouble. I trusted Allen to protect her until I got there, and when I got there, I pulled in right behind Glen Holloway's SUV.

This is the hardest part to learn and to write. By the time I got inside, Glen was telling Allen, "I never asked her to do anything violent. That was all her."

I wasn't sure what to believe, but the evidence pointed to Kris being behind many of the evil things that had been happening. Had that tendency always been in her? In what ways had I nurtured it? I had always judged the other mothers, believing they were raising monsters with their carelessness, with their selfishness. Had I been the worst mother of all?

I had sworn to finally write the truth. No more Time Between Time and no more spiders. The truth is: bracelets and Plasticware cannot hold the projected blame that is meant to be shouldered by the women in my social circle. And by the daughters that they are training to surpass them in sheer deviousness and lack of fear of repercussions.

The truth is: cancer is rampant on Cape Cod. It could be due to toxic plumes that filter into the drinking water. It could be due to the proximity of the power plant. Melanie's entire life was like an accident: the constant financial struggles, the bad marriage, the cancer. She was only lucky when it came to winning Plasticware and bracelets, so I managed to tie those events into the tragedies that struck her later. It is no surprise she turned on P.P.; the woman had psychically eviscerated her.

The truth is: Nash could not stop pilfering the drugs she meant to sell. At first she took them for weight control, then she just took them to feel out of control in her very controlled world. The drugs had a hallucinatory effect, causing Nash to hear voices. Dinah's voice was the one she heard most often, instructing her to get the bracelet party in motion. Dinah had hired the actor to pose as a bracelet salesman and she and the girls had used their prior experience with jewelry craft kits and bedazzling to create an array of products. Dinah had rigged one bracelet in particular. Despite spying on the event, she had lost track of the bracelet and had relied on the salesman to get it into the right hands. He had failed.

It had been frightening to see the indestructible Nashville DeCota falling apart before our very eyes, strung out and failing at the game of hygiene. Nash was the Island Impaler. Dinah was the Tooth Snatcher. They were both probably so much more and so much worse. It just felt good to pin these crimes on the self-righteous Sylvie, who was guilty of several vicious crimes of her own. Mostly of having a treacherous husband who was more narcissistic than she.

The truth is, P.P. had hired Danen to hit Marjorie's car so she could steal her jewelry. No one could ever figure out why she wanted the worthless trinkets; we determined it was just another layer of her rivalry with Melanie. A contract for the accident had been found in Danen's room. Nash had taught the boy well.

The truth is: Nash and Danen died in what was labelled a murder/suicide. It was never determined which was which. Ballistics tests were inconclusive because a welder had been used on the gun barrel, and their bodies had been found after animals and insects (but not spiders) had contaminated them and rendered them difficult to study. Nash had never made it to the cold operating table, and the suicide note, it was concluded, had been crafted by someone who was neither Nash nor Danen. The note had been found in one of Nash's Plasticware containers. The two had not engaged in any type of relationship beyond benefactor and recipient. The entire case was a mystery and one that I would eventually be commissioned to write about, but my daughter knew more about the anonymous suicide note than she should, and I needed to keep the spotlight off her.

I later found out that Glen Holloway had not been Kristianne's first lover. That honor had gone to Danen. He had broken her heart, explaining that he could not commit to anyone when he had so much work to do on himself. She had been jealous of the time he spent with Nash, and that was all that she has ever been willing to divulge regarding those two.

She had also had a brief tryst with Kayleigh's boyfriend, Billy. She was afraid she would be forced to run the gauntlet if it were discovered. She tried to cover by going along with everything Kayleigh said and did—basically kissing up to the girl constantly. Kayleigh and Dinah were the ones who began the Sylvie hate. Kris' infatuation with Glen took it to a deadly level.

The truth is: the man selling the bracelets was a bad actor and a worse liar. He ratted out Glen and the girls without a moment's hesitation. No one could blame him. His check had been cashed and he had no affiliation with anyone involved. Following his roles as Marsh Man (which had required impressive stunts and holographic projections) and bracelet salesman, he went on to a commercial for male pattern baldness. I am not sure how he got his lustrous hair to look so thin in the "before" shots, but the "after" shots were the man-bun man in all his glory.

The truth is: something bad came from the marsh. Kristianne confirmed this when I met with her at her new collaborative school. She was signing to me, as there was always someone listening: a social worker, usually. "I had been coming home from cheer practice. It was so hot that I decided to take a quick dip. Even though I hate the marsh and the way it smells and makes my hair smell. It was just so hot. I felt like I wanted to cool off everywhere, every part of me. So, I just took off my clothes, even though I didn't have a bathing suit with me. I didn't think anyone else would be there. But, then Glen—"

It was weird to see her sign his first name.

"He was there. He saw me." Kristianne sighed. "At first, it was like a nightmare. You know the ones, where you are naked in school or whatever?"

I nodded.

Her face turned red and I could tell that this next part was difficult for her. "He got into the water with me."

Even though I am deaf, I could hear a roaring sound moving through my head. I think it was my blood pressure. I didn't know what to do, or say, or how to react. When I had originally written this scene, I had placed a teen-aged Melanie in the water with a Marsh Person. It was the only way I could deal with it. Thinking of Glen with my daughter, I could only imagine him as a monster.

"He is a bad man, Mom. He gave us drinks that had stuff in them. We gave the same stuff to other girls so we could take their pictures. He hired that man that Dinah had used to play tricks on us and on other girls. He wanted to record our reactions. He had this thing with apples, too. I think he was obsessed with the Tooth Snatcher."

"That was obvious at that assembly. He was rubbing it in our faces, too." I hated that we had sat there, his captive audience, while he smugly flaunted his power over our children.

"Dinah caught us together, so Glen blackmailed her. Stuff about her and stuff about her mother. She went along with everything, even put a leech on herself—"

"—Yes, I know."

"Then Glen figured out that she was the Tooth Snatcher. He became obsessed with her. I felt like I had to do something, had to keep his interest on me. I did some very bad things."

The truth is, Glen got away with it. More than that, he garnered sympathy for being the single parent of the Cape Quints. The videos of Sylvie's wrongdoings helped Kristianne's case, which was why she ended up in a collaborative as opposed to jail. Sylvie's was the only case tied to Kris and I was going to do everything in my power to keep it that way. But now, Kris and I are both ready for the truth to set us free.

Allen and I ran into Glen at an event for "The Blessing of the Boats" in which people lined up their watercrafts for a dousing of holy water before shrink wrapping them for the winter. Allen gave Glen the cold shoulder, as did I, but Glen wanted to have the final word.

"It was research, Allen, you have understand that." His smile was as smug as ever.

"Messing with young girls' minds is not research. There was nothing scholarly about what you did."

I could barely look at Glen, but he was not going to let me get away without a final bit of torture.

"I got a contract, from a real publishing house. That was the point with the girls. It was a study. It would lead to a book. A real one, with a tour." Glen leaned in so close that I could smell his cologne. "A contract is a thing of beauty."

Elaine Pascale is the author of *If Nothing Else, Eve, We've Enjoyed the Fruit; The Blood Lights; The Language of Crows;* and the soon to be released *The Solstice.* She is the co-editor of *Dancing in the Shadows: A Tribute to Anne Rice* and a regular contributor to Pen of the Damned and the Ladies of Horror. When not writing, Elaine can be found on her paddleboard or casting spells beneath the stars.

Milton Keynes UK
Ingram Content Group UK Ltd.
UKHW050032190624
444315UK00015B/917